MW00338387

Praise for FINAL NOTICE

"Van Fleisher could join the ranks of James Patterson and Tom Clancy with the quality of writing that I found in Final Notice. More importantly, he took a simple idea and elevated it into a thrilling, fast paced read that never once slackened." **Samantha Coville for Readers' Favorite**

***

"... A fiction novel that is not that far from reality. My attention never wavered while reading this novel. The characters are likable and multidimensional ... the plot was perfectly paced .... (and) I kept on tuning the pages because I was impatient to see how each character who received a final notice would react. I have to congratulate the author on the ability to surprise me multiple times throughout the story." **Sarah Khan for OnlineBookClub.org.**

***

"It is original, with biting humor, and well executed; Final Notice is a great read. Final Notice by Van Fleisher is a thrilling novel that includes strong elements of sci-fi to provide readers with an awesome reading experience. The story is intelligently plotted, featuring a lot of suspense and grim humor, and forces readers to consider what they would do if they knew when they would die. Van Fleisher has a powerful sense of setting and readers will feel as though they are navigating the physical and spiritual landscapes of the novel alongside the characters. Final Notice is a great read." **Romuald Dzemo for Readers' Favorite.**

***

"... A powerful and engrossing set of tales incorporating social and political commentary... . While the underlying premise may come from science fiction, the ultimate impact lies in their social perspectives, which leads readers to think about future desires, the consequences of actions when

death is an imminent certainty, and issues ranging from gun rights to senior citizens' quality of life." **D. Donovan, Senior Reviewer, Midwest Book Review**

***

"Van Fleisher is a master entertainer... . Final Notice by Van Fleisher is an intelligently imagined and expertly crafted novel with an original concept. Combining dark and biting humor, satire, and suspense, Van Fleisher creates a story with characters who are sophisticated and reveal a lot about human nature. There is an unpredictability in the plot that makes it intriguing and exciting, with surprises that readers won't see coming. You can't stop reading this book once you start it." **Divine Zape, Readers' Favorite.**

***

And from Amazon Readers ...

"Shocking Reality of Gun Ownership in the wrong hands and the Consequences."

"Fantastic Present-Day Intriguing Story!"

"Final Notice is an incredible political thriller that discusses the issue of gun control in America."

"This story is imaginative and unique and draws attention to provocative topics that America is in the midst of ..."

"Great political satire!"

"A 'must read' book for right now!"

"What a thrill ride! From start to finish, this book kept me engaged and entertained with its fascinating concepts."

FINAL NOTICE

A Novel

VAN FLEISHER

FINAL NOTICE, A Novel

VAN FLEISHER

"The characters and events in this book are fictitious. Any similarity to real persons, living or dead, is unfortunate."

Copyright © 2017 Van Fleisher
Cover design by BookBaby

All rights reserved. In accordance with the U.S. Copyright Act of 1976, the scanning, uploading, and electronic sharing of any part of this book without the permission of the Author constitutes unlawful piracy and theft of the Author's intellectual property. If you would like to use material from the book (other than for review purposes), prior written permission must be obtained from the Author at van@finalnoticebook.com. Thank you for your support of this.

First printing: November 2017
Second printing: May 2018

The Author is not responsible for websites (or their content) that are not owned by the Author.

ISBN (Print Edition): 978-1-7320833-0-1
ISBN (eBook Edition): 978-1-54391-412-2

TABLE OF CONTENTS

FORWARD

My initial intent was to call attention to the way that senior citizens are perceived and dealt with in the United States, mixing that with our seemingly insatiable appetite for guns. Driving that appetite is our political process, feeding our fears and hunger for guns; so, I felt compelled to bring that aspect into the story.

Although the book presents a number of murders, I have used these crimes solely as a way of highlighting what I believe is a serious and growing national concern. In no way do I condone murder, even when the act may benefit the majority.

I am pledging at least 10% of my net income from this book to be donated to a variety of organizations working for a better country (see my website at www.finalnoticebook.com for details). Better healthcare for all, better education for all, better job opportunities for all, better government for all, and fewer guns for fewer people. I am not anti-gun, per se, but until we embrace sensible safeguards to regulate who can and cannot have a gun, I believe the Second Amendment is being abused.

* * *

PROLOGUE

WHAT WOULD YOU DO IF YOU KNEW - FOR CERTAIN - THAT YOU HAD ONE WEEK TO LIVE?

Some would spend the time getting their legal affairs in order, revising wills, and writing out detailed instructions. Others would spend much of that time calling, writing or e-mailing family, friends, lovers and ex-lovers. Some might try to squeeze in something they have always wanted to do or visit or make an exceptional donation. Still others might clean out the refrigerator, dust the furniture, wash the floors and do the laundry. And some ... might kill.

* * *

CHAPTER 1 - IN THE BEGINNING …

Pasadena, California. It was an extremely unnerved Vince Fuller who returned to his comfortable home in Pasadena's historic Highlands. His hands were still shaking as he fumbled with the back-door key. Luckily, Trudi would not hear him, he thought with relief, as he caught the strains of his wife's guitar and voice coming from the den. She was caught up in one of her new folk songs. But Miles, their little Corgi, certainly heard him come in and came running to greet him. Vince gave him a quick scratch between his oversized ears, and went quickly and quietly to their master suite, where he washed the dirt from his hands and changed out of his soiled clothes. He felt guilty for this act of stealth although he had done nothing wrong.

Only then did he knock on the den door, out of courtesy, and Trudi shouted, "Hi, Honey!" as she stopped playing and placed the guitar back in its stand. Folk music was a passion of Trudi's and she had been doing it for over 50 years, mostly for her own enjoyment, with friends, at song circles, and the occasional low-profile, coffee house gig. She had even recorded a couple of CDs, which, despite favorable reviews, managed to gross just over $500 … total. Folk music, it often seemed, was yesterday's music and the only people who liked and appreciated it were, literally, a dying breed. Vince liked it though, and always enjoyed hearing her humming and strumming around the house.

Trudi gave Vince a quick hug and kiss. "I'm sorry, Honey. I didn't realize what time it was. I think dinner will be a bit late... and a lot simpler. How was your day? Any luck with finding your ideal coffee maker?"

Vince was trying to be upbeat and calm. "No. Close but not perfect." He had been searching for a coffee maker that could make espresso, coffee, and lattes without using pre-packaged products. "I'll take Miles around the block for a quick walk while you whip up a late and simple supper, as long as simple doesn't mean without wine!"

Miles saw the leash in Vince's hand and responded with a marked increase in the wag speed of his stump of a tail. Walks, head scratches and belly rubs were right up there with food, and that was saying something. Some people know Corgis as the Queen's dogs (as in Queen Elizabeth of England): jaunty little dogs that are "little" only in terms of their legs, which are almost shorter than their pointy ears. But Miles was something of a character – friendly and fearless, with enough speed, swagger and "attitude" to outstrip a dog twice his size. So, not surprisingly, he attracted a lot of attention.

It was late afternoon and there were a fair number of people out and enjoying the day. In the past, their reactions when they saw Miles always amused Vince, but today his head was in a different place altogether.

Vince had recently turned 70, and although he was physically fit, carried his 165 pounds well on his six-foot frame, and didn't feel 70, the reality was unavoidable and today was proof. Well, so were the reading glasses, thinning hair and stiffness in the morning. He was getting old, if not already there. He knew what he would have done to that hopped-up piece of shit who knocked him down at the Mall today had that happened even 20 years ago. And if it had occurred when he was playing college football ... well, the truth is, it wouldn't have happened. It had happened today only because he was old, and that asshole knew he could get away with it. And that's what really ate at Vince. Being knocked down hadn't physically hurt him, but his pride and ego had suffered a blow. He still heard that menacing, mocking voice say, "Get the fuck out of my way, old man." And there was nothing he could do about it.

After dinner, Vince and Trudi cleaned up the aftermath of the quinoa-kale stir fry and retired to the living room to watch the evening news, with a glass of red wine in hand, and Miles at their feet. It had become a ritual of sorts, one that had been adopted and refined after Vince's retirement from his job as an international management consultant, two years earlier.

Trudi was poised on the couch, petite, fit, auburn hair (with some help from her hair dresser), green-framed glasses assisting her 65-year-old green eyes, with one leg curled up beneath her and the other on the magazine-strewn coffee table, while Vince shifted in his overstuffed chair, navigating the thousand channels with practiced expertise. Vince and Trudi bought this house and much of its furniture 40 years ago. The furniture had been recovered and re-upholstered a few times, and they loved the comfort that comes with good quality and age. They had watched their neighborhood change over time as families moved in and out, generally white middle class leaving and ethnic upper-middle-class moving in; but

Vince couldn't figure out how anyone could afford to buy a house at today's prices.

Surfing the channels, he stopped at Fox News – an occasional practice to "see how the other half thinks."

The TV spokesman said, "We're going to take a short break and when we come back, Fox News will present another real life, true story about a grave threat – no pun intended – (laughing) to senior citizens."

Vince cringed and was tempted to switch channels but instead just muted it as a commercial began. Ignoring the muted commercial, Trudi said, "Wow, they really know their audience, don't they?"

He tried to smile but this wasn't helping his mood.

Perhaps Trudi sensed his low spirits and added, "I spoke with Alma today and she is going to check dates with Ahmed to have us over for dinner."

The ploy worked, and Vince smiled, genuinely, for the first time. Alma Khan was a great cook and she and her husband, Ahmed, were good friends of theirs. "What's the occasion?"

"Nothing. We were just catching up on stuff and realized it had been too long."

Vince had met Ahmed Khan almost 20 years ago when he was doing a consulting project at Cal Tech, where Ahmed worked. Vince recognized the unique qualities in Ahmed that enabled him to see the bigger picture instead of being solely focused on the technical issues. They stayed in touch over the years and then the Khans moved to Pasadena, not far from the Fullers, and their connection turned into a friendship.

Vince's significant time working in over 30 countries around the world made him more than comfortable with people from different cultures. He also had great admiration for the degree of openness and generosity in most cultures as compared with his own country. He knew that there were good and bad people everywhere, but his experience made him realize that the good in other cultures was every bit as deep, if not deeper, than the good in his own.

Vince was getting pretty adept at recognizing the end of commercials and was about to unmute when another commercial started. "I hope she's cooking her lamb recipe. That has to be the best dish I've ever had."

"Better than my quinoa-kale stir fry?"

Vince was finally relaxing, and his usual good humor returned as he danced around Trudi's question until the Fox News host returned.

"Our guest this evening is Dwayne LaPlant, Executive Vice President of Marketing for the NRA, the National Rifle Association. Good evening, Dwayne, and thank you for joining us."

"Thank you, Sean, for having me."

"As you know, Dwayne, we've been running a series of segments about the random acts of violence that seem to have spread from racial and ethnic attacks to attacks on the elderly and women. What's your take on this phenomenon?"

Vince squirmed in his chair.

"Well, Sean, it's clearly opportunistic. Older people and women are less able to fight back and defend themselves so naturally they're more vulnerable to these physical attacks. Same with children. That's why we advocate being able to protect yourself through responsible gun ownership."

"But in the case of the elderly, aren't you concerned about an increase of accidental shootings? You know, forgetting to use the safety mechanism or not seeing clearly?"

"We get some of that, even with younger people," LaPlant replied with a laugh. "Our studies have shown that with adequate training, almost anyone can be a responsible gun owner. That's why we introduced the NRA Armed Seniors Discount Program. If more old-timers packed heat, it might make thugs think twice before bullying them."

Vince felt a weight on his chest, as if they were talking directly to and about him. He was overcome with guilt, embarrassment and rage ... but guns?

Sean agreed. "Good point. How's that program going, by the way?"

"Pretty amazing. We've sold more guns under that program than Obama sold health policies. (He laughed again.) In fact, we're planning a big event to celebrate our millionth sale."

"A million guns? Just to seniors?"

"Yep."

"And have there been any repercussions?"

"Nothing unusual. A few isolated incidents."

8

"It seems that we've been hearing about more than just a few. Do you have any statistics?"

"No. We don't track that, but it stands to reason that if the normal accident rate is applied to a million more guns and users, there could be an increase. But seniors are not exactly an aggressive group, so it is probably even less than normal.

We just think that if we armed all seniors, people would think twice about taking advantage of them."

"Like having armed guards in all schools?"

"Exactly."

"Do you have any advice for seniors about how to avoid problems?"

"Good question, Sean. There are over 40 million seniors over 65 in the United States. So, even a million new gun users won't make that much of an impact. First of all, we plan to continue the discount so that more responsible seniors can protect themselves and enjoy the lives they've worked so hard for. We are also planning a series of training videos that will be promoted on our website that will help seniors avoid problems."

"Can you give me an example, Dwayne?"

"Sure. Most seniors with guns will probably be open carrying, and we suggest that they make the weapon as visible as possible. Even if you are licensed for concealed carry, make your gun visible from time to time, especially in situations where there are a lot of people around, to make the most impact. Ladies can take their guns out of their purses and put them on the counter when checking out. When that piece of steel hits the counter top, everyone around will know that this is someone you don't want to mess with.

"In addition to the visibility aspect, over 30 states have passed 'Stand Your Ground' laws, allowing people feeling threatened to brandish or even use their guns, in public, in cars, and at home. These laws vary from state to state so we urge you to become familiar with the laws in your state to see when you are within your rights to defend yourself."

"Thanks for those tips, Dwayne. I'll bear all this in mind the next time I have the urge to knock down an old lady." (Sean and Dwayne laugh.)

Vince was angry, upset and confused as he replayed the afternoon incident over and over in his mind. "If I had been carrying a gun, that wouldn't have happened, would it?" Or, "If it happened and I had a gun, would I have used it? Could I stand my ground?" Then he mentally re-enacted the scene where the guy knocked him down, but this time with him pulling out a gun and saying, "OK, asshole, so now how tough do you feel?"

Vince muted the TV. "I've had enough of this. And what kind of a name is Dwayne? 'What's your name? Duh … Wayne.' A million, armed senior citizens? God help us all!"

Trudi countered by saying that a number of her friends talk about incidents they have seen or experienced, and that some are even thinking about getting a gun.

"But that's crazy! A bunch of armed geriatrics who can't see or hold their hands steady?" It was almost as if Vince was arguing with himself.

Surprised by the intensity of Vince's reaction, Trudi asked, "Want some more wine?"

"Sure, just a bit," he said, as he switched to CNN with the remote.

Trudi poured the dark red wine. "But you know, if some tattooed skinhead asshole knocked me down, and then sneered at me, he'd have one more hole to sneer from if I had a gun."

Vince quickly looked at her to see if she knew what happened to him, "What? Where is that coming from?"

Trudi laughed. "Flashbacks from my sixties' Berkeley days, I guess. But I'm kidding. I don't want a gun." And then, laughing at the news anchor's name on the screen, added, "Well at least you found someone with a normal name: Wolf Blitzer!" (Both laughed.)

TV: "This just in from Arizona. As many as 12 residents at a Senior Citizen home outside of Tucson have been shot. Authorities are saying it was not an act of terrorism. I repeat, it was NOT an act of terrorism. Reports coming in say that an 89-year-old resident of the home wheeled himself into the dining room and just started shooting the other residents as they sat at their tables. The facility's armed security guard shot and killed the gunman. Details have not yet been released pending notification of next of kin. So far, there is no apparent motive. Four of the 12 shot are dead, and six are in critical condition. A spokesman for the NRA praised the security guard's action and pointed out that this validated the policy of deploying armed guards in schools and healthcare facilities.

"In other news, the President's relationship with Russia..."

Vince hit the mute button, "Twelve people? Must have had two guns or big clips. Sounds like a good shot though, getting 12."

"Are you praising him?"

"No, just thinking that he's 89 and did that. I don't even know how to load a gun, and I'm almost 20 years younger than he is."

"How hard can it be? You hear some of these good ol' boys talk and they don't sound like the brightest sparks, but they sure know how to handle a gun. Excuse me, I need to go to the bathroom."

Vince thought to himself, I know nothing about guns ... what kind of guns there are, what they cost, how to load them and how to shoot them. If I had a gun, would I have used it today? A million, armed seniors? Am I that far out of the loop?

Trudi returned. "Are you sleeping?"

"Not yet. I was just thinking that we seem to have fallen out of the loop, or at least I have. We watch the news most nights, but then I hear about a million seniors getting guns and it shocks me. We're seniors. Should we have guns?"

Trudi settled down on the couch, "Don't be ridiculous, Vince! I was just kidding about blowing away the skinhead. Really. Guns are not the answer to anything! And just because a lot of people are going along with something doesn't make it right."

"Well, that's true. I guess I just feel out of it. I'm not ready to get old but I'm afraid it might be too late."

"You're not old. 70 is the new 50, remember?"

"Yes, I do. Sometimes I forget how good a memory I have." Vince looked squarely at Trudi. He knew she loved him, even if a big piece of shit knocked him down in the parking lot. He also knew that she was concerned about him, about his anger and distance that night. And he knew that he loved her and that together, things were good. "Thanks for your patience tonight. I had a rough day. But I know that you're here for me and you make me happy."

"That's why you married me!"

"You got that right, Trudi James, although your dazzling smile and amazing voice helped."

"Let's go to bed while you're still thinking of me in the past ... as in way past!"

Vince laughed. "OK. Come on, Miles, let's get you outside for your evening business. See you in a minute, Hon."

* * *

San Diego, California. Stan Mason had just hung-up the phone with police in Tucson who had called him about his father. His mind was a sea of confusion with new questions popping up like popcorn in a microwave. "Why?" was the one that popped up over and over again. He had just spoken with his dad three days ago and all seemed good. Or was that what Stan wanted to hear? He said his health was good, but he always said that. Was he perhaps a bit more maudlin, morose, even fatalistic? He tried to remember the conversation but couldn't.

He didn't think his dad mentioned any issues with the Home or people there. Stan knew he wasn't happy at Green Valley, never had been, and hadn't made any friends there; but given his loss of mobility, there weren't any real alternatives. Stan's place was too small and, with the stairs, impossible for his father to navigate.

Stan scrolled back in his mind and being honest, his father had not been happy since his wife died – 53 – years together and then he was on his own. He'd had a successful career in banking, starting as a teller and rising to vice-president, but he had a difficult time adjusting to retirement. He didn't have any hobbies or special interests and the big change from being an important person in the organization to a "nobody" was hard. When his wife died, and along with her, the "honey-do" list, he felt completely irrelevant. As Stan thought about his father's mental state, suicide wouldn't have been so difficult to understand; but killing people?

And the guns! His dad had told him, about three weeks ago he thought, that the Home had planned a field trip to a nearby gun show because there was interest amongst the residents, in part, due to an NRA discount. But his father never mentioned it again. Then the police told him that his dad had two guns with extended magazines. That blew his mind. His dad had been in the Army but that was a long time ago. They never had guns while he was growing up. Ever. And the police report detailed that there was no apparent motive, pattern or specific targets. Just the closest and most accessible.

The police asked Stan if he could come to Green Valley and go through his father's possessions to help them find some possible trigger to the carnage. They would be interviewing witnesses and other residents in the meantime. Stan couldn't imagine what he'd find, but he knew he'd just acquired two guns, although the police told him that he couldn't take them just yet. And then his mind exploded again with questions, disbelief, and confusion.

* * *

CHAPTER 2 – THE NRA DISCOUNT

Pasadena, California. The next day, Vince woke up at 6:30 AM as he had done for the past 40 years. Old habits die hard and although he had retired over two years ago, he still woke up at the same time, with or without an alarm. Of course, he had some help from Miles, who was even better than an alarm clock. Wagging his stub of a tail, Miles led the way to the back door, his portal to the outdoors, waiting for Vince to assist him. Vince opened the door and mused again – for the thousandth time – if they should install a doggie-door; and then the thought immediately receded as a parade of past arguments against it began to swirl through his head.

Passing back through the house, he went to the front door and emerged into another cloudless California day, framed by the towering San Gabriel Mountains. His copy of The Los Angeles Times rested on the walk, protected from the mostly non- existent rain by its sheath of plastic film. As he now did each morning, he looked at the masthead to see what day of the week it was, since without the ritual of a Monday to Friday job, the days all seemed the same. Today, the Sunday paper's bulk was a giveaway.

He took in the headline, *"Ill-Prepared for Dangers Ahead,"* a story about migrants coming up from South America and trying to reach the United States. There was another front-page story about inner city gang shootings, and a couple more about politics. Not finding anything of immediate interest, he began to thumb through the paper, allowing the slowly rising sun to warm his back.

As Vince scanned the pages for anything of interest, he spotted an article in the USA NEWS section, reiterating last night's news:

"Arizona Retirement Home Shooting Claims 6 Lives.

Twelve people were shot, six have died and four others remain in critical condition as a result of a mass shooting yesterday at the Lazy Pines Retirement Home in Green Valley, Arizona, outside of Tucson. A police report stated that a lone gunman and resident of the Home, John Mason, 89 years old, opened fire in the dining room of the facility before he was shot dead by the Home's security guard. Mr. Mason had lived at Lazy Pines for five years. He had two guns with extended magazines and enough spares to hurt many more people. An investigation is ongoing and at this stage, a motive has not been established."

And Vince thought for the second time, "An 89-year-old gunman." That thought was interrupted by Miles' bark from the back yard ... time for Miles' breakfast and Vince's coffee.

* * *

Miles lay there licking his lips in a futile search for some remaining crumbs as Vince poured himself his first cup of the day. There would be two to three more as the day wore on ... another habit from his working days. And although she retired, along with Vince, Trudi appeared, right on cue in her robe and slippers, proving that her habits don't recognize Sundays, either.

"Hi honey. Did you sleep well?"

Giving her a kiss on the cheek, "Yes, how about you? Ready for a cup?"

"Yes, please!" Miles waddled over to her for his morning scratch between the ears. Seeing the paper on the table she asked, "Anything of interest today?"

"Not much. There was an article about that retirement home shooting we saw on TV last night. Six people killed. Four still in critical condition. Guy had two guns and was armed to the teeth with extended ammunition clips, so it's a good thing the guard got him when he did. An 89-year-old mass killer!" He handed her a cup of the strong coffee, laced with a squeeze of agave.

"Thanks. Did they say what prompted him? Was he crazy?"

"No. Not much more than what we heard last night, but it sure seems like something snapped. I was wondering if he had two guns because he got the NRA Senior Discount," he said, smiling.

"Vince. That's not funny. Six people, like us, died."

"Sorry. There was an article about a gang shooting and my imagination shifted into high gear. Imagine rival gangs of senior citizens shooting each other with their senior-discounted guns for the best tables at the early-bird specials."

Trudi had to smile as she shared that thought and added, "Maybe as members of the notorious Gray Panthers ... or new splinter groups, like the Gray Jets or Gray Sharks."

"You're showing your age there. Actually, the Gray Whales might be more appropriate."

"Now that's really not politically correct!" But she laughed just the same.

After breakfast, Trudi ran out to the store to pick up a couple of things for their Sunday lunch. Vince finished the paper and noticed a copy of the AARP magazine, "Real Possibilities," lying on the coffee table. He'd glanced at the occasional copy, but for some reason, he never enjoyed it. Perhaps it was too much like proof that he was a real senior citizen; and the fact that virtually all the people featured in it looked far better than he did, even when they were far older: Warren Beatty, James Taylor, Mick Jagger. Well, Jagger didn't look better. But he was loaded and still enjoyed a high-octane life. The parking lot incident returned, and he tried to ignore it.

Turning the pages and scanning the advertisements – mostly for stair-lifts, walk-in bathtubs, hearing aids, life alert devices, drugs, phones with large number keys, and life insurance – didn't cheer him up either. And there it was, the NRA advertisement:

"It's Not Too Late To Protect Yourself And Your Loved Ones.
"You haven't worked your entire life to suffer injuries or death by predators who see you as an easy target. Even more horrific is the possibility that someone might harm your spouse,

children and grandchildren while you stand by helplessly, unable to defend them.

"At the NRA, our motto is 'Never fight if you can avoid it, but when you must fight, don't lose!'

"The NRA is on your side and we are offering AARP members a discount on the purchase of qualified guns along with an NRA discounted membership, so you can support the fight for Freedom and your 2nd Amendment Rights."

Vince was still processing the ad when he heard Trudi return. "Need any help with the groceries, honey?"

"No thanks. Just this one bag. What have you been doing?"

"Not much. Just reading the paper," Vince said, putting down the magazine.

"Find anything else of interest?"

"Not really." For some reason, he didn't want to mention the NRA senior ad. There was something about the concept that both thrilled and scared him. Appealing and abhorrent at the same time, and he couldn't let go of it.

Vince recalled his thoughts of last night. He didn't know a thing about guns. The only guns he'd ever fired, even held, were those pellet guns at carnivals, knocking down swimming ducks … or trying to. He remembered that he wasn't very good at it. Perhaps it was this knowledge gap and his natural curiosity that drove the intrigue. He knew generally that there were rifles and handguns, but that was about it. How much did they cost? What were the different types? Could he even have one in California? And if he had one, would he, could he, have used it yesterday?

It was this association of questions that made Vince realize, once again, that since his retirement, his access to information was limited to what the TV or LA Times chose to share with him. There was no coffee break banter to catch up on hot topics or ask questions in a relatively safe environment. Trudi was actually better-connected through her frequent get-togethers with her friends, but even that was limited. He received so few emails now that he rarely fired up his old laptop, and simply used his iPhone. He couldn't even remember the last time he used his laptop after giving back the company-issued one. His PC was so slow. He thought of his son's amazement and disbelief when he discovered that they hardly ever used it. "Dad, you've been using a computer at work since I was born. Why don't you use it now? We could chat, FaceTime or Skype, and use Facebook."

"Vince? HELLO!" Trudi appealed in a louder than usual voice. "What planet are you on?"

Vince jumped. "Sorry. Yes, off in space. I was just thinking about computers and how a new one might improve our lives and connectivity. We could do Facebook with Dave and Barb and at least see pictures of Caleb."

Caleb was their 5-year-old grandson and Barb and Dave were their daughter-in-law and son. Barb was a school administrator and Dave a teacher in Austin, Texas, so they didn't see as much of them as Vince and Trudi would have liked.

Trudi asked, "That sounds like a good idea. Why do we need a new one? Doesn't our old laptop work?"

"It works, or probably does, but it's so old, doesn't have much memory, and can't handle a lot of the newer technology."

"Sounds like us!" she quipped. And they both laughed.

But Trudi, putting some groceries away, continued. "What made you think about Dave, Barb and Facebook?"

"I don't know. Just thinking about them and as busy as they are, I hate to bother them with calls." Vince drained his now cold coffee, bringing the cup to the sink. "Just a way to keep in touch, casually. It was Dave's idea." Vince felt vaguely guilty and transparent using their son as a pretense for getting a new computer, but there was an element of truth about keeping in touch.

Folding the now empty bag and putting it near the back door, Trudi said, "OK. I have to go into town tomorrow and there's an Apple store right next to Payless Shoes, where I'm going. We can go together."

"I hadn't thought about a Mac. Am I too old to start all over?"

Trudi scoffed. "Too old? Remember, 70 is the new 50. And you were a computer wizard at work. They can't be that different. Even I know that they can connect with each other."

"And how do you know that, Ms. Gates?" he smiled.

Trudi, hands on hips, "C'mon, Vince. Seriously. Everyone I've ever known who has switched to a Mac loves it."

Vince chuckled. "Sure, I'll come along and look at the Macs. I have to admit, I'm intrigued by their reputation and loyal following."

"Great. Let me get going on fixing lunch." Trudi was the main cook in the house, but Vince served as sous-chef and chief bottle washer. He also had a number of specialties that he liked to try out on Trudi. She appreciated the effort and even if some of his experiments didn't succeed, she kept her mouth shut and said, "Yummm." She wasn't about to look a gift horse in the mouth.

Vince smiled, "OK. And I'll get dressed."

* * *

Green Valley, Arizona. Stan Mason had been going through his father's sparse collection of possessions at the Lazy Pines Home apartment. As the police had already advised him, the guns weren't there; they would be held until all forensic tests had been completed. There was, however, a copy of the receipt for the guns, clips and ammunition from the Crosshairs Gun Show in Tucson: Two used Glock-19, 9mm handguns with ten-round clips (one at $350 and the other at $300). Two fifteen-round 9mm clips. One box of fifty 9mm shells. An NRA Senior Citizen discount of 20% had been applied to the guns.

Even if someone had been there for him to talk with, he'd be speechless. The same disbelief and confusion he'd gone through when he first received the phone call from the police flooded his brain. Why two guns? Why one gun? And why extra clips? Coupled with the fact that these all played a role in a heinous mass killing, 17 days after he purchased them, made it more than a coincidence.

His thoughts were interrupted by a loud knock at the door. Thankful for even the smallest diversion from the dark thoughts bouncing around his head, he opened the door to a waiting Inspector Zack Dallas from Tucson Homicide.

"Stan Mason?"

"Yes," he said almost happily because it was one thing he was sure of. Actually, it was the only thing he was sure of at the moment, as he looked at the tall, well-built, African-American man.

"Inspector Dallas from Tucson Homicide. Thanks for making the trek to Green Valley and talking with me."

"Of course." Stan realized that this was the first time he had ever spoken with someone from the police. Stan, being white, thought about the large number of recent news articles about police killings, usually white police and black men, making him a bit uncomfortable; but Inspector Dallas had a calm and almost friendly demeanor, helping to put Stan at ease.

"Have you found anything of interest or out of the ordinary?" Inspector Dallas asked. He had a soothing, almost Morgan Freeman kind of voice.

"I'm still in shock looking at the receipt for the guns. Dad told me he was going to a gun show, but I thought it was just to have something to do. He never had anything to do with guns when I was growing up. He was in the Army but that was before I was born, and he never talked about it."

Inspector Dallas jotted a note on a small notepad. "Did he ever say anything about anyone here?"

"Not really. Nothing specific. I know he wasn't happy here and he hadn't made any friends, but he didn't think anyone else was happy here either. That all of them were sent here to die."

Inspector Dallas jotted another note and added, "The staff and residents have all said that he was a loner and didn't have friends. Nobody really knew him. They would only see him for meals. Seems like he ate alone, although some people tried to engage with him. He pushed them away and refused to join in."

Stan asked, "Did you find out anything that might help explain what triggered this?"

"Nothing whatsoever. We were hoping you knew something. The only aspect of this case that has any degree of logic is the timing of the gun purchase and the shooting. Do you think there could be a link?"

"I don't know. I've been wondering, did he want to buy a gun with a thought in mind or did something happen after he purchased the guns?"

"That's a good question. You're sure there's nothing he said the last time you spoke?"

"There was nothing. But maybe I wasn't listening as well as I should," Stan said guiltily. There were many times when he spoke with his father that his mind drifted, especially when his father complained. Pangs of regret welled up.

"And is there anything else in his possessions that surprised you or was unexpected?"

"An iPhone and a sport watch. I'm surprised my dad would have an iPhone, but a sport watch for someone in a wheelchair seems really odd ... "

Inspector Dallas jotted again and said, "We looked at the phone, but it doesn't seem like there were any calls except for that one from you. Email hadn't even been set up."

"No. My dad wasn't a techie. So, what's next, Inspector?"

"As far as we're concerned, it's an open and shut case. More than a dozen witnesses identified your father as the lone shooter and the guns were his. We don't have a motive, but we really don't need one to close the file. So, you're free to take or dispose of his possessions. Here's a Tucson Police receipt for the guns. We'll let you know when we can release them."

"I don't want them. What can I do with them?"

"You live in California. Hmm. Not sure about the legality of these or if you can sell them there. Think about what you want to do with them – you know, sell them or keep them – and in the meantime, I'll ask around the department and see if anyone might be interested. Your dad got them for a good price, so unless you want to make profit, they're a bargain at what he paid."

"So, I'm not liable for anything – you know, for the people who were killed? I mean, I've never felt so awful in my whole life."

"Unless you were legally your father's guardian, I don't think you can be held responsible. If anyone other than your father is responsible, it would be Lazy Pines and perhaps the people who sold the guns to your father."

"Hmm. OK. Thanks, Inspector."

"Here's my card and direct line. Thank you and please get in touch if you think of anything else. I'm really sorry, Mr. Mason. And if we find out anything else, we'll be sure to let you know."

* * *

CHAPTER 3 – INTO THE UNKNOWN

Pasadena, California. Vince was actually pretty jazzed about seeing the Apple store. For years he had heard about Apple and its loyal legions of followers. He always had the feeling that Mac users looked down a bit at people who used Windows … like they used tin cans and strings or calculators. Well, he was about to find out what, if anything, was behind the smugness.

Wishing Trudi luck with her shoe shopping, he split off and entered the Apple store. Despite the early hour, it was already pretty busy. He was met by a techie-looking greeter armed with an iPad and headset, who asked him the reason for his visit.

"I'm looking for a new computer," Vince replied, trying to sound confident but not too interested.

"OK. Desktop or laptop?"

"Laptop."

"What's your name?"

"Vince Fuller."

"OK, Vince. Shouldn't be long. The laptops are over here. Have a browse and there's also a video showing the various models and their features. We'll have someone with you in a moment."

"Thanks." Vince went to one of the tables with laptops and began looking them over.

Within an hour, a rather surprised Vince walked out carrying a large plastic Apple bag containing a brand-new MacBook Pro. If you'd asked him before going in, he would have told you there wasn't a chance he would switch to a Mac after all these years in Microsoft's clutches; but Kevin, the young guy helping him, made it seem so simple and convinced Vince to opt for the Microsoft Office for Mac package, as he was used to the Microsoft software. Vince did resist the suggestion to upgrade his iPhone, proving to himself, if no one else, that he wasn't a pushover.

Checking in on Trudi at the shoe store, Vince found her still trying on different pairs, so they agreed to meet at Starbucks, a few stores down the street. As he walked through Starbucks to the counter, carrying the familiar plastic Apple logo'd bag, Vince thought he caught a few looks of approval from the mostly younger crowd, typing away at their mostly Apple keyboards.

After ordering and receiving his coffee – a tall, dark roast – Vince found an open table. Proudly unpacking his new laptop, he thought about his experience at Apple. How did he buy that laptop so easily? Was Kevin a great salesman? He did explain things well and asked questions and wasn't at all smug when Vince told him about his singular Windows' experience. That was part of it. Kevin wasn't at all disdainful of Vince's age and lack of knowledge, as evidenced by Vince's questions. He had sometimes felt a dismissive attitude in a lot of other younger people he dealt with and he had to admit, it was hurtful and added to the burden of growing old. Irrelevance was painful. Not physically, as in his parking lot experience, but hurtful, nonetheless.

Vince's laptop started up as quickly for him as it had for Kevin. He now had an icloud.com email address, but nobody except him and Apple knew that, and he was more interested in surfing than corresponding. So, he postponed the uncertain task of setting up his current g-mail account on his Mac. Besides, since he retired, he rarely got anything other than political mail, begging for money. Clicking on Safari, Vince stepped into the unknown; and as the internet can do, he began to realize, more than ever, how much he didn't know and how much he'd like to know. At the moment, the most burning questions on his mind stemmed from his conversation with Trudi ... about guns.

Vince typed in, "What is the cost range of a handgun?" Almost instantly, the screen blinked, and he was looking at a screen showing the first dozen or so of "About 674,000 results (.84 seconds)." He paused to think about what just happened. He had used the internet at work, but it was generally for very specific searches, like typing in a known company's website address. He had never really done broad searches, or surfed, as they called it. There was a site called Cabelas that looked hopeful, and it was – listing 113 handguns ranging from $169.99 to $4,499.88. He doubted many seniors bought $5,000 guns, even with a discount, but how prevalent was senior citizen gun ownership? He typed into the Safari search box, "How many people over 65 have a gun?" and was rewarded with "About 179 million results (.55 seconds)." He clicked on the first listing, *"Gun Ownership and The Elderly: People Over 65 Have Highest Rates Of Ownership And Dementia,"* published in Medical Daily.com. I wonder if defense lawyers have used this, he mused: "My client doesn't remember killing him." Maybe that guy in Arizona had dementia and wouldn't remember killing those six people? We'll never know.

Vince began reading the article. "What many people do not know is that people over the age of 65 have the highest rate of firearm ownership in the nation … yet they also have a high prevalence of dementia, depression, and suicide, as well. Clearly, on the wrong day, this combination of odd factors could potentially lead to a lethal situation and for this reason, gun safety among the elderly is a pressing, if unnoticed, issue."

Surely, that is a possibility in the retirement home shooting, Vince thought, thinking at the same time that the NRA was hoping it stayed unnoticed.

"I see you've fitted into the coffeehouse scene quickly. Sipping lattes and surfing on your Apple," said Trudi, as she dropped a couple of large bags onto the floor next to Vince's table.

"Hi. And it looks like you were successful after all," Vince replied, closing his laptop.

"Yes. And I found some new trainers to replace my aging Nikes."

"Good. Do you want a coffee or would you rather go home?"

"A coffee would be nice. Thanks."

Vince returned with her coffee, "Here ya go."

"Thank you, sir," Trudi replied formally. "So, are you having fun with your new toy?"

"I am. It's very easy to use and very fast. No time to lose your train of thought like I did with the old laptop, while it ground away with its processing."

"What have you been surfing, and please don't tell me porn?"

Vince laughed. "Not yet! But I did learn that people over the age of 65 have the most guns … and dementia. So that guy's comments on TV about older people buying guns seem to be accurate."

"Still, that's surprising. Not the dementia part."

"I was wondering if that guy who killed those people in Arizona might have had dementia. The article I read mentioned depression and suicide, as well."

"Could be, but it seems like shooters never just get wounded, so we can't find out what they were thinking."

* * *

That evening Vince and Trudi sat down with the laptop and Vince showed Trudi the speed of surfing with their new machine. She took to it like a duck to water and loved it. The world was at her agile fingertips.

Their first "just out of curiosity" search – for shootings by senior citizens – didn't yield much fruit, but they learned a lot about guns:

Over 13,000 people had been killed in the United States during the past year in gun homicides and unintentional shootings, excluding suicides.

36 Americans were killed each day by gunshots, excluding suicides.

Over 50,000 gun incidents were reported last year.

There were 20,000 suicides with guns last year.

Over the past 10 years, 71 Americans have been killed by terrorism versus 302,000 by gun violence.

And the trend was definitely upwards.

"We really are out of touch," said Vince, shaking his head. "Do we even know anyone who has been shot, or know anyone who knows someone who has?"

"I don't."

"Do any of your friends have guns?" Vince asked.

"Not that I know of. The Martins might. But he hunts, doesn't he?"

"I think so. And Rueben Martinez is an ex-cop. He probably has a gun."

"You're not really thinking we should get a gun?"

"I don't know. For protection, maybe. In case someone tries to burgle our house and we're here." He briefly thought about the guy in the parking lot.

Trudi scoffed. "And what, shoot them? We'd have to be pretty lucky for that to happen."

"Pretty lucky to have burglars?"

"No. Be in a lucky situation where they didn't have a gun and we had a real easy shot. Even then, I'm not sure you can just shoot someone if they're not armed."

"Well, let's see," said Vince. "Type in, 'Can we shoot an intruder in our own home in California?' "

And sure enough, in 1.24 seconds, Trudi had 1,620,000 results. "Here it is. California law protects us if we shoot a burglar in our home. Still, it wouldn't help if we didn't hear them until they burst into the room. I can't see either one of us having the presence of mind to reach for the gun, roll out of bed and blast away. What are you smiling at?"

"At the image of you doing just that!"

"Hey. I've been watching Angelina Jolie and I think I can manage the moves."

"Enough about guns for today. Let's go watch the news and see what my bearded buddy, Blitzer, has for us."

"OK, as long as it's not another shooting!"

CHAPTER 4 - VITALTECH

Quincy, Massachusetts. Vijay Patel was one of those people who might be described by others as someone whose brain was too big for their head. He came to the USA from Mumbai, India, to study advanced mathematics at MIT. As he was completing his PhD in Spectral Graph Theory, Numerical Linear Algebra and Machine Learning, he became interested in medicine and enrolled at Harvard Medical School. Upon graduation, "Dr. Dr. Patel," as he could legitimately be called, entered the field of Internal Medicine. And for most people, that would be more than enough.

But Vijay was also an athlete, regularly qualifying and running in the Boston Marathon with times that placed him amongst the top 15% of finishers. He might have been even better except for the fact that there are only 24 hours in a day, and even Vijay hadn't been able to alter that formula, having already reduced his 'borderline minimum' of required sleep.

Possessing a strong techie streak along with his fiercely competitive nature, he was on a constant search for training aids and devices that would help him improve his fitness and athletic performance. This search, combined with his background in mathematics and medicine, led him into the research and development of a new monitoring device that would do much more than the current generation of "sport watches." And now he was on the cusp of something very big.

Initially, Vijay and a small team had developed a new proprietary form of non-invasive optical blood measurement and analysis which went far beyond any current devices available – measuring and analyzing hemoglobin, pulse- rate, oximetry, and other chemical concentrations. In layman's terms, he had developed a sports watch that could measure, analyze, diagnose and even predict complex health issues. The commercial value of his creation was potentially enormous, and he was now being guided, behind the scenes, by one of the top underwriting companies and one of the top private equity companies in the world, on a path that was expected to lead to one of the largest IPOs in recent years.

Technically, the device was a dream. Accurate, consistent, easy to use and understand, and relatively easy and inexpensive to manufacture. It was so far ahead of anything else available that the biggest questions were centered on marketing, pricing and the rollout of upgrades and new features. Their private equity backer had assembled a team of top technology marketers with deep experience in companies such as Apple, Samsung, Fitbit and others, along with clinical advisors from some of the foremost medical centers in the country. And the legal considerations, given the clinical capability and features of the device, had required a large team of lawyers. Vijay had managed to develop the prototype at a modest cost, which he funded himself. But when he realized the enormous amount of work (and millions of dollars in costs) required to actually launch a product of this type – even before production and promotion – he knew that he would need outside assistance. The thought pained him, as that also meant losing some control, but he didn't fully realize how much of an understatement that was.

Based on a number of focus groups and research, the team wanted to include as many features as possible to price the device at a significant premium while attracting optimum demand. But throwing too much in at the start might complicate the offering. On one hand, saving features for subsequent roll-outs offered the possibility of upgrade pricing. On the other hand, it also increased the potential for competing products. As smart and educated as Vijay was, this was a very different world for him.

One area of fierce debate amongst the disparate team members was the initial inclusion of a revolutionary and controversial capability: that of predicting death, based on the highly sophisticated monitoring, analysis and diagnostic capability of the device. Infinitesimally small changes and trends detected in the blood were instantly analyzed, and when the analysis showed an irreversible trend, a "Final Notice" could be issued, advising the user of certain death within a 'user selected' number of days. The marketers seized upon this capability, actually a by-product of the device's processing ability, as a powerful feature. The arguments centered on whether or not to include it and, if included, how much advance time – in days or weeks – should the Final Notice provide. Longer periods would have less accuracy, but shorter periods contained more shock value and would not afford the user time to get his or her affairs in order. In fact, a complementary add-on product was being discussed that would catalog, notify and even execute orders to help next of kin cope. Users could program their watch to ready and update any requests or required actions as soon as they received their Final Notice; and the device would put everything into motion when it determined that death had occurred.

The clinical and legal advisors were much more reluctant to include the Final Notice option, but the marketers cited the very high desirability aspect, as demonstrated in the focus groups. The focus group findings were so enthusiastic and the process so thorough, that the clinicians' and lawyers' arguments were difficult to sustain. Vijay was torn between the two arguments but Konig, Konig & Litt, their private equity backer, believed that its inclusion created a huge advantage over other similar products; and given the sheer market size in the USA alone, this would be a blockbuster launch. The money spoke, and it was decided to include the Final Notice option.

The team had decided to go with an older age, alpha test group on the basis that they would have more medical issues, therefore testing the product's capability more comprehensively. A secondary consideration was that the older group would be less tech-savvy, therefore better testing the watch's user interface and friendliness. The range of the Final Notice feature could be set between 1-30 days, but it was decided, for simplicity and better comparison, to 'hard set' the alpha test Notice periods to one week. An earlier prototype, called the VT1, incorporated an emergency Notice that would alert users to call 911 as soon as possible in the event of an urgent life-threatening physiological event. The new model had the capability to automatically call 911 and others if authorized by the user, such as children and close relatives. That would enable faster first responder attendance as the cell phone's location could be easily traced. Because of concerns for potential bugs and mistakes, however, the automatic 911 call was not activated on the alpha test users' devices.

One hundred participants between the ages of 65 and 90 were chosen from around the country, with the help of clinical team members interacting with cooperating physicians. None of the participants had been diagnosed with terminal diseases or clinical depression, and all were in relatively good health, given their ages. Although it was never cited as a reason for the high age upper limit, most of the team hoped that the Final Notice feature would be tested. They were sensitive, however, not to seem too enthusiastic in that hope when explaining the 90-year upper age limit.

In the meantime, production plans and supply-chain elements were developed and a manufacturing/assembling facility in India was selected, due to Vijay's insistence. Preliminary marketing material, packaging and customer service plans were also created. In addition to field-testing, ongoing market research was being carried out to help peg the base price level of the device, to be known as the VitalTech2 or VT2, the flagship and launch product of VitalTech Industries. Assuming a good result from the alpha testing and high margin potential based on market research, the underwriters, Credit Suisse, would begin to execute and hype the blockbuster IPO.

* * *

J. Edward Konig was a self-made man, if you discounted his privileged start in life. The only son of a New York banking titan, J. Edward, or Mr. Konig, as he preferred to be called – the 'J' had supplanted his first name Jacobson, which came from an old ancestor whom no one could quite remember – had attended New York City's best schools. He fit in well with his classmates, whose parents included movers and shakers from around the world: businessmen, politicians, athletes, entertainers, and plain "old money."

He graduated from Harvard Law School, although not with academic distinction, followed by a stint at arguably the top New York corporate law firm of Pearson, Spector & Litt. Although his intellect and knowledge of corporate law was acknowledged, he had a reputation for cutting corners and turning a blind eye from time to time. He was also lazy and resented the hours he needed to work in order to move up through the ranks. And so, after three years, he launched the private equity firm of KKL, Konig, Konig & Litt, having enticed his former Harvard classmate Lawrence Litt, son of Louis Litt (senior partner at Pearson, Spector & Litt), to join him. The other Konig was simply his name again, which he explained as an effort to make the firm sound larger and more substantial. The truth is, it was his ego ... and his need to make sure Lawrence knew that he was actually not second in command.

Thanks to J. Edward's father's deep connections in the financial world, KKL was able to build a significant fund to rocket to the top of the PE world. They became the rock stars of private equity at a very propitious time in the economic cycle. They had backed a couple of billion-dollar-plus social media start-ups; and the profits from the IPO made J. Edward's titan father's efforts look paltry by comparison. As luck would have it, the VitalTech launch fell into his lap via a new employee, Jennifer Andrews.

Jennifer had joined KKL when both J. Edward and Lawrence realized that they would have to get off their butts and hustle business. This recognition, however, didn't make them get off their butts and hustle. Instead, they decided to hire a business development executive. The executive search firm put together a very short list (at KKL's request – they wanted to keep it simple) of qualified candidates. As seemed to be typical for the KKL principals, their luck continued when they hired the first candidate presented. Why bother to waste time when she seemed to fit the bill? Jennifer was smart, independent, a problem solver, highly organized, personable, high-energy, had financial know-how and possessed an ability for process-oriented thinking. That was what the search firm summary said, but J. Edward and Lawrence, coming from an antiquated, somewhat primitive mindset, looked no further than the photo and thought ... "She's drop-dead gorgeous."

Jennifer Andrews had attended Stanford for her undergraduate degree in finance and Harvard for an MBA. She had been drawn to the excitement of the PE industry and had been a serious rainmaker at two smaller PE firms. Now she wanted to compete at the top. She quickly realized that finding mega-deals would be a lot harder than hooking the big and medium-size ones she had previously brought in for her other firms. However, J. Edward and Lawrence did have a significant contact base that she was able to loosen from the recesses of their memories and, armed with their endorsement, she set out to shake the branches.

At Stanford, she had been a very competent athlete, setting a number of distance records for the Cardinal Track & Field team, and almost qualifying for the US Olympic team. Since leaving school, she had found the time to train and perform well at marathons and other distance races around the country, and it was at the Boston Marathon that she had met Vijay Patel.

In their own ways, they both stood out in crowds. Vijay was very tall and well-muscled, like a lithe wide receiver, with a full head of rich dark hair, honey-hued skin, deep dark eyes, and a smile that would make an orthodontist proud, had there been one. Think tall, dark and handsome. Jennifer was his blond, light-eyed counterpart: tall and extremely fit, along with a matching – although in her case, orthodontist-assisted – smile. Think California girl, plus the powerful intellect that shone from her earnest grey eyes.

Their after-race encounter had led to conversation and dinner, which they wisely postponed until the following day. (Even well-conditioned athletes sleep early and well after a two- to three-hour competitive run.) During dinner, Vijay led the way with personal history discovery, and when he heard that Jennifer was with a private equity firm, he almost believed that the gods, all 33 of them, had conspired to bring the two of them together. As he explained what he and his team had been working on, it wasn't her finely honed business development instincts but her sincere interest in the product that grabbed his attention. Vijay didn't even realize that KKL was the hottest PE firm in the country at the moment. All he cared about that evening was that this might in some way bind him and this amazing young woman together. He needn't have worried.

***

CHAPTER 5 – LOGICAL OUTCOME

Boynton Beach, Florida. It was another hot and humid day in Florida, but Earl Hoover was used to it. He'd lived in the area for over 30 years, moving here right after his discharge from the Army when the Vietnam War ended, at least for the United States and Earl. And today was just another day, just as it had been for 30 years. Another day. One at a time, all blurred together into one 30-year day.

It was his birthday and he sat there reflecting on his life. He grew up in the southwest area of Miami, which was little more than miles and miles of flat sandy soil and scrub brush, with straight grid-style roads, many simply constructed of crushed coral rock. Life was simple in those days. You'd call it very low-tech now. Some kids had bikes and at 14 you could drive a motor scooter, and even a car if you had a 16-year-old in the front seat. He smiled, thinking about the lack of wisdom in that rule, as he recalled his 16-year-old friends egging him on to go faster and faster.

Back in those days it was easy to get beer, either with a fake ID or getting an older guy (black guys were the nicest) to buy you a six-pack. Everyone had a fake ID thanks to Georgia. At their Department of Motor Vehicles offices there were stacks of blank licenses. You actually filled them out by hand, and when you passed the driving test and were processed, they put a big embossed stamp on the card. Nobody using them as fake IDs ever got to the last two steps. You simply cut off the bottom of the card with the all capital letters stating, "NOT VALID WITHOUT AN OFFICAL SEAL." The staff at liquor stores in Florida didn't have Georgia driving licenses, not that they even cared. You might get the wry smile when, as a 14-year-old, you presented your license showing your age as 21, but that was all. They didn't care.

The combination of drinking and driving at a young age did not, however, appear to create safety issues. With low traffic levels and almost entirely straight roads in southwest Miami, there were very few incidents, and only scratches and small dents when they occurred. Safety with sex was another story. A number of girls at Earl's high school and even junior high left school mysteriously after they started to gain weight. And the father of one of his friends was widely, but quietly, known as an abortion specialist.

High school was probably the high point of Earl's life. There was a lot of freedom for kids in those days, and Earl was even freer as his parents weren't really in the game. His dad was usually drunk when he was home, and, in hindsight, Earl realized that his mom was probably depressed for most of his growing-up years. She committed suicide when Earl was in Nam. His Sergeant asked if he wanted to go home for the funeral, but he declined. He hadn't stayed in touch and didn't even know if his father was alive or not. And he really didn't care.

High school was all about girls and sports, especially football. Florida may not have taken their high school football to Texas' Friday Night Lights level, but it was important, and almost necessary, if you wanted to get laid. He'd had a few girlfriends, but they didn't last long. Dates usually involved parties and parties involved drinking and for Earl, that meant drinking too much and then saying or doing the wrong thing. Still, there were lots of girls around and he was a solid member of the football team. It was also the last time he was somebody. Upon joining the Army, right after graduation, he became a number, and ever since, he'd been one more statistic.

He was one of the lucky ones, however, as he was assigned to the Motorized Infantry, giving him practical experience – teaching him to drive and maintain a wide range of trucks and vehicles. As an American GI, he was never short of female companionship during his leaves as long as he had a few dollars to spend. It was probably the second-best time of his life. Structured, very little decision making, food and shelter. Earl actually enjoyed it.

After his discharge, Earl was easily able to get jobs – some long term and many short term – driving everything from auto haulers, boat haulers, dry vans, flat beds, reefers and tankers. He did local, regional and even interstate hauls. Those were his favorites as he got to see a lot of the country, at least along the highways. He enjoyed the ephemeral camaraderie of his fellow truckers, even if it was only for a quick bite and longer beers. Rarely did he see anyone twice.

Earl could never seem to accumulate enough money to get his own rig, and more often than not, he bounced from job to job, haul to haul. He never married and his friends, if you could call them that, were the regulars in the few down market bars in his neighborhood who knew each other's first names, or at least the names they went by. His current month-to-month apartment was sparse and devoid of any personal touches. It looked more like a cheap motel room.

A month ago, he had experienced severe stomach pain, bad enough that he drove himself to the emergency room of the closest hospital. He had to wait a long time and they wouldn't give him anything for the pain because they didn't want to mask the issue. That was easy for them to say because they weren't having the excruciating pain. When he was finally seen, the doctor couldn't find a cause and they gave him a stomach relaxant. Another doctor then called him into an office, asked him a few questions and then asked if he'd be interested in taking part in testing a new product. He would be one of a small group of people using a watch-like device that would analyze his vital signs. The doctor explained that he was being invited, not solely because of the stomach issue – it might help identify the cause if it reappeared – but also because he fit the demographic for the test group. He would need to answer some questions from the manufacturer from time to time and he would receive a small fee for his time.

Earl was still not sure why he said yes. Perhaps it was the money, but perhaps it was because he was being included in a small group, made to feel special and belonging to something. The requirements had been simple, and they gave him a watch, although it did a lot of things that Earl didn't understand. They also gave him a pay-as-you-go smartphone. It had been a while since he'd had a cell phone. After he turned 65, his Social Security pension and Veteran's Benefit were enough to live on if he watched his spending, and a few extra beers were more important than a big cell phone bill, especially since he rarely used it. The doctor helped him set up the VT2 App which would capture the watch readings and transmit data to the manufacturer. Earl asked Sally Ann, the apartment complex manager, to help him set up the internet connection.

Sally Ann and Earl got along well, even very well from time to time, although she didn't want anyone to know it. It suited him just fine. He didn't need a social entanglement, just sex, and he was pretty sure Sally Ann felt the same way. Lately, though, he didn't feel like either. His stomach pain re-occurred a few times, even worse than before, but the doctor had prescribed a number of the relaxant pills on the initial visit and he never used them all, so he coped without needing to go back to the ER.

As he sat there on his 66th birthday, Earl felt his watch buzz. He looked at the message scrolling across the watch screen: "This is your FINAL NOTICE. You have 1 week. Call your doctor." If you had asked Earl, he wouldn't be able to tell you his exact feelings at that point. Was it fear? Loss? Relief? He remembered talking with a woman from VT2 that if this notice appeared, he should call his doctor to see if help was available as his final days passed. At about the same time, Earl's stomach began contracting and the pain was far worse than ever. He grabbed the pill bottle and swallowed the remaining two. He then took a beer from the fridge, even if it was before noon, and chugged it as best he could with the pain raging.

He sat there breathing deeply as the pills began their magic. Another beer was opened and downed. Earl went into the bedroom and removed his pistol from the bedside table drawer. It was one of his few possessions, a souvenir from Nam that he had purchased during one of Saigon's calmer days, a MAC Mle1950 pistol that had been used by the French Army when they took their beating from the Cong. He shot it on rare occasions and it was well taken care of, as he had few other things to look after. He carried the gun out to the kitchen, downed his last beer. He switched off the safety, put the barrel in his mouth and ended what was left of his life.

It was three days later before Sally Ann used her master key to check on Earl after she repeatedly got no response to her knocks. She found him slumped over a kitchen table covered in dry, almost blackish blood. She was sorry, but not surprised. She liked Earl. Liked him a lot, but he would never let her get close. Or was that her? They were like two magnets that could attract and repel, depending on the alignment. When the police asked her if she had any thoughts about why he did it, she simply said, "It was the logical outcome."

The police left with the gun, VT2 watch and smart phone, which, other than Earl's very small collection of clothes, represented all of his possessions.

* * *

Pasadena, California. Vince was surfing, looking for geriatric hit men, when he came across the following article, headlined: **"85-Year Old Man Kills Store Cashier."** He read on. *"An 85-year old man shot and killed a 25-year old cashier at a local store in Joplin, Missouri on Saturday. Witnesses said the man walked into the store, shot the cashier, and walked out. It did not appear to be a robbery nor was there any altercation between the man, identified as Quentin Moore, and the cashier, Stephen Kinsead."*

"According to a Joplin Police spokesperson, although Moore left the store, a witness identified him and police were dispatched to his home. He was found dead. The family doctor, called to the home, said it appeared to be from natural causes, possibly a heart attack. The weapon was found and it was matched to the fatal shooting.

"Sharon Moore, the suspect's wife, said that her husband had been looking at his smartphone and then suddenly said, 'I need to go out for a little while.' He seemed upset. When he returned, he went straight to their bedroom saying that he needed to lie down.

"Police are questioning witnesses, looking for a possible motive."

"Trudi, come read this article."

"What is it?"

"Read it. 85-year old man kills store cashier." Vince turned the laptop around.

Trudi sat down, adjusted her glasses and read the article. When she finished, she sat there silently, thoughts swirling through her head.

Impatiently, Vince asked, "Well, what do you think?"

"I feel overwhelmed, like I'm on the inside of something that nobody is getting. First the talk amongst my friends about getting guns. Then that man in Arizona, and now this?"

"It's probably just coincidence. There are just these two incidents."

"You're probably right, but when I read that article, a strange feeling came over me like I knew something. An intuition."

"I'll do some more surfing today and see if I can find anything. Any more incidents."

"Good idea, but we need to set up a schedule, so I get some surf time."

"Seriously? But remember, I can search your browsing history to see if you're looking up porn."

"I don't need porn. I get together with my friends all the time for some great Chippendale parties!" Trudi parried playfully.

Vince stood up abruptly, "I'm outta here. I'll take Miles for a walk to try and clear my head of that vision!"

"Even if it were true, what would be wrong with that?"

"What if I stop off at that adult bar in Sepulveda with the all-college-girl lap dancers?"

"They really have that? College girl lap-dancers? I wonder if they get a scholarship or something?"

"I think the 'or something' is a job as a lap dancer."

They both laughed, and Trudi said, "Have a nice walk and Miles, you keep your Daddy out of trouble." Miles stayed neutral and refused to comment.

"Thanks. The Mac is all yours!"

FBI Headquarters, Washington, DC. Adam Winters was an analyst with the Violent Crime section of the FBI. Guns played a big role in violent crime and one of Adam's tasks was to try to keep the FBI ahead of issues, rather than simply tracking down suspects after a crime had been committed. Two items recently flagged his attention in his continual news search: the NRA Senior Discount for guns, and a move by a number of states to eliminate a history of mental illness as a disqualification for gun ownership. Adam knew that the 'over 65' ownership of guns was the largest demographic segment in the country and that ageing brings along with it additional mental issues. Current information on the prevalence of gun mishaps amongst seniors was not available and Adam was concerned that the combination of these two moves would result in an increase of problems.

Not long after he had put a watching brief on any news involving guns and seniors, news of two occurrences was picked up: One in Arizona and one in Missouri. As Missouri was one of the states moving to liberalize gun ownership to include those with mental health histories, it was decided to have the Kansas City field office pick up the lead.

* * *

CHAPTER 6 - FBI NOTES: QUENTIN MOORE

Joplin, Missouri. FBI Special Agent Zoe Brouet thought about the Joplin incident one more time before getting out of her rental car: an 85-year-old man walks into a store and shoots and kills a 25-year-old cashier in Joplin, Missouri on Saturday. According to witnesses and corroborated by the surveillance video, the man walked in, shot the cashier and walked out. There was no interaction between the two and it did not appear to be a robbery attempt.

Police found the suspect dead at his home, from natural causes, possibly a heart attack. A weapon found at the suspect's home matched the murder weapon.

The suspect's wife told the police that her husband had looked at his phone, went up to their bedroom, and then left suddenly. When he returned, he seemed upset, saying that he needed to lie down.

Zoe gathered her thoughts and her briefcase and rang the bell of Mrs. Sharon Moore's neat, light green bungalow.

Sharon Moore opened the door to see a striking young woman. She was short but very athletic looking, with tawny-colored skin, almost black hair and exotic, dark, almond-shaped eyes.

"Hello Mrs. Moore. I'm Agent Zoe Brouet, FBI. I'm sorry to bother you and I know you've been questioned a lot by the local police. I have transcripts of all that, so we don't have to waste your time going over everything again, but I have some additional questions."

Agent Brouet had all the details that the Joplin PD had gathered. Address of the shooting, time, names of shooter, victim and witnesses, weapon used, etc. But there didn't appear to be a motive and well, there were a couple of other concerns. There was, of course, the FBI's ongoing concern about the effect of the NRA Senior Discount; and about Missouri's recent legislation removing virtually any requirement for a background check to obtain a concealed carry permit. And then, there was the comment about looking at his phone.

Mrs. Moore replied, as she let Zoe in and led her to the living room, "OK, but I've told them everything that happened."

"I'm sure you have and thank you for your help. You told the police that your husband was looking at his phone and seemed upset. When we checked his emails and messages, there did not appear to be anything that would trigger a reaction like that. Correct?"

"Yes, that's correct, but it seemed like he was looking at his phone a lot more recently."

"Did he say anything about why or what it might be?"

"No. It could have something to do with a new watch he got. His increased attention to his phone seemed to coincide with his getting the watch."

"A watch?"

"Yes. One of those sport watches."

"Can I see it?"

"Sure. Let me get it."

"Do you have his phone, too?"

"Yes, I'll bring it down."

Mrs. Moore returned with a black watch and the latest iPhone. Zoe eyed the phone and tried to frame her question tactfully. She recalled the difficulty she and others had when her department switched over to an ultra-hi-tech paperless system. "I'm impressed. This is the latest iPhone and your husband was 85. How did he learn or keep up with the new technology?"

"Quentin was one of the digital pioneers and was always working on the next big thing. He was one of Apple's top engineers before he retired and moved here."

Zoe examined the sport watch. She knew they could do a number of calculations like count steps, distances, stopwatch functions, etc., but that's as far as it went. The brand or logo was VT2. Both the watch and iPhone were dead after a week without charging. Zoe asked, "Can I take these with me to have our techies check them out?"

"Sure. What do you think you'll find?"

Zoe didn't really know, but Mrs. Moore's comment that her husband seemed attentive to the watch and phone around the time of the shooting had piqued her interest. "Not sure, but there are a lot of unanswered questions with respect to your husband's actions and we want to get to the bottom of it. Is there anything else you can add about what happened? Had you or your husband been to the KwikServe store on Joplin Avenue before the incident?"

"Yes, and now that you mention it, that was odd."

"Odd? In what sense?"

"About three months ago, Quentin came home after buying a few things at KwikServe. He was furious and muttering about a young cashier there who had insulted him. Apparently when Quentin tried to pay his bill with "Apple Pay," there was a problem. The cashier called him an old geezer who shouldn't be playing with new technology. Quentin exploded and told the kid that he was involved with developing it. He was so upset that I made him promise me that he would never go back there."

"And did he stick with his promise?"

"Yes, as far as I was aware, at least before the last time." She teared up and wiped her nose with a tissue.

"Do you know if the cashier that Quentin shot was the same one that upset him earlier?"

"I have no idea. I hadn't thought about that."

"Mrs. Moore, was Quentin depressed or did he show any signs of ... unusual behavior?"

"Perhaps he was a bit more withdrawn, but otherwise, I didn't notice anything different about him."

"Is there any way you can tell me what date Quentin had the encounter with the clerk, that made him so angry?"

"Unless the problem he had with Apple Pay caused him to pay cash, he probably charged it, so I can check our credit card bills. I'll have to dig around, so can I do it later and get back with you?"

"Sure. Here's my card and number. Before I go, one more question. In addition to the gun that Quentin used, the police found another gun. The one he used is very new, purchased just last month and the other one is over 10 years old. Do you know why Quentin bought a new gun?"

"You know, I think he was motivated because of an NRA Seniors promotion. There was a big discount for seniors and he was a sucker for new things and good deals. I remember kidding Quentin about buying something just because there was a discount and told him that I hoped Harley Davidson didn't come up with a big promotion on motorcycles."

They both smiled.

"And sorry, one last one and I'm gone. How was Quentin's health?"

"He had congestive heart failure, which sounds pretty scary, but it seemed to be under control through his medication. Dr. Felder, our family doctor, saw him regularly and said the rate of deterioration was slow."

"I plan to see Dr. Felder, but you felt he was OK? Were you surprised then, at his sudden death?"

"Well, yes, but I guess I felt whatever happened that made him do that, that shooting, pushed him over the edge medically, as well."

"Thank you very much, Mrs. Moore. You've been a big help. We'll check the watch and phone out and get them back to you as soon as possible. And in the meantime, if you think of anything else, please give me a call." She gave Mrs. Moore a receipt for the watch and iPhone.

Looking at her card, Sharon said, "I will, Special Agent Brouet. Good bye."

As Zoe walked out, she felt her pulse rise with excitement. She looked at her watch and decided to try to see Dr. Felder before she returned to Kansas City.

Zoe told Dr. Felder's receptionist that it was important that she speak with the doctor and that it wouldn't take long. The receptionist said she'd be right back, returning almost immediately to say that Dr. Felder would see her as soon as he finished with his current patient.

Not more than 15 minutes later, Zoe was shown in to the Doctor's office. Felder looked to be in his late 60's or early 70's. Handing him her card and receiving a strong handshake, Zoe said, "Thanks, Dr. Felder, for squeezing me in. I'm FBI Special

Agent Brouet and I'd like to ask a few questions about Quentin Moore."

Shaking his head, Felder said, "Poor Quentin. I'm still baffled by what he did."

"You had no reason to believe he was ... confused or suffering from dementia, depression?"

"Maybe a bit of depression, but not really at a clinical level requiring treatment. He was getting old. Had congestive heart failure and, like all of us, was going to die. But shooting someone for no apparent reason. Way outside my reasonable expectation."

"How long had you known Quentin?"

"Almost 20 years. Right after he retired from Apple. Nice guy. We were practically friends."

"You weren't surprised about his cause of death?"

"Not really, although it came a lot sooner than I thought. Sooner than Quentin thought, too, I think."

"Why do you say that?"

"Congestive heart failure is a process with a more or less predictable trajectory ... unless something else gets you first. Quentin's coronary capacity was declining, but slowly. Medication was working, and surgical options were not a good match for his condition and age. Quentin always wanted me to tell him how much longer he had, but although the outcome was assured, the timing and rate of decline was not something that I liked predicting, but I told him that in my opinion, if nothing substantially changed his current state of health, he could live to 90 or more. Both his parents made it into their 90s and Quentin wasn't a smoker or drinker and kept himself pretty fit."

"When was the last time you saw Quentin ... I mean the last time before you examined him after his death?"

Tapping some keys on his computer and looking at the screen, ... "Sorry, but this computer stuff is all new to me. Emails, patient records. All very complicated. Let's see ... exactly two months ago. In fact, he was due for a routine visit next week." Looking at his screen again, "Hmm, I forgot to mention the watch."

"Watch?" Zoe asked as she tried to keep calm.

"Yes. As part of a field test, I had received a new watch prototype to pass along to a patient - it monitors vital signs, I think. Quentin enjoyed technology, so I gave it to him to try out. It's supposed to be the latest and greatest but I'm still in the analog age, I'm afraid."

"Could the watch, or the information it fed back, have influenced Quentin's behavior?"

"I don't know, but I remember now. The watch had just come in and it was still on my desk, unopened, when Quentin came in for his appointment. I had read the cover letter and, knowing he liked new technical things, I just gave him the box with the watch in it. I assumed it had documentation inside. I don't even remember the name of the company. I don't put much faith into all these new gadgets, but I knew Quentin did."

Zoe jotted down a note and asked, "Does VT2 ring a bell?"

"No."

"Are you aware that Quentin had two guns?"

"I knew he had one, that's right here in his file, but it was there before legislation was passed that prevents us from asking that question anymore, so I wouldn't know about a second one unless he volunteered that info."

"He bought a second gun two months ago. He didn't mention it?"

"No. Do you think there's a connection between that purchase and the shooting?"

"I don't know. It just seems odd. Dr. Feldman, thank you for your time. I'll let you get back to your patients. If you think of anything else, please give me a call."

"Sure thing. Good-bye."

Zoe left thinking that she may have made a bit of progress, but there were still so many questions. But now she had some hard evidence that might answer some of them and give her some working leads.

Checking for messages, Zoe saw that Sharon Moore had left a voicemail with the date when her husband had the altercation at KwikServe. Looking in her notebook, she called the number of the Joplin Avenue KwikServe store and was put through to the manager.

"Good afternoon, Mr. Reynolds, my name is Zoe Brouet, Special Agent for the FBI, and I'm looking into the recent shooting of one of your cashiers, Stephen Kinsead."

"Good afternoon, Ma'am. How can I help you?"

"Can you tell me who was working the cashier position on the afternoon of November 10th?"

"I should be able to. Just a moment." Zoe heard the sound of clicking keys. "Rhyana, that's R-H-Y-A-N-A Adams and Stephen Kinsead. Both were on duty from 3:00 to 9:00 PM."

"Thank you", Zoe replied, trying to tone down her excitement. "That's all I need. Bye for now."

Zoe thought, "This is a link, but what exactly does it mean? They had a history, but it would be pretty unusual for someone to blow someone away for a simple angry encounter, and Moore didn't have a history of aggression. There's something else we don't know. Let's see if the lab can pry something out of these things," glancing at the evidence bags with the watch and iPhone. "In the meantime, I need to get back to the office, write up my reports and fly out to San Diego."

* * *

San Diego, California. Zoe rang the bell at Stan Mason's townhouse in the Chula Vista suburb of San Diego. Stan answered and let her into his ground floor living room. Zoe had a single purpose for this trip and she was pleased to see the VT2 watch and iPhone sitting on the coffee table when Stan invited her to have a seat on one of his modern, but surprisingly comfortable, chairs.

"Here is the watch and iPhone. As I mentioned on the phone, I was surprised to find them amongst my dad's possessions and I'm even more surprised that you think they may be a clue as to why he did what he did."

Zoe pulled the watch and phone closer and looked at the watch to verify it was a VT2. "We're not entirely sure yet but after we analyze the watch and associated app, it may help our understanding into what triggered your father to do something so out of character."

Zoe asked if Stan had any additional thoughts since his interview with the Tucson police. He hadn't, but Zoe now had two matching possessions of the two killers. She hoped that her techies could find something in common with the two VT2's that would give them some insight into what triggered violent reactions in what appeared to be normal, non-violent people. She gave Stan a receipt for the items and returned to San Diego International Airport.

* * *

CHAPTER 7 – DINNER & GUNS

Pasadena, California. As Trudi and Vince were getting ready to leave for the Khan's, Vince asked, "I wonder how they feel about the talk and suggestions about banning Muslims from entering the country? Would it be rude to ask them?"

"I don't think so. They're a poster family for why immigration is good."

"I'll say. They're nothing short of laudable Americans and their kids, wow! Talk about success stories!"

"You like them because Alma cooks that amazing lamb dish," Trudi joked.

"Yeah, but she tempers my affection by thrashing me in ping pong! Maybe I'll feign an injury if she asks me to play."

"She actually likes playing with you because you give her a good game. And she actually doesn't slaughter you as much as very consistently beats you."

"Like, every time!"

The Khans had immigrated to the USA when Ahmed secured a position with CalTech Labs. He had been a computer engineer doing things that nobody outside of the (very) high tech community would ever understand, and now he was a department head. Alma was a nurse by profession but before she could get qualified in the US, she became pregnant with the first of their two children. Their son, Aziz, was currently finishing up a post-graduate degree at Stanford and had already been accepted at Google when he graduated. Their daughter, Fatima, graduated from the US Naval Academy and was a Navy pilot.

"Well, we better get moving if we don't want to be late. And don't forget the wine." The Khans didn't drink but welcomed them to bring something if they wanted.

They arrived a few minutes late and when Ahmed opened the door, Vince gave a sigh of pleasure as he breathed in the mouth-watering aroma of Alma's lamb dish.

"Trudi, Vince, welcome!" Ahmed greeted them warmly, giving Trudi a hug and Vince a bro-shake. "How are you two? It's been too long!"

Trudi replied, "I know. How can retired people be so busy?" Vince added, "Was it the Anderson's Christmas party when we saw you both last?"

Ahmed thought and replied, "I think you're right."

"How have you two been, and how are Fatima and Aziz?" Trudi asked.

"Alma and I are fine, and the kids are both doing very well, but come on in. We've invited the Martinezes, too."

Trudi and Vince were pleased that Rueben and Doris Martinez were there. Their enthusiasm for the occasion raised even a few more notches. They had been introduced to them through the Khans and they were a warm and very down to earth couple. Rueben's experiences as a police officer were always interesting conversation points.

Ahmed led them into the living room as Rueben and Doris rose to greet them.

Trudi stepped forward and gave Doris a hug and kiss on the cheek as Vince gave Rueben a hearty greeting, before switching partners for polite but warm hugs.

"Is Alma slaving away in the kitchen?" Trudi asked. When Rueben confirmed her guess, Trudi grabbed Doris' hand and said, "Let's go invade her space."

Ahmed asked Vince if he'd like something to drink, "Some water, apple or orange juice or shall I open your wine?"

"Or a beer?" added Rueben.

Vince noticed that there was a glass of beer where Rueben had been sitting and assumed he had brought that. "A glass of wine. Thanks, Ahmed," he said, as Ahmed disappeared in the direction of the kitchen.

"How have you been, Vince? Retirement agreeing with you?"

"I'm surviving it. Miles helps keep me fit and on schedule, Trudi watches my weight, and I've been re-immersing myself into technology with a new toy from Apple."

"A toy? Literally?"

"No. Not literally," chuckled Vince. "No, after a lifetime of using Windows machines and software, I bought a Mac and both Trudi and I are having fun with it. In fact, I may have to get Trudi one of her own, or an iPad, we're both using it so much."

"Boy, when they began introducing computers into the department, there wasn't much enjoyment going around."

"That was a long time ago and they weren't any fun then, even for work. The new ones, although I can only speak for the Apple machines now, are really very user friendly and intuitive. And so fast! I can recall my old machine taking so long I could go get a cup of coffee ... from Starbucks!"

"Yeah, and that was when the closest Starbucks was eight blocks away! But everything was being re-invented at the Force at the same time. The computers allowed us to change our entire process, create and change existing forms, and learn what had been a foreign language, all at once. It did get better, and in time, easier."

Ahmed returned with a glass of wine, followed by the ladies. Vince greeted Alma with polite affection and gushed, "Alma, it smells wonderful. Is it your lamb recipe?"

"Yes, and I won't even make you play ping pong for it tonight!" "Whew!" Vince parried.

Doris turned to Rueben. "The lamb recipe is from her family who have a famous restaurant in Pakistan called Salloos. There's one in London, too."

Alma added, "A meal at the one in London will cost almost 20 times as much as the one in Lahore. Probably safer though," she smiled.

Rueben replied, "I agree with Vince. It smells delicious!"

To which Alma replied, "It's ready now, so why don't we go to the dining room and see if you like it."

They did, and Alma basked in the warm glow of compliments.

**

They had finished their dinner, followed by mango kulfi, and were just sipping their coffees, when Vince asked the question he had mentioned to Trudi earlier.

"I hope this isn't too awkward, but we consider you good friends and we were hurt and embarrassed by the talk that Muslims might be banned from entering the country. We think it's awful, but I can only imagine how you must feel about it!"

Ahmed spoke first, "I wish I could slough it off and say, 'consider the source,' but that sentiment is coming from a much broader number of people, which has me concerned. It may be my imagination, but it feels like people are looking at me differently, in a wary and suspicious way. Not even surreptitiously."

Rueben chimed in, "Well, I'm not Muslim, but I'm the other group that's being vilified. I have definitely seen a difference since I've taken off the uniform. And it's like you said, Ahmed ... people look at me as if to say, 'I'm watching you.'"

Vince asked, "Are you hearing anything from your ex-department colleagues about how, if at all, the talk has morphed into incidents?"

Alma, eyes down, interjected. "I saw something yesterday at the store. A Muslim woman wearing a hijab was checking out ahead of me in the same line, and although I didn't see or hear what caused it, the cashier shouted at her and told her to 'Go back to where she came from.' I left the line, pretending to have forgotten to get something, and returned to a different line. I was scared."

Sympathetically, Ahmed said, "Why didn't you tell me?"

"You would have gone down there and made it worse."

"But the cashier shouldn't get away with that."

Rueben said, "You asked about incidents, and yes, they are on the rise. Small ones like what Alma saw and bigger ones, too. And I'm not saying small means unimportant, but my friends on the force tell me they are seeing physical incidents, property damage and even shootings. Someone shot a man the other day because they thought he was stealing from a K-Mart. He wasn't stealing but he was guilty of being of Mexican descent."

"At CalTech, most of us are immigrants of some sort, mostly with darker skin, so it's not an issue there; but once we leave the lab, it's open season. In fact, Rueben, I wanted to ask your opinion on having a gun." Vince perked up at Ahmed's question as Rueben replied.

"Are you serious? Hmmm. OK, but this is my opinion and not what a nationwide survey of police think. I've carried a gun most of my life now. Fortunately, I never had to use it, but if I had, I was well trained, and except for the last ten years, I really didn't assume that everyone had a gun, unless a report came in that a suspect was armed. That change in assumption has created – again, this is my opinion – a change in the way police go about our jobs and interact with people. We now assume everyone is armed and this escalates the interaction. Some of us are better than others in trying to keep emotions low, but when you are on high alert to keep from getting shot, mistakes happen, as we've seen, over and over in the news.

"But let's be clear, it's not just racial incidents that are increasing. Violent crime in general is increasing. Break-ins, senseless beatings, and shootings are on the rise. So, even if I hadn't been a cop, I would want to have a decent chance to protect my wife and family, and perhaps because I was a cop and am comfortable and trained in handling a gun, I have one."

"Are you carrying now?" asked Ahmed, smiling at his own use of jargon.

"Yes." And when everyone looked at him to see if they could see it, he added, "It's in my jacket over there," pointing to the windbreaker on a chair.

Vince asked, "If I wanted to get a gun, what kind of training should I get?"

Trudi, surprised, said, "Are you really thinking about getting one?"

"It's just a hypothetical question."

Rueben replied to Vince's question calmly. "OK, but before you even think about training, I want you both," looking at Ahmed as well, "to think about something else: If you have a gun, and we're talking about protection, not hunting, you need to be very clear that if the time ever comes ... that you are prepared to shoot someone. Simply waving a gun without the will to use it can cause a situation to escalate beyond what it might have been."

"That's a very good question. Trudi and I need to consider that before we decide if we should go ahead."

Trudi shot Vince a quick disapproving glance.

"As for training," Rueben continued, "I'm glad you said 'should' instead of 'need.' It's actually embarrassing because you don't 'need' any training to buy a gun; you just have to have an HSC, Handgun Safety Certificate. That involves answering 75% of 30 questions correctly. Getting a concealed carry permit in California is pretty difficult, although you'd be amazed at how often that detail is flaunted, even by otherwise law-abiding citizens."

Vince remarked, "Ergo your assumption that everyone is armed."

"Exactly, although it's a fact that concealed carrying is not as prevalent in California as in states that routinely allow it. So, an assumption that everyone is armed, at least in California, is wrong and may lead us to overreact.

"But getting back to your question about training – shooting itself isn't that hard, although it takes a lot of time and practice to be a marksman. But we're talking self-defense, with a handgun, and typically at short range, so being a crack shot isn't the goal."

Trudi asked, "What *is* the goal?"

"First of all, safety. Safety for the shooter and for those around him that he or she doesn't want to shoot." This evoked some chuckles from the group, but Rueben went on. "You'd be surprised at how often innocent people are shot when a 'good guy,' even an experienced gun owner, starts shooting. There is always a risk that your shot will miss, just graze your target, or even ricochet, and the bullet continues and hits someone else. Experienced shooters take this into account and often will not take a shot if there's a risk of hitting someone other than the intended target."

Alma added, "I read about someone accidentally shooting a person in an apartment next door when the bullet went through a wall."

"Wouldn't surprise me. You can get beginner's training for two hours. Guns are pretty simple to operate. That's why they give them to cops," he said as he laughed. "But seriously, the hardest thing to do is shoot under pressure, and if there's a break-in and someone has a gun, believe me, there's pressure. Worse than the difference between shooting baskets on your own or shooting baskets with a 7-footer waving his arms in your face."

The group fell silent for a moment before Rueben added, "If any of you want to take the step, let me know and I'll be happy to give you advice on buying one. Some ranges require a two- person minimum for safety, although a class session would be different."

Vince continued with his concern about immigrant prejudice, "Thanks, Rueben, I may take you up on that. But getting back to what we were talking about a few minutes ago about racial and immigrant profiling and prejudice, how do all of you feel about that? I mean your two families epitomize the dreams that this country was built on. You've told me, Rueben, about your parents coming here to work on farms and how proud they were seeing you go through school, college and then the police department."

Doris spoke up, blue eyes flashing in angry memory. "When I started going out with Rueben, most of my family was against it. Some said as much and others didn't need to say anything. You could see it."

Rueben was smiling, "It was pretty uncomfortable, especially with her father. He scared me at first but my feelings for Doris made all that unimportant. But you know, in all fairness, my family wasn't a whole lot better."

Doris continued, "It was really only my mom who was truly supportive. Everyone else gave me all the reasons why it was a huge mistake, including how awful it would be for our children, being from a 'mixed marriage.' " That made everyone smile. Ricky Martinez had been the captain of his high school's football and baseball teams, was voted the most popular boy in his class, and won an academic scholarship to USC.

Vince, getting back on track, continued, "And that's why I'm at a loss about the attitudes of bigoted people. Does anyone really think that any of you, or your children, took jobs from some more worthy Revolutionary War descendants?" There were chuckles and smiles all around. "Seriously, you got those jobs because you were better qualified than the other candidates, and why else would it be? That process makes our country better. Makes everyone up their game. That's the American way. I've worked in other countries where nepotism is rife, and it holds them back. In the Middle East they have western assistants to many of the top local executives because the local execs are not capable. Instead of recognizing history and appreciating the facts, we seem to be going backwards."

"That's why I desperately wanted to come to the USA," said Ahmed. "The 'American Dream' is something we all knew about in Pakistan and for many of us, we bought into that dream, worked hard to reach it, and realized it. When I think of my kids, I know it's still alive. There are just some people, who, for whatever reason, haven't been able to keep up and need someone to blame. They need to lash out to make themselves feel better. It's not rational. They don't want to pick strawberries. But they also don't want to go to college for six or more years ... and in some cases, they lack the ability, the vision or the resources to do that."

"And then there are the politicians who take advantage of those people," added Trudi. "I have little respect for politicians in general, with a few exceptions. The vast majority of them are in it for themselves and one party is just a little better or worse than the other. Occasionally, I see an article about the wealth of someone when they enter politics and how much they're worth a few years later. How does that happen on their salaries?" Trudi asked rhetorically, getting more emotional as she spoke.

Alma added, "Not only do the politicians take advantage, but they set the tone. Building walls, banning people based on religion, preventing groups of people from voting. Even if some of their rhetoric is simply that, it's a rallying cry to their followers to think this or believe that."

"And nowadays, it's hard to even know what to believe," said Ahmed sadly. "This whole fake news situation, including blatant lies and misinformation from our President, makes it very difficult to believe anything without doing some very thorough research. We might be better off watching the comedy news programs and reading The Onion."

That sentiment was fully endorsed by all, but Vince sobered up the group. "My concern is that two or three things will happen that can lead to some disasters, and I'm not even talking about international or terrorist-inspired events. First of all, I'm concerned about healthcare, social programs and the economy as it affects the large majority of people. If the progress made with healthcare is reversed, if Medicare, Medicaid or Social Security is tightened or scaled back, and if controls on banks and businesses are removed, along with aggressive trade barriers, everyone except the top 1-2% will suffer financially, even more than at the moment.

"Secondly, if the real news sources are bullied and tarnished with loud and powerful allegations that they are, in fact, the fake news, then fewer and fewer people will really know what's going on. And if that lack of facts pushes or leads people into increasingly bigoted positions, that lack of knowledge will lead to fear ... which leads to my third point." A quiet gloom had settled on the table, but Vince was too immersed in his diatribe to notice.

"Violence and a growing appetite for guns. Trudi and I just heard that a million more guns are being purchased by seniors because of a discount! So, a 'perfect storm' is not impossible and could be disastrous."

"I sure hope you're wrong!" said Alma.

Vince hadn't meant to deliver such a heavy thought at the end of a very nice evening ... but he had, and nothing he could say could erase his prognosis of doom. Watches were looked at and Rueben led the breakup of the evening. "Doris and I walked over so we better get started before it gets too dark."

Vince, craving redemption, said, "We can drop you off."

"That's OK. We always walk off our dinner and this one deserves a walk, even a short one. Thank you very much, Alma, for an absolutely delicious meal. We plan to reciprocate soon, although it will be tough competition."

"Are you kidding me? I'll run all the way for your guacamole and duck enchiladas."

Trudi said, "We'd best be off, too. Thank you both so much for the fabulous meal, even if the last conversation topics were much less enjoyable." She avoided looking at Vince, but he could feel her unspoken reproach.

"Hey, the topics are reality. The meal, an escape. It was great to see all of you again," said Ahmed, sincerely.

Vince, sheepishly, "I'm sorry. I led us into the dark valley and I certainly didn't mean to throw cold water on a great evening."

Ahmed again, "Don't be silly. You made us think about some things that we shouldn't ignore."

"OK. Thanks, and thank you both for tonight. Alma, I'll even play ping pong with you next time ... if you spot me a few points."

"No way!"

After the farewell hugs, the Fullers and Martinezes made their way to the street and Rueben said, "Vince, let me know if you do decide on a gun. I know my way around them and I'd be happy to help."

"Thanks. I'll do that. Goodnight."

* * *

CHAPTER 8 – TWO DECISIONS

Pasadena, California. Vince and Trudi drove the short distance to their home in complete silence, knowing that they would be up for a while discussing their dinner conversation.

After letting Miles out, Trudi made some tea and Vince poured himself another glass of wine to calm down.

Trudi came in with her tea and launched what would be a fairly long discussion. "Are you seriously thinking of getting a gun?"

"I'm more serious than I was before this evening. My remarks near the end of dinner were formed as we discussed the course our culture has taken, and I'm concerned about a breakdown of what we've considered normal. Maybe it's just the steady march of culture that we've experienced during our lifetime. Way back when we were kids, our parents didn't lock our doors all the time. Then, we started locking our doors when we became adults, and now people are buying guns. If my worst fears begin to become real, I'd like to be ready. Are you OK with it?"

"What if the people breaking in get our gun first? I've heard that happens."

"We'll get a special locked box that only responds to our fingerprints."

"They make those?"

"Yes. I've been researching guns and options. They make biometric ones that open by fingerprint recognition. We could have both our prints programmed."

"But I hate the idea that our country is becoming a nation of gun toters and I hate the way the NRA stirs people up about losing their gun rights. I've never seen anything to suggest that the government wants to take away our guns ... just put in place reasonable controls. Even Reagan supported the Brady Act. But every time a politician from either party even hints at controls of any kind, the NRA uses its muscle to stop them. Their reaction to Sandy Hook sickened me, and instead of doing anything to control who has guns, they and the politicians in their pockets are now trying to arm all teachers. Barb and Dave may both have guns before we do."

"We don't know that they don't have guns already. Teachers and school administrators in Texas may already be armed. And while I don't really want to have a gun in the house, I'd never forgive myself if something happened that having a gun might have prevented."

"Well, I hope you'll take Rueben up on his offer of assistance. He's been around guns for a long time and knows what's what."

"I will, but I also thought we could do this together. Look at guns and get one that at least feels OK in your hand, and then go to training together. Besides, being in this together is a good safety idea so we both have equal knowledge and understanding of the gun and safety."

"I like the doing it together aspect, but it's a bit sickening to think about having a gun in the house."

"Hopefully, we'll forget we even have it, like the fire extinguisher. By the way, where is that?"

They both laughed, and Trudi added, "Far left cupboard in the kitchen. Hmm, I wonder if it even works? So, when would you want to do this? And where?"

"Let me do some more research, we can continue to think about it, and then we can call Rueben to get his advice. I'm not expecting any burglars soon."

"Well, I'm having a hard time with the idea, but do some more research. In the meantime, back to the other aspect of the culture issue, I can't even imagine how the Khans and Martinezes feel when they hear ethnic slurs, from the President and leading politicians, no less! It was bad enough when it was mostly African-Americans who felt the historical prejudice and bigotry. Now we still have that and a lot more. What does that do to people? In my lifetime, there have been a couple of times when I knew people didn't like me or looked down at me for some reason. It was very uncomfortable but very rare and short lived, plus I could usually avoid those people in the future. Black people, Muslims and Latinos can't avoid the general public; but it must take incredible strength, maybe even bravery, to simply go to the store."

"Yeah. I'm thinking about the woman Alma mentioned. How will she feel the next time she has to go to that store, or will she choose another store, which may be less convenient or more expensive? I guess all minorities have always faced discrimination, which is why they lived in groups. Chinatown, Koreatown, Olvera Street, Little Tokyo, Little India, etc., haven't developed to make ethnic shopping easier. It's for inclusion and protection."

"Who could look down on the Khans or Martinezes? They're intelligent, accomplished, good-hearted, and just wonderful people! I feel proud and honored to have them as friends. Maybe I – or we – need to get more involved."

"In what?"

"I don't know. Move-On, Color of Change, Brady Campaign. Marches, petitions, phone calls."

"Seriously? I'm not unconcerned, but what can be done? Bigotry and prejudice are tough belief systems to change."

"I know, but I do remember Berkeley – don't laugh! We did help change things."

"Yes, the results were positive, but look at us now. When I was younger the dream of world peace was easy to imagine; but now, so much seems worse than ever," said Vince, sadly. Then, with a lighter tone, sighed, "It's getting too late tonight to fix the world, so how about we go to bed?"

"Sounds good to me. Don't forget Miles."

"Whoops. Thanks. See you upstairs."

Vince went to the back door and walked out past Miles, who was curled up on the mat. The stars were out in full force and a thin slice of moon shone in the clear night sky. As he gazed starward, he wondered if he could shoot someone? Even in self-defense. He felt Miles rub his nose against his leg and he leaned down and scratched his head between his pointy ears. "Dogs don't have to worry about things like this. I guess that's where the expression comes from, 'Lucky Dog.' "

* * *

The next day, Vince called Rueben. "Hi, Rueben. It was really nice to see you and Doris last night and sorry for raising the subject of guns and cultural tension."

"No problem. 'D' and I actually enjoyed the conversation. Too often these things are left unspoken; but with good friends, we know we're safe and can be open."

"Oh good. I was afraid I'd ruined the great meal."

"Not many things could ruin Alma's lamb dinners!" he laughed.

"That's for sure. And since you're so smart, I wanted to get your advice on getting a gun."

"Is Trudi OK with that?"

"Well, we haven't fully decided, but we've agreed to get trained together if we do. What do you think?"

"Perfect. That way you've got four hands and you both understand the working and safety aspects of it."

"That's what I thought, too. Good. So how would we start?"

"Well, first, each of you needs to have an HSC ... Handgun Safety Certificate. You can download the manual, which is what the written test will be based on. Once you pass it, and it's not hard, you can legally purchase a gun, and that's important because you'll know, or at least be more certain, that the gun you get doesn't have a criminal past."

"OK, I'm just Googling Handgun Safety Certificate now. OK, here it is. I'll download it after I hang up. So, when we get our certificates, where would you suggest going to look at guns?"

"There are a couple of good stores not far away and depending on timing and location, gun shows can be fun, and you might have better luck picking up a good used gun from a reputable dealer. You can probably check out gun shows on your computer, Mister Techie."

Vince laughed. "Hardly a techie, but I'll give it a go."

"You'll need to take the test and get your HSCs first, otherwise your trips to stores and fairs won't get you much. On the other hand, most gun stores administer the test and if you buy a gun from them, you often get a discount on the test. But let me know when you want to go and I'll go with you. 'D' won't go. She hates guns. Always has."

"Thanks, Rueben. I'll give you a call as soon as we decide."

"Sounds like a plan. Happy studying!"

Vince impatiently downloaded the Handgun Safety Certificate Study Guide issued by the California Department of Justice. Scanning the Table of Contents of the 56-page booklet, he noticed a number of self-tests and scrolled to each. Looking at the questions he realized that it wouldn't take long to study adequately, as he answered all the True-False questions correctly simply by using common sense. The fill -in and technical questions would need to be studied, but this was far simpler than the DMV test. He printed two copies and went in search of Trudi.

She was in the den, just finishing up the ironing. There wasn't much of it any more since Vince retired. But she actually enjoyed the relatively mindless task that gave her some mental private time. And she was thinking that, like Vince, she needed to get her head more back in the game. Her relatively few glimpses at the wide world offered by the internet had hooked her and she wanted more. Problem was that Vince was on his machine so much that she didn't have access. And so, when Vince entered the den, she immediately said what was on her mind. "Hey, I've been thinking that we should get another laptop. You're using that one most of your waking day."

Caught a bit off stride because he was on a mission, he said, "Oh, sure, honey. We can do that. Or, if it's mostly for surfing, you may like an iPad."

"That's one of those tablet things? I've seen a couple of my friends with them. What are the pros and cons?"

"Typing is not as easy as it's an on-screen keyboard, although you can get external keyboards to interface. But you can also use it like a Kindle, to read books online. Other than that, not a lot of practical difference. We can go to the Apple store tomorrow and you can try one out."

"OK." And then seeing the printed papers in his hand, she asked, "Whatcha got?"

"Our HSC Study Guides!"

"HSC?"

"Handgun Safety Certificates. I spoke with Rueben and he suggested getting that step out of the way. I've looked at the questions and it shouldn't take long to prepare for the test. And Rueben will come with us to give advice about choosing a gun. If we buy one, we'll have a 10-day wait before we can bring it home. California laws are much more restrictive than other states. In many, you don't need a permit, nor do you have to have your gun registered. And that's amazing, given that guns are lethal weapons and bullets can be traced back to a gun, like a fingerprint."

"Slow down. I thought we were going to continue to think about this."

"This is just part of the decision process. We're not taking any tangible steps yet, just getting ready in case we want to … pull the trigger."

Trudi faked a groan. "Vince Fuller. It's a good thing I don't have a gun right now!" But she was too pleased about her upcoming iPad to give him an argument.

***

CHAPTER 9—WRINKLES

Quincy, Massachusetts. A few weeks into the alpha test, Maria Moon, VitalTech's PR Director and Drew Pierson, Director of Research and Development, bumped into each other in the VitalTech coffee lounge.

"Hi, Drew. Long time no see."

"Hi, Maria. Yeah, like all of us these days, I've been chained to my desk."

"Not surprised. I've seen most of the top line alpha test results, but what's your take?"

"Overall, I'd say it's going well. The watch is doing its job, as I knew it would, and the user interface has been better than anything I've been involved with before."

"That's saying something, coming from an ex-Apple guy."

Drew looked uncomfortable and scanned the room. Spying a table in the corner, away from everyone else, he asked, "Do you have a minute?"

"Sure. I have a long chain right now."

Drew forced a smile as they sat down at the table. "Can we keep this confidential?"

Maria replied warily, "OK. What's going on? You're not leaving us, are you?"

"No. Nothing like that. Of the 100 participants in the alpha test, three have been involved with gun incidents. Two have killed people, including a multiple killing, and one, the youngest, has committed suicide, and we're barely into the test period."

Maria said nothing as she absorbed what Drew had just told her, wondering if it was coincidental or within a norm of some sort. Then she remembered the last top line alpha test results. "Are these the three with Final Notices?"

"Yes."

"Who else knows this?"

"I don't know. The guy who killed six people was shot and killed. It's possible the clinical team picked up on it if the VT2 analysis and prediction were different than expected. I'm not sure what kind of follow up they do. Plus, he was the first and it didn't really raise any alarms. The second guy actually died of natural causes almost a week before his Notice date, but he shot and killed someone between the time of his Notice and his death.

"How do you know that?"

"I got a call from the FBI last week asking about the VT2 and she told me that before dying, our test user shot and killed someone."

"Jesus. Does Vijay know this?"

"No. He was away last week, and I am seeing him later today. When I bumped into you, I thought I'd get your reaction and advice about how to handle it."

"Gee, thanks. What do we know about the suicide?"

"Nothing unusual, except that he received a one-week Final Notice earlier on the day he shot and killed himself."

"After what you've told me, I expect it would be considered unusual. Any suicide note?"

"I don't know. The user didn't register any next of kin or emergency contact, so short of calling the police and asking …"

"Yeah. Probably not a good idea. How do you know he committed suicide?"

"A call from the police. This guy was pretty much a loner with a few casual acquaintances. The guy hadn't password protected his app so when the cops looked at the phone, they saw no phone activity and no emails, just a few standard apps and the VT2 app. When they opened it, they saw that the 'Last Activity' date on the app Welcome screen was the date of the suicide and they called the Help Line number. They didn't know what the app was, so they didn't ask good questions, but they told Debbie on the Help Desk that he had shot and killed himself."

"I recall that the Notice feature was really liked by the focus groups. Was there any talk about adverse reactions? The suicide guy could have been depressed so that's almost normal, but the killings?"

"I know. How do you think I should handle it with Vijay?"

"You know him as well as I do. Tell him straight out what's happened. And what you think. Drew, what do you think?"

Drew hesitated for a moment. "Not sure. The depression angle is certainly logical. And we won't really know how that will play out over time, but as you said, the killings are the big worry. We don't have the details on either of the two except the bare facts. One guy shoots a dozen people, killing six, before he's killed. The other guy walks into a store, shoots the cashier, walks out, goes home and dies. Revenge? Retribution of some kind? Nothing to lose?"

Maria spoke with great urgency. "When are you seeing Vijay?"

"I was going to catch up with him later."

"No. Do it now. I'll come with you if you'd like. What you just said is a PR disaster waiting to happen and I don't care how good the VT2 is. This could be our Final Notice."

"Thanks. I'll get my notes and swing by your office on the way."

* * *

Not long afterwards, Maria and Drew met with Vijay. Vijay was in a good mood. All the pieces seemed to be falling into place with the planned production set up and both KKL and Credit Suisse were increasingly bullish about the IPO.

Vijay couldn't wait to share the news from his meetings with Credit Suisse and KKL. "I'm not going to start throwing numbers out yet, because you guys will start spending all your time thinking about what you're going to do with all your money, but suffice it to say, everything is looking good for a very successful IPO. The product is right, and our timing is perfect."

Drew and Maria looked at each other and Drew swallowed hard. "Vijay, we may have a problem."

"What do you mean? What kind of problem?"

Drew repeated what he told Maria earlier, "Of the 100 participants in the alpha test, three have been involved with gun incidents. Two have killed people, including a multiple killing, and one, the youngest, has committed suicide."

Vijay looked pale. "Holy shit!! Sorry, Maria. What do we know about the deaths?"

Drew took Vijay through what he knew about the Tucson killings. "I haven't had time to check with Clinical to see if their readings indicated that he died from an outside cause or how long he began shooting after his Notice."

"How did we find out?"

"I saw it reported on TV and at first it didn't register but for some reason it made me think, so I checked the test file later and saw that the name and address matched the news report. He was the first, so it didn't stand out as important.

"OK. Tell me about the second shooting."

"The second one was an 85-year-old man who shot and killed a store cashier after he had received his Notice. He then went home and died of natural causes, so it may not have raised any alarms in Clinical, but it appears that he died before the day given in the Notice. Again, I haven't spoken with them yet to see if they detected anything unusual, or to correlate the Notice timing with the time of the shooting."

"How do we know about this one?

I got a call from the FBI asking about the VT2."

"What? The FBI called? What did you tell him?"

"It was a her, but just the basics. That it was a holistic fitness/health monitor and that the user was part of a test group helping to ensure that the application functioned as planned."

"What kind of questions did she ask?"

"Hmm, I'm trying to recall. That's right, she asked if the watch had diagnostic capabilities that could cause the user to become depressed."

"What did you say?"

"I gave her a high-level overview of the Final Notice function, which she seemed very interested in. She also asked for access codes to the app and any documentation."

"And did you give it to her?"

"Yes. The User Name and Password. I also sent her the standard documentation."

"Did you check it out with Legal?"

"No. It was the FBI and I verified that by calling her back at their listed main number."

"OK, good. That should be OK but going forward we need to set up a process. I'll get the team together first thing after lunch, so we can discuss it. Tell me about the suicide."

"I got a call from the police."

Vijay grimaced.

Drew told him the details he had shared with Maria earlier.

"OK. I'll get Liz and Patsy to meet with us at 1:00. I'll ask Patsy to bring the file logs, so we can determine the Final Notice time stamps. Do we know the dates and times of the shootings?"

Drew replied, "No, but I can call and find out."

"No, not yet. The first one is easy. We know the time of the Notice and death if he was still wearing the device. Maybe Patsy can tell based on the final readings. The suicide is easy, too. We just need some more info regarding the second one. Maybe Liz has a legal connection that can casually check police records. But let's keep this between the five of us for the time being. Thanks. See you both at 1:00."

As Drew and Maria walked down the hall, Drew asked, "How do you think Vijay took it?"

"I think he was shaken, but I have confidence in him and us to figure out the right solution."

"But it sounds like he doesn't want the IPO managers involved yet. Do you think he'll try to hide it?"

"No. My guess is that he wants to know the details and develop a plan before he involves them."

"You're probably right. Thanks. See you at 1:00."

* * *

Vijay sat back in his chair and re-read the email from his younger brother, Sanjay. Twelve years younger than Vijay, Sanjay was bright, but not in the same way as Vijay. Nonetheless, he attended the well-respected Indian Institute of Technology in Mumbai. But when their father became ill, Sanjay dropped out to help with the family store. His parents were furious at Sanjay's decision, but he was resolute. 'Store' was a euphemism for the canvas and corrugated metal lean-to/shack where they had lived and sold fruit and vegetables to the local residents. Vijay had been able to get them into a real house several years ago, but his father would never give up the store. He would rather have died than sit around and have Vijay support them.

Soon, Vijay thought, I'll be able to get them out of there completely and set them up somewhere, so they can enjoy their remaining years in luxury, or at least tranquility, given his father's ascetic nature. He was also hoping that he could help out Sanjay, even get him involved with the VT2 manufacturing operations. That would go a long way to assuage his guilt for having his brother give up his goals while he was fulfilling his own.

As he reread the email though, his hope turned to worry, as it might all be too late ... especially if the VT2 launch was delayed, or worse yet, cancelled because of the killings he'd just learned about. His father had suffered a seizure several months ago, and although he seemed to recover, as a medical doctor, Vijay knew it wasn't a good sign. That's why, in addition to the 100 VT2s in the alpha test, Vijay had given out three others – to his father, his mother and Sanjay. All three were programmed for 30 days, which would give Vijay time to get things in order at VitalTech and get to India. He had also programmed the relay alert feature on his father's VT2 to alert both himself and Sanjay. Perhaps when the alpha test was finished and a little more progress was made with the production plans, he could make a quick trip to India.

Was his last visit really almost five years ago? Where had the time gone? More guilt washed over him as he compared his life with that of his parents and brother. He lived in a luxury apartment in Boston and commuted to his office in Quincy in his high-end Tesla. His parents lived in a suburb of Mumbai, next door to a sprawling slum. They walked or hired a three- wheeler – the ubiquitous, noisy, smelly (and wide open to smells) auto rickshaws that are like bugs in constant motion, 24 hours a day.

Vijay had stayed in a Marriott hotel on the beach when he last visited, although to be fair, there really wasn't room for him at his parents' house, he told himself. When his family came to the hotel for dinner, it was like entering a palace, and their discomfort was palpable, not just because of the elegance of the surroundings, but the looks from the staff. Even when Vijay explained to them that almost all of the hotel staff lived in slums and poor conditions, it was hard to believe, looking at their smart, freshly laundered and pressed uniforms.

His father had complained about the food. Tasteless and foreign, even though it appeared to be Indian cuisine. Oddly, he didn't mention the price. Perhaps he didn't realize that numbers that big were prices for the food. If he had known, Vijay was sure he wouldn't have eaten.

He was rescued from another wave of guilt as Maureen buzzed him to announce that his colleagues had arrived, but he wasn't looking forward to this either.

* * *

CHAPTER 10 – CONSEQUENCES

Quincy, Massachusetts. Drew, Maria, Patsy Carter, VitalTech's Head of Clinical Affairs, and Liz Glass, VitalTech's Legal Counsel, assembled in Vijay's conference room. Vijay had just cleared his head of his thoughts and guilt with respect to his parents and Sanjay.

Grabbing his notes, he opened the door to the conference room. "Hi guys." (Even though there was only one guy.) "Thanks for clearing your schedules. We may have a problem."

Liz and Patsy looked puzzled. Liz asked, "What kind of a problem?"

"Drew. Please give them an update of our conversation."

Drew took them through the circumstances of the three users and the shootings, including the brief involvement of the police and the FBI.

Patsy responded, "It doesn't surprise me, in a way. We all knew that one of the big unknowns was how users would handle the Notice feature. What Drew hasn't mentioned, because we just updated the logs, is that two users have died within the past week of natural causes and the Final Notice prediction was consistent with their actual deaths. We'll need to check and see if there were any unusual incidents associated with these two."

"Unusual as in shootings?" asked Drew.

"Yes, or harming people in other ways. There was another natural death a week earlier and he might be the one that shot the cashier, which also might explain the anomaly with the Notice timing."

Vijay was absolutely focused on what Patsy had just said.

"What anomaly?"

"The user received his Notice for a week, but then the system issued an urgent 911 Notice five days before the week ended. We didn't understand why that would change. But if the Notice triggered extreme stress and/or anger – which could be why he shot the cashier – or if the stress was a result of shooting the cashier, that could explain his accelerated death."

Vijay recapped, "So, out of our group of 100, we have a total of 5 deaths, including one suicide. And under the circumstances, the suicide is almost normal. Let's face it, knowing you have a week to live might make suicide seem like a good way to go, depending on your illness and pain levels. Two others involve some type of anger or revenge; and two more appear uncomplicated.

"The issue is the Notice. Nothing else with respect to the VT2 would trigger aggressive behavior. Drew, will you follow up with these two most recent deaths and verify that they were indeed uncomplicated with respect to guns or other violence?"

"Got it."

"And while you're at it, see if they had guns or easy access to one. In fact, see if we can find out the total number of alpha testers who have or had access to guns. Liz, I wanted you here in case we have or may have a legal issue."

Liz took a breath and replied, "I don't think we do at the moment, but we need to give some additional thought to the set-up of the beta test, to take some precautions and ensure we don't have legal issues going forward. Obviously, unless Drew's search turns up information that the two users he's following up on killed people using baseball bats, guns seem to be the big variable. We may need to ascertain which users have guns and ensure we have representative numbers with and without."

Patsy added, "Since we involve a doctor in the enrollment process, they can ask that question."

"Not in Florida, Missouri and Montana. Other states are considering passing legislation as well," Liz retorted.

Vijay almost shouted, "What the hell is that about?"

Liz weighed in, "The NRA. That's how all this legislation gets started. Even the tobacco industry put up with restrictions for minors, but if the NRA had its way, kids would get a gun instead of a cup or rattle as a birth present. And when election time comes around, the NRA takes care of its own, and by that, I mean, they support politicians that push for gun liberalization."

"This country drives me crazy with its obsession with guns. Perhaps the Notice is too much to handle. We should consider scrapping it or maybe diluting it to a notice that you should see your doctor asap. We need to get the full team together. OK, here's a list of my takeaways from today:

"Drew, follow up with the two recent natural causes as well as the gun access sub-group and get back with me. What's your target? You've got the next action, too, so don't over-commit."

"Close of business tomorrow, or sooner," Drew quickly responded. "Some of it might be easy, but I'll keep you posted if I'm delayed."

"OK, good. Next. We need to start planning the beta test. That's you again, Drew, and take Liz's suggestion regarding gun ownership or access into account. I'd like to have some with guns and some without."

"Are we still going with the same age group?"

"I think it's time to broaden the group and include representative samples down to 20 years. The VT2 is more about everything else it can do ... not just the Final Notice. And if there are additional deaths ... well, we won't have a Final Notice."

The four attendees looked at each other with shock and concern, but Drew brought them back when he asked, "What's our volume capacity?"

"Today? 200, but that will be growing rapidly as we finalize production set-up. When can you have a discussion draft ready for us to review?"

"How about the end of next week. Thursday or Friday?"

"I'll ask Maureen to set it up for Thursday afternoon with the full team. That OK for you guys?"

Silence while they checked their phones, iPads and calendars followed by OKs all around.

"Maria, can you draft a simple procedure for distribution to everyone, including the reception desk, on how to handle inquiries from the public regarding the VT2? We need it as soon as possible in case we have any more alpha issues, and we can incorporate it into the beta test program from day one.

"Include procedures to handle and capture questions from test users, consumer interest, retailer/wholesaler interest, clinical, law enforcement, legal questions or concerns, and any others you can think of. I'd like a daily recap, too."

Maria assured him, "I think I know what you want. I'll have a draft to you by midday tomorrow."

"And run it by Liz, too," he said, looking in Liz's direction.

"Liz, Patsy, you've escaped this time, but you'll soon have your hands full. Thanks all. See you later." Vijay was energized, back in control, yet there was a feeling that a dark cloud had just settled in. He hoped the two natural deaths were indeed simply deaths, with no complications.

* * *

Midland, Texas. Billy Roy Hunter watched Marla, his third wife, storm away from him in a huff. She was still mighty fine to look at but she'd become a first-class bitch. All she ever wanted any more was … everything: a new car like Darlene's, a bigger boat like Shirley Anne and Ed's, a bigger ring like Suzie's, and on and on. But this time she wanted Billy Roy to get her son, Grant, into Yale. Shit, the kid would be lucky to get into a correspondence course, in something easy, let alone Yale. And Marla was right, he could do it, but it would cost him big time with a contribution of the size that he would notice.

Billy Roy had made some very big bucks – on top of the fortune his father had left him. He had friends in very high places, including an old classmate at Yale. Well, actually, they attended Yale at the same time; classmates would imply that Billy Roy actually went to class. He and his Ivy League buddy did a lot of business together before his friend got that big job in DC, and even more business after that.

So, when it came to Yale and the bribe, or 'donation,' as it would be called, Billy Roy was not exactly financially challenged. He was a friend of the Dean at Yale, too, so he was in a position to help Grant out; but the Dean would need a hefty donation to fight off the Yale academic establishment if he pulled those kinds of strings. And the fact was, Billy Roy didn't like Grant at all … a real mealy-mouthed mama's boy.

100

He and Marla had been married for almost two years and he'd known her for two years and a month. Thirty-two years younger than him, she was arm candy enough to make everyone he knew, or everyone who'd seen her, green with envy. And as long as she didn't say anything, she was perfect. That was the problem. Oh, she was all quiet and sweet at first, but it didn't take too long for her greed and want-it-all genes to start working overtime. He still couldn't figure out how she could spend money that fast. He tried talking with her but that didn't work; tried putting caps on her credit cards but she told her friends what a cheapskate he was and that maybe he wasn't as rich as he pretended to be. That really pissed him off.

His buddy and lawyer, Luther Holmes, told him that if he divorced her (unlike the first two times), it could cost him; reminding him yet again that he should have waited for him to draft a pre-nup. More than an expensive divorce, lots of things might come out into the open when his finances were looked into, and that's the part that Billy Roy Hunter did not want to happen. Which is why he had retained a detective to see if they could get something on her.

He poured himself a Jack Daniels from a bottle on the credenza, lit a Marlboro and thought about his situation. Only 71 years old and the doctor told him that he might not have many more. Too many cigarettes, too much booze, too much food, and too little exercise. Billy Roy reflected briefly on the sins of his past, downed his bourbon and decided that if given another chance, he'd do it exactly the same ... except the marrying Marla part. That mistake might see him leaving a sizeable fortune to her and her worthless son. The thought of that alone might kill him, and as he thought about it, he poured himself another drink and lit another cigarette.

In the distance he heard doors slamming and Marla's unintelligible screaming. This wasn't the first time this scene had been played, but the intensity seemed greater this time, and his involvement was more than as a half-amused spectator. In the past, her demands were easily satisfied, he would give in and she would reward him with the only thing he wanted from her. This time, all he felt was a growing rage, his face getting hotter, and his breathing got more shallow and labored.

He heard the front door open and a voice call out, "Mom. It's me!" Billy Roy thought he could have also added, "your worthless, piece of shit son." Grant came into the living room, weaving and slurring his words. He seemed drunk and almost surprised to see Billy Roy in his own house.

"You cheap, vindictive son of a bitch! Mom told me you wouldn't help get me into Yale. You've always hated me, and this was your chance to prove it."

"Well, baby boy Grant. That's pretty harsh talk from a mama's boy. Looks like drinking makes you pretty brave. But the word 'hate' would imply that I even give a shit about you," he said, his rage boiling.

Grant reached into his jacket and pulled out a gun, pointing it wildly in the direction of Billy Roy, and discharged a shot that wasn't even close, shattering a window. This seemed to cause a number of things to occur at more or less the same time. Billy Roy's breathing grew more uneven; his face was reddish purple and his VT2 watch buzzed with an "Imminent 911 Final Notice" warning. Grant had turned white, watching the rage boiling up over Billy Roy. He was weaving about and his hand was shaking so much he could hardly hold the large revolver, let alone shoot it again.

Billy Roy looked at his VT2 watch, smiled, and turned. Steadying himself with one hand against the credenza, he opened a drawer with the other hand, and when he turned around he was pointing a S&W 357 magnum at Grant. He discharged two shots, killing Grant with either the first or second round. Marla ran screaming into the room as Grant crumpled to the floor. Billy Roy only needed one shot to kill Marla, and it was the last shot he ever fired, just before falling to the floor, dead, from a massive heart attack. As he fell, the gun careened off the credenza and landed a few feet away, behind an overstuffed chair.

* * *

The following morning, Juanita, the housekeeper, had a bit more work when she arrived and found three dead gringos. She circled the three dead bodies as far away as she could, eyes and mouth aghast. She didn't see the gun and tripped over it. Picking it up, and functioning on habit and instincts, she returned it to the open drawer and closed it. And then it hit home that this tragedy was causing a wider ring of ripples. Juanita was working illegally, so calling the police was not a great option. Leaving the scene of a crime wasn't either, and Juanita realized that if she simply disappeared and it was discovered that she worked there, she could be implicated. Regardless of what she did, they would probably come looking for her, even if only to find out what she knew. She decided to call her nephew, Hernando. He would know what to do.

Juanita had never used the house phone before, as Señor Hunter didn't allow it. However, as he was lying there, quite dead, she decided it would be OK. It would be the least of her problems. After quite a few rings, she got Hernando's answering machine and in Spanish she cried out, "¡Ayudame Hernando! ¡Tengo tres gringos muertos y no se que hacer!" (Help me Hernando. I've got three dead gringos and I don't know what to do.) She dialed the number again and Hernando answered, "¿Quién es?" (Who is this?) Juanita explained her situation. Hernando asked for the address and said he would be there pronto to help her.

Juanita was paralyzed with fear and didn't know if she should go about her tasks or just sit and wait for Hernando. While she was pondering what to do, she almost jumped out of the chair when the doorbell chimed. Hernando couldn't have come that quickly. Should she answer or not? She ran to the utility room closet and brought out the big, noisy Kirby vacuum cleaner. It would be her excuse for not hearing the doorbell. And it would have worked if she hadn't started on the family room at the back of the house, because she found herself face to face, on opposite sides of a sliding glass door, with a large, grizzled man she had never seen before. He tried to open the door, found it locked and motioned for her to open it. She hesitated. She didn't know who he was, why he was there or what he wanted, and under normal circumstances – hell, she didn't know what was normal anymore.

She decided to shout through the glass that Señor Hunter was not home. In a way that was true. "Señor Hunter no home now!" she blurted out. Miraculously, he said OK and left so she returned the vacuum cleaner to the closet. Shortly afterwards, Hernando showed up and took stock of the situation. He asked her what she had touched, and she looked around and told him the gun, telephone, utility closet door and the Kirby. Hernando instructed Juanita to get in his car. He decided that the prints on the closet door and Kirby would be normal, but he wiped the gun, phone and front doorknob and drove his aunt to the house of a friend who would smuggle her back to Mexico that night.

* * *

It doesn't really matter who finally found the dead trio, or when, but it is worthy to note that the case remains unsolved to this day. What the police know is that three people, identified as Billy Roy Hunter, his wife, Mrs. Marla Hunter, and her son Grant Thornton, were dead. Mrs. Hunter and Grant Thornton died from gunshot wounds. Mr. Hunter died from natural causes. The gun that fired the fatal shots, an 8-shot Smith & Wesson 357 magnum, Model 327, was in a closed drawer and wiped clean of prints. Three shots had been fired.

A second gun, another S&W 357 magnum, 6-shot Model 27, had been fired once. It was assumed that the shot exited the broken window, but the bullet was never found. The prints on the Model 27 matched the younger, male victim. Both guns were registered to Billy Roy Hunter, which would have pissed him off even more, knowing that Marla or Grant had taken it. There were no prints on the front door, which was unlocked. The last calls made from the phone, which was wiped clean of prints were to a 'pay as you go' phone that was untraceable. It appeared that part of the carpet in the family room had recently been vacuumed. A set of prints on the utility room closet door, the Kirby and other cleaning articles had matching prints that did not belong to the victims. There was another set of unique prints on the outside of the family room sliding glass door belonging to an ex-cop and now a private investigator in Florida. He has not yet been located and the case is still open.

What the police did find out eventually, however, was that the VT2 watch that Billy Roy was wearing was of great interest to the FBI.

* * *

CHAPTER 11 - ZOE BROUET

Kansas City, Missouri. Zoe was a rising star in the Bureau. Double major Psychology and Criminal Justice at Michigan State in East Lansing and a law degree from the University of New Mexico in Albuquerque. Her parents had immigrated to the US from France before Zoe was born. Her father was French and her mother, Tunisian. Zoe was a tomboy and excelled at soccer and academics. As a senior at Michigan State, she helped take her team to the Soccer Championships.

Like many immigrants, her parents viewed the law as something that must be complied with, in all respects. "Even speed limits," her mother would always remind her. And so, Zoe's interest in the law carried forth and an FBI recruiter on campus convinced her to join the Bureau. After graduating at the top of her mixed-gender class from the FBI 18-week Academy program, she was assigned to the Kansas City office, where she sat, alone, looking at three files on her desk. She wished they had visually unique shapes, so she could put the pieces together in the right way to solve the puzzle more easily than she was doing at the moment. What did she know?

Quentin Moore, 85 years old, Joplin, Missouri shot and killed a convenience store cashier with whom he'd had an argument, three months earlier. Motive: Depression, Revenge?

Moore had a VT2 watch and shot the cashier after receiving his Final Notice. He died later that day of natural causes. Had owned a gun for a while and had purchased another just prior to the shooting using an NRA Senior Discount.

John Mason, 89 years old, Green Valley, Arizona, shot 12 people, killing 6, at a retirement home. No motive. Possibly depression. Her visit to San Diego to interview Mason's son yielded another VT2 watch, again showing a Final Notice.

Mason was killed by a security guard. Purchased two guns just prior to the shootings using an NRA Senior Discount.

And now, another one: Billy Roy Hunter, 71, Midland Texas. The case was still open, and it was uncertain who the shooter was, as the prints had been wiped. It was Hunter's gun that he'd had for a while that killed his wife and stepson. Hunter died of a heart attack virtually concurrent with his Final Notice.

The three deceased shooters were taking part in a field test ("alpha test," they called it) using a new health monitor watch, which they were all wearing at the time of death. Guns had been involved in all three incidents. The FBI techies had established that the watch and its associated app represented a highly advanced health monitor that went far beyond the capability of other sports/health type watches. The techies had also ascertained that the VT2 could be set to advise the user of their predicted time of death, within certain ranges. All of the deceased received such a notice.

A logical conclusion is that the three deceased, after receiving the notice, went into such deep and immediate depression that they killed someone.

In any case, her upcoming meeting on Wednesday with VitalTech's founder, Vijay Patel, might help get to the bottom of it and head off any more unnecessary deaths.

* * *

Pasadena, California. On Tuesday evening, Vince opened his laptop and went to one of his favorite bookmarked sites, Daily Kos Gunfail. He had found the site while researching gun incidents and he really enjoyed the Gunfail blog. And a brand-new entry entitled, *"Two Guns, Four Shots, Three Dead, Two Shot"* immediately caught his eye:

"Midland, Texas. Police are baffled following the discovery of three members of a prominent Texas family found dead in their sprawling Midland home. Billy Roy Hunter (71), his wife, Marla (39), and his stepson, Grant Thornton (18) were found dead on Monday. Raul Gomez, the family's gardener, called the police after repeatedly trying to get someone to answer the door.

"The police are still investigating the shooting, however the spokesman revealed that Mrs. Hunter and Mr. Thornton were shot with the same pistol and Mr. Hunter had died of natural causes. The coroner estimates the times of death as the same for all, two to three days earlier. There were two guns involved but only one was responsible for the deaths. The investigation continues."

Vince was struck by the age of one of the deceased, 71. Could this in some way be related to the other recent deaths in Arizona and Missouri? Would he ever know?

* * *

Quincy, Massachusetts. The industrial park containing VitalTech was unimpressive, and the building, very low key. It stood in marked contrast to the dossier on Vijay Patel, whom Zoe would be meeting with soon: PhD from MIT, Harvard Med School graduate, accomplished athlete, and founder of VitalTech. She hoped that this meeting would reveal more clues as to why the three people, bound together through their common membership in the VT2 alpha test, were involved in at least 12 deaths.

Agent Brouet was met in the lobby by Maureen Singer, Vijay Patel's secretary, whom she had watched descend the single-story staircase.

"Good morning, Ms. Brouet, or is it Special Agent Brouet? I'm Maureen Singer, Vijay Patel's secretary."

"Good morning, Ms. Singer," Zoe smiled. "You can call me Zoe or Agent Brouet." As Zoe handed Maureen her card, she thought they were about the same age, but Maureen was taller and had beautiful red hair.

Maureen smiled back, "It's Maureen. Did you find us OK?"

"Yes, thanks to the miracle of GPS. How long have you been here?"

"About a year. Let me take you up to see Vijay."

"Does he prefer 'Vijay' or 'Dr. Patel'?" They both smiled at the 'what's your name?' theme of their conversation.

"Everyone calls him Vijay. He's a great guy," she added, as they climbed the stairs.

"Vijay, this is Zoe Brouet with the FBI." Maureen handed Vijay Zoe's card.

"Special Agent Brouet," he said aloud, reading Zoe's card. "It's nice to meet you."

"You can call me Zoe. And the pleasure is mine," she replied. She was surprised at how tall he was, but that experience was not uncommon for her.

"How can we help you today?"

"I'm charged with investigating the mysterious, and frankly, motiveless shootings that have involved three of your alpha test participants."

"That was fast. We just put two and two together ourselves and realized that two of our users had been involved in shootings and one committed suicide." Vijay replied, with high regard that they had figured it out.

Zoe was confused. "One of your users committed suicide? Who was that?"

Vijay looked at his computer screen and tapped a few keys. "Earl Hoover in Boynton Beach, Florida. You said three shootings. The others were" ... again looking at his screen ... "John Mason in Arizona and Quentin Moore in Missouri. Right?"

Zoe scribbled the information about Earl Hoover, "We didn't know about the suicide and perhaps you haven't heard about the latest incident. It happened over the past weekend, although the bodies weren't discovered until Monday."

"Bodies?"

"Yes, it's complicated. Two people were shot and the third, one of your alpha testers, died of natural causes. It appeared to be a heart attack."

"And the alpha tester shot the other two?"

"Good question. It was his gun, but the prints were wiped so we don't know for sure. The police are carrying out tests and looking for additional evidence."

"Wow! Zoe, I want to do all I can to help you with your investigation. Four out of 100 test-users seem more than a coincidence. How can I help?"

Zoe scribbled a note. "Well, you've just started. I now know that you had 100 people enrolled in your test and one committed suicide. And yes, that would be more than coincidental, given that shootings were involved with all the deaths. How were the test participants selected?"

"This was an initial test, so we chose older participants, 65-90 years old, as they might have more medical issues, therefore putting the VT2 through its paces. None, to the best of our knowledge, had life-threatening illnesses or were clinically depressed. We believe they were in generally good health, given their age. And, to test user friendliness, their age would make them less tech savvy."

Zoe jotted some notes and thought to herself that Quentin Moore was a poor choice in that regard and said, "I spoke with Quentin Moore's physician. Quentin was the one that shot a cashier and then died shortly thereafter at home of natural causes. And he mentioned congestive heart failure as the possible cause of death."

"I can check on that but if neither we nor the physician dropped the ball, it's possible that he had early stage congestive heart failure and that his condition didn't automatically put him at risk of death within the next year or two."

"So, something happened to accelerate his condition?"

"Yes, if the original diagnosis was correct. But you need to understand that the human body is often a mystery, and while there are many people who live much longer than we, as doctors, believe they should, given their condition, there are others who don't last as long as we expect."

"Fair enough. Tell me about the notice feature, 'Final Notice,' I believe you call it."

"Appropriate question, given my comment about predicting accurately," Vijay replied, smiling outwardly, but now beset with inner turmoil. "The VitalTech team has developed a unique, powerful and very accurate set of analytical functions that are administered through the VT2. I'm a medical doctor and I can say with full confidence that our technology is superior to going into a laboratory for ongoing testing, as every minute, all day, every day, the VT2 is carrying out those tests. The unique suite of data and analytics behind it has consistently and accurately predicted death during all our tests for the past three months. For simplicity of analysis, we decided to set the Final Notice to one week."

Zoe jotted down a note. "What are the possible time frame ranges?"

"We're very confident up to 30 days."

Zoe wrote again and asked, "Have there been any adverse effects during your tests, other than the shootings?"

Vijay squirmed uncomfortably in his chair. "None. However, our earlier tests and these 'alpha' field tests are very different. For example, we carried out the initial tests in hospital environments where there was care and support when people learned they would die within a week. Most of the alpha field test people live much more independent lives.

"Importantly, too, in the context of your visit, none of our initial test subjects in hospitals had access to guns. And possibly, the tests in the hospitals were with people who were perhaps more prepared or conditioned to the fact that they would be dying soon. That is not the case with our field test participants."

"Why is the Notice feature important to include?"

"Well, the answer that our Focus Groups gave us centered on the ability and time to get their affairs in order – including reaching out to loved ones and friends and clearing their consciences of loose ends. Many people are unprepared with respect to wills, etc. and even those who are prepared can benefit from the little details and updates that are missed. But mostly – as scary as it might be – the Notice gives people the opportunity to say goodbye."

Emotion crashed over Zoe like an ocean breaker that she never saw coming and her eyes welled up. She took a deep breath and as calmly as she could, replied, "My father died, and we had a lot of unfinished business and reconciliation left. His death was unexpected, and I was at a critical point in my FBI training and couldn't even attend his funeral. I wish he'd had a VT2."

Now it was Vijay's turn for emotion. He had been leaning in favor of changing the Notice but after hearing Zoe's comment, he was unsure. Didn't he give a VT2 to his father for that very reason? "But if the Final Notice is causing senseless deaths, is it worth it?"

"I'm not a psychologist but I've studied the subject and seen a lot of 'human nature' and as distressing as these deaths are, they are the result of actions from a small percentage of people – with or without guns – who have chosen to take advantage of the system. What you don't know or hear about are the other stories, and I'd be willing to bet that the percentage of these is far higher, where the Notice has enabled far more noble outcomes."

Vijay was moved by the sincerity of this young woman and it helped to keep the dark cloud at bay.

Zoe had recovered from her emotional tumble. She took a deep breath and continued, "Dr. Patel ... Vijay ... given what you know about the deaths and gun incidents of the four test subjects, what is your educated explanation, from a doctor's perspective, for what may have happened?"

"Knowing – for sure – that you will die within a known period of time will affect different people in different ways, as we've seen. Some might be relieved, like perhaps the suicide victim, by the ability to avoid more pain or helplessness during their final days. This already happens much more than is documented. Others are angry, and that anger may be aimed at individuals or groups. The man in the retirement home seemed to be angry with his fellow residents for some reason. Perhaps the man who shot the cashier was angry at him or even at the store itself."

Zoe interrupted, "He did have an angry altercation with the cashier earlier, in fact."

"Aha. So, yes, there are a number of reasons, but in all these cases it was access to guns that created an outcome different than our experiences so far. I don't know enough about the last victim, but I can find out. What was his name?"

"Billy Roy Hunter in Midland, Texas."

Vijay picked up the phone and pressed a few keys. "Patsy, hi. Can you pull the alpha test logs for Billy Roy Hunter in Midland and bring them here? I need them, asap. ... Thanks."

"Patsy Carter, our Clinical Head, will be here shortly. Tell me about the Midland shooting."

"I don't know much more than what I told you. We know that Billy Roy was wearing a VT2 watch and that the coroner's estimate of death was Friday or Saturday. Will your logs pinpoint the exact time of death?"

"Yes, they should. Oh, here's Patsy, now. Zoe, this is Dr. Patsy Carter, our Clinical Head. Zoe is a Special Agent from the FBI and has been investigating the links between the VT2 and shootings we discussed last week. Apparently, there has been another gun incident involving one of our test participants."

"Good to meet you, Zoe. I just looked at these and Mr. Billy Roy Hunter died on Friday at 4:36 PM, CST. The data indicates heart failure as the cause of death. And the supporting analytics confirm that was the case, as opposed to a gunshot wound."

"Thanks, Dr. Carter. He wasn't shot, so that's a plus for your analytics. What else can the data tell us?"

Looking at the print-out and graphs, "It seems like from about 4:00 PM until death, there were significant negative changes: increased stress level, increased blood pressure, reduced blood flow, reduced oxygen intake, and increased blood sugar."

"As doctors, in your opinion, what might have caused those changes?"

"Patsy?" Vijay deferred.

"Severe stress could be the catalyst for all of this. That could have come about through sudden exertion but judging from the length of time and Mr. Hunter's physical condition, 35 minutes of physical exertion is unlikely. Given the rapid and significant change, I would say an argument, or arguments, could have been the trigger."

"Why did you say 'or arguments?' "

"If you look closely at this graph – we can enlarge it to see more detail – there was a steady build up from about 4:00 PM until about 4:30 PM when the trend stabilized and even began to normalize. Then it suddenly spiked up again until death. So somehow, the first argument abated, followed by round two."

They sat in silence for a moment, each lost in their own disparate thoughts.

Zoe broke the silence, "Thank you, Dr. Carter. See if this scenario would fit your data. Hunter and his wife argue from 4:00 PM until about 4:30 PM. She leaves, and he pours himself a drink. Would that support the normalizing trend?"

"In my opinion, yes. Alcohol and even cigarettes could have a short-term positive influence."

Zoe looked at her file and said, "In addition to a half empty glass of bourbon, there were cigarettes. One stubbed out and the other one halfway burned down."

"And the second spike?" asked Vijay.

"The third victim was Mrs. Hunter's son from a previous marriage. He didn't live there. So, what if Hunter is calming down after a big argument with his wife, his wife's son comes in, and argument two starts? We know that a gun with the son's prints had fired one shot which exited a window."

"That would definitely support the readings."

"Hunter reacts to the missed shot; his stress levels spike and he receives his Final Notice; shoots the son and his wife before dying of a heart attack."

Both Patsy and Vijay were chilled by the plausible depiction of the murders. Patsy replied, "Very possible, yet almost unbelievable coincidences."

Seeing an opportunity to get a second objective opinion, Zoe asked, "Dr. Carter, Dr. Patel has given me his opinion about why someone receiving their Final Notice might be motivated to kill someone. As you know, prior to the Hunter shooting, two other test participants have shot and killed others. Could I ask your opinion?"

Patsy thought momentarily. "Revenge, settling old scores before it's too late. If you know, for sure, that you're going to die in a day, two days, a week, there'll be no repercussions and it could even make you feel better. Hell, although I don't have a gun, nor am I sure I could use one if I did, I could think of a few people I would like to take out if I knew I was dying in a couple days. Take them out and make the world a better place."

Vijay interceded, "Patsy, let's not get into politics." All three cracked up laughing.

Zoe brought the conversation back. "Dr. Patel, you indicated that this current alpha test is an initial field test. Do you plan additional tests and, if so, how and when will you launch them?"

"Another good question, and yes, we are planning a beta test and are working through the details now. Drew Pierson, our head of Research & Development, looked into how many of our alpha test users have guns or access to them and he came up with 60. We can't be 100% certain of that number, as the question of gun ownership can't be asked in all states, but let's assume it's correct. 60% is higher than the national average so we will set the beta test at 50%, which is closer to reality. By the way, Drew also confirmed that two recent deaths following Final Notices were uneventful. And one of those users had a gun."

Zoe replied, "Yes, I've spoken with Drew on the phone and that's good news that everyone with a gun doesn't use it after receiving their Notice. How large will the beta test be?"

"We haven't agreed on that number yet, but certainly between 200 and 500, maybe more if production can support it. But Agent Brouet," (consciously reverting to a more formal tone), "in your opinion, do we have a legal or even moral responsibility to do anything about a VT2 user's actions after receiving their Final Notice?"

Zoe was still running the probabilities of more shootings through her head, given the beta test size. "I have a law degree, but I couldn't say for sure about your legal responsibility. The Final Notice function is really no different than a doctor telling someone that they have x number of days or weeks to live, and that's not illegal. As for a moral responsibility, I may be an exception in the law enforcement community, but I'm not a big fan of armed citizens. If there's a moral responsibility somewhere, I'd start with the NRA. I got involved in this investigation because the NRA is giving senior citizens discounts on guns. And states are making it easier and easier to buy guns. There are only 14 states that require a permit to purchase one, and unless you check the box that says you are mentally unstable and/or a convicted felon, it's 'thank you for your business and good luck!' "

"OK," said Vijay. "I'll need to check with our legal department, but here is what I'd like to do. For our next test group, we'll ask each participant if they have a gun. I understand that in some states doctors can't ask about guns. But we will go with a 50/50 gun/no gun test population as best as we can determine. And if I don't get push back from legal, we'll give you a user list, showing the gun status. I don't want to emulate Big Brother, but I don't want more innocent people killed, either."

"That's a good idea, and I'll be honest with you. After my bosses receive my report, they may issue a demand to have that list anyway. In fact, can you give me a list of your alpha users with the information Drew found as having gun access?"

Vijay pondered and replied, "I think we can, but let me check with legal. If they are OK with it, I'll send it today or at least let you know if there's an issue."

"Thanks. It's easier and better for you to volunteer. If you don't, I may be forced to demand it and that doesn't sit well with me. Let me know what your guys come up with."

"Will do. Anything else we can help you with?"

"Not right now. I may need to come back, but for the moment, I'm good. Thank you both very much."

They shook hands all round they said their goodbyes.

Zoe stopped by Maureen's desk on her way out. "Bye, Maureen. You were right. Your boss is a really nice guy. Thanks for your help."

* * *

CHAPTER 12 — GRETA JOHANSSON

Seattle, Washington. Greta Johansson was looking at her late husband's collection of guns. There were six handguns. Some looked older and some new. She didn't know much about any of them except that they could kill someone. As a former teacher, she'd wept many times upon hearing reports of school shootings like the big ones at Columbine, Red Lake, Virginia Tech, Oikos University, Sandy Hook, and Umpqua. She wept for each of the smaller ones, too. And she was angry. Angry at parents and a system that produced kids who carried out the carnage; angry at the NRA and their zeal to sell guns to anyone; and angrier still at politicians who did the NRA's bidding. So now she was going to do a small part to help stop or at least slow down the deaths.

Greta received her Final Notice five days ago. She had called her only child, Monika, her daughter in San Francisco, a rising star in technology, and told her the news. Monika had flown up immediately and they'd spent the last day and a half together before Greta insisted that she leave. She preferred to die alone.

They discussed Greta's Will but Monika was too busy with a huge project, was making big money, and did not want to be troubled with the disposal of Greta's car, house and possessions. She did take away a few photos and pieces of her mother's jewelry, but that was all she wanted. It was, given the situation, a nice visit. Nicer than many they'd had in the past. Calm and loving. And now Greta was going to wrap up the last loose ends.

At 78, she was still fit enough, had good eyesight with her glasses, and moved and acted like someone in a lot better health than she was. She packed the guns in a carryall bag along with the ammunition and was relieved when she found she could still lift it. Grabbing her purse with her other hand she headed for her car. It was the first time since her Notice that she drove, and she hoped nothing would happen on her short errands today. It also felt strange to think that this might be the last time she would drive.

Greta made the short trip to Olive Way in the Capitol Hill area and parked in the small area reserved for clients. She pushed open the heavy wood and brass door of King, Newton & White and entered the rich and impressive lobby, with its oak- paneled walls and lush furniture. The smartly dressed and coiffed receptionist greeted her by name and Greta was impressed, but then reflected that it had only been a few months earlier that she was here on a number of occasions after William's death. He'd be rolling over in his grave if he knew what she was doing with his guns. Moments later Henry Newton emerged from one of the large oak doors and guided her to his office. Henry had been their lawyer for almost 40 years, but he still looked far younger than he was.

"Good afternoon Greta. How are you?" Henry asked, sincerely.

"Well, Henry, that's the reason for my visit, but thanks for asking. Actually, I'm pretty sure that I will die very shortly so I wanted to get a few things in order. You may not agree with me, but I am committed to my, what you might call, unorthodox path. I want to change my will."

Henry was a bit taken back by Greta's aggressive posture. It seems that just a few months ago she was a babbling brook of tears. "Of course, what would you like to do?"

"I want to leave my house, car, and all my financial assets to charity. And I want you to decide which charities to leave them to. My conditions are that they are highly rated with respect to efficiency and that more than 90% of the funds will reach the intended beneficiaries. Secondly, that they benefit disadvantaged children's education and well-being.

I want all my clothes, which William always joked about insofar as quantity, to be given as directly as possible to homeless women in Seattle. And I'd like all my other possessions and anything I leave behind to be donated directly to families that need the items. And finally, I'd like any tax receipts for the donations sent to my daughter. Is that clear?"

Henry had been writing furiously and when Greta stopped, he looked up. "Yes, I think so, but why do you think you'll be dying soon? You look very well."

"Trust me. I know. And I mean days, not weeks or months. When can you give me a plan? I don't need numbers. I know you'll need to have the property appraised, but what charities would you recommend? I would feel ever-so-much better if I knew beforehand."

Henry was clearly confused by this sudden sense of urgency, but he managed to get out, "Is tomorrow OK?"

"Perhaps," said Greta, getting up from her chair. "Now I have one more important task to do before it's too late." And it was the one she was most nervous about.

"I'll see you out."

"I'd rather you get to work on the charities. I can find my own way out." And she left both the office and a very perplexed Henry.

Greta drove the short distance to 1519 12th Avenue and miraculously found a 15-minute-only parking spot, just down the street. Fifteen minutes should be plenty of time, she thought, and if it's not, it probably won't matter. Lifting the heavy carryall bag of guns and ammunition, she walked the few yards and climbed a few steps, entering the building and expecting to see more policemen than she did. There was an unmanned desk with a phone and sign that read, "Lift receiver to reach your party." Greta lifted the receiver and an operator asked her whom she wished to see. Greta didn't expect to be talking on the phone. She wanted a personal interaction now more than ever. She replied, "I want to see someone about gun control." The operator asked her name, said that someone will be with her shortly, and suggested taking a seat.

Greta took a seat with a full view of the interior door, but also close to the outside door. She partially unzipped the bag, taking a final look at the contents. A few minutes later the interior door opened and a young man, who seemed much too young to be a policeman even though he was dressed as one, approached her. "Mrs. Johansson?"

Greta rose from her seat and replied, "Yes." She moved her right hand up from the bag ... taking the officer's outstretched hand.

Shaking her hand firmly, but gently, the officer said, "Hello, I'm Officer John Huston. How can I help you today?"

Greta reached down and lifted the bag onto a chair. "I want to make sure that these guns and ammunition are never used to kill children. I understand that you can have them melted down."

Officer Huston smiled and said, "Yes we can."

"How much will it cost for six?"

"Actually, if you have six, we'll give you $600 in Amazon coupons. Amazon is helping to sponsor the gun buyback program."

Greta laughed and said, "I was afraid it would cost a lot and that I might not carry through with my plan to destroy them. Can I give you an address to send the coupons, Officer ... ?"

"Huston, Ma'am. Where would you like them sent?"

Greta gave him Henry Newton's details and asked him to enclose a note that the coupons belonged to Mrs. Johansson's estate as possessions.

"Thank you, Mrs. Johansson. Please have a seat and I'll be right back with a receipt."

She sat down and a feeling of relief ... and tiredness ... swept over her. William's guns would never hurt anyone now. When Officer Huston returned a few minutes later, she had dozed off and he had to gently roust her from a pleasant dream. As she left the East Precinct Police Station, Seattle's liquid sunshine was misting down, refreshing her enough to make the short drive home. She placed the car keys in plain view on the entry hall table, along with the spare set. Greta hung up her coat, changed into her nightgown and robe, and made herself a simple, light dinner of spaghetti with an easy clam sauce using canned clams. She poured herself a small glass of New Zealand Sauvignon Blanc, turned her cd player on and listened to a Maria Muldaur album while she enjoyed her meal. She washed and put away the dishes and went to bed ... for the last time.

***

Zoe was right and sadly, neither she nor VitalTech would ever see the good side of the Final Notice as displayed by Greta Johansson; nor would they know about other acts of generosity prompted by the Final Notice from dozens of other people, including: Waylon Dalton, Justine Henderson, Abdullah Farooq, Marcus Cruz, Thalia Cobb, Mathias Little, Eddie Randolph, Angela Walker, Lia Shelton, Hadassah Hartman, Joanna Shaffer, Jonathon Sanchez, and many others.

* * *

Midland, Texas. Zoe landed at Midland International Airport and was met by Sheriff Bruce "Bull" Johnson. Zoe had heard the nickname and pictured a short muscular guy with a big mustache and cowboy hat; and except for the fact

128

that he was tall, lanky and clean-shaven, she would have been right. Sheriff Johnson had a deep booming voice, so perhaps that was the root of the nickname, but Zoe never found out. He gave her Billy Roy's VT2 and iPhone and had her sign for them, explaining, too, that both the watch and phone were dead, and password protected, so they would let Zoe and her team try to hack them. He asked if she needed the guns, but she declined. Over coffee at the airport coffee shop he told her that they had made a little progress in that they had found the private investigator, who told them about a woman in the house on Saturday who was vacuuming the carpet. She had told him that Hunter wasn't home, and he added that she had an accent.

Given the inexact time of death, it's not known what role, if any, she played. Hunter's gardener told police that a cleaning person named Juanita was employed but he didn't know her last name or where she could be found and no further leads on her whereabouts were uncovered.

Sheriff Johnson had also interviewed Billy Roy Hunter's lawyer, Luther Holmes. Holmes stated that things were not good between Hunter and his wife and that his relationship with her son was even worse. Importantly, Johnson added that they eventually found gunshot residue on Hunter, so it was pretty certain who the second shooter was, although the absence of prints on the gun was puzzling. Zoe told Johnson about her meeting with VitalTech and the scenario they had discussed, as well as sharing the exact time and day of death. Johnson was skeptical about the role of the watch, but he accepted the information and description of the events that Zoe laid out as reasonable. He had sincere doubts of the maid's involvement, both from a motive and character appraisal of the many Latina women he'd seen in cleaning jobs. Their joint input was sufficient to at least put aside the case, if not formally close it. There were still some unanswered questions, but they were satisfied.

* * *

Pasadena, California. Vince had helped Trudi come to terms with her new iPad and the differences between it and a laptop. She was definitely hooked. They had decided on a locked AT&T version because of the price. Trudi could get her emails at home or on the road and be able to read them without a magnifying glass. She was also feeling good because she donated their old Toshiba laptop to a charity, after doing a complete machine reset and full data wipe.

She began to surf progressive organizations, being careful not to accept notifications or sign up for newsletters, as Vince had suggested. Giving out your details to even one, he warned, will result in an onslaught of emails begging for money, as many organizations share their donor lists. Like Vince, she found the Daily Kos an interesting site, and although it was obviously biased to the left, she fact-checked the stories that seemed far-fetched and found them to be accurate.

But apart from her new pastime, she increasingly found that the happy little California bubble she lived in was just that: a bubble with a very real and different world on the outside. She also found that her Berkeley protest roots were alive and well, and she began re-connecting with her music of the past, creating more strident songs of protest.

Trudi had been an accomplished folk-blues-Americana singer/songwriter during her college years and early in her marriage. But she scaled back on playing out when Dave was born. After he grew up and went off to college, she returned to songwriting, joining a song circle in a local art gallery, and enjoying the safe haven that it offered. She also serenaded Vince from time to time, knowing he liked her music.

* * *

CHAPTER 13 – VIJAY'S DILEMMA

Quincy, Massachusetts. The VitalTech team was assembled to discuss and agree on the beta test parameters. At the conference room table were Drew, Maria, Liz, Patsy, plus Wade Thomas, COO, Don Casey, VP Marketing, and Ganesh Desai, CFO.

Vijay formally kicked off the meeting. "I have asked you all to participate in this discussion about the ultimate design of the VT2 beta test. This is an extremely exciting and important step of the VT2 launch. We are pleased, overall, with the outcome of the alpha test; but as most of you know, there has been a dark side as well, and it relates to the Final Notice feature.

"One of the unexpected consequences of the Final Notice is that a number of people, specifically people with guns, have killed people, knowing they will die within a week. I have spoken with the FBI, and Liz has consulted with our outside counsel, who assure us that we cannot be held accountable; but that doesn't make me feel any better. So, I want you all to consider this issue as we discuss the beta test parameters and keep an open mind with respect to the Final Notice, including scrapping it altogether or changing it to a 'Contact your doctor ASAP' alert." A small murmur spread through the room.

Don Casey asked, "What does KKL think about that?" Don knew that KKL shared his enthusiasm for the feature and feeling that it represented a major unique selling proposition.

"I mentioned it to them and we'll be meeting this afternoon to discuss it and check on the IPO progress," replied Vijay. "I'd like you, Liz, Maria and Ganesh to attend. It's at two. So, let's get the discussion underway by having Drew and Patsy present the findings of the alpha test."

Drew and Patsy presented the alpha test results to date, with Drew elaborating on the shooting complications. His additional research determined that of the 100 participants, 61 had access to guns, and of those 61, six received Final Notices. Of those, there was one suicide and three crimes committed, resulting in nine people being killed. Drew concluded, "Taking these crimes into account, we will be designing the beta test fifty/fifty – those with access to guns and those without."

Ganesh asked, "Do we believe that this 50% outcome – three crimes out of six with guns – would hold for the entire future population of users?"

Patsy responded, "Jesus, I hope not. Everyone in this test will die if they wear it long enough. If 50% kill one or more people … that would be a big problem. But a hundred is a small sample and it's skewed toward an older user base. The beta test is planned to have a much wider age range. What the study gives us is the knowledge, and therefore the ability, to call attention to the potential issue. Doctors can be made aware of the dangers and be on the look-out for behavior that could result in an incident."

Liz chimed in, "That might help with the beta test, but in a full roll out, doctors won't necessarily be involved."

Patsy parried back, "That's true. But here's a thought. Just as we've used doctors as the source for our alpha users ... and will do so again with the beta testers ... perhaps we could link the unlocking of the Final Notice to some kind of registration and acknowledgement from a user's doctor."

Don quickly jumped in. "That would over-complicate the sales and marketing process and potentially hurt sales. It may not even be legal. But for the beta test, it's OK."

Liz again spoke: "I don't think it would have legal implications in that sense, but certainly we'd have to take any additional requirement into account for sales and marketing activities to ensure clarity and full disclosure for the users."

Vijay interjected, "The FBI would like to receive both our alpha list and beta list, along with the information as to the user's gun access. As the alpha test is coming to a close, I spoke with Liz and she agreed it's OK, especially since the FBI would most likely be successful in forcing us to share it. So I did it voluntarily. How should we handle the request for the beta list, Liz?

"Where will we get the gun info?"

Drew answered, "I checked with the doctors who were involved with the VT2's in the alpha test to identify the 61 users with guns. We were thinking of including a short questionnaire for users in the beta test that would state gun ownership status and also provide a doctor's assessment of the user's physical and mental health."

Liz voiced concern. "I'm not sure about the questionnaire. Let me run that by our outside guys as well as the question about releasing the list."

Ganesh asked, "Patsy, how big is our beta test group?"

"We're planning 100 in the first wave and then after 2 weeks, another 100 per week until we get to 500. If all is going well, we'll then add a final 500."

"Wade, presumably you've been involved with this and can cover these volumes?"

"Oh yeah. The production set up has gone very smoothly. We even got a nice grant from the Indian government, who are trying to energize their manufacturing for export capability. Those volumes are nothing. We're just chomping at the bit, waiting for the bell so we can show off our stuff," he said with a big smile. "And speaking of grants and Indian manufacturing ... Liz, Ganesh, what's the potential for a big surprise from this administration of slapping a big import tax on us?"

"Ganesh and I have been talking with our outside counsel and as we never manufactured in the USA, and aren't shipping jobs abroad, they don't see an immediate concern, but then again ... "

"Thanks. Looking at it another way, I'm almost positive that nobody with similar products makes their stuff in the USA, so we'd all be in the same boat."

Then Vijay asked the big question: "I'd like to hear from each of you ... your view on the Final Notice. Keep it or not? Or something in between. Patsy, since you've been privy to this before today, what's your view?"

"I look at it from a doctor's point of view and the benefits of the VT2 are indisputable. As a doctor, I have also witnessed the suffering, both emotional and financial, of ... I can't think of a better way of saying it, a messy end to one's life. Life insurance benefits not discussed and often lost to the beneficiaries. Wills not complete or updated, leading to all sorts of problems. I accept that the Notice may give some users a feeling that they can do what they want with impunity, but that's someone's unique moral code and we can't be responsible for that. If we did, cars wouldn't be able to break the speed limit. I say it stays. For the full post-beta test rollout, perhaps with an option and some encouragement to register it with their doctor. I also suggest that we activate the optional Notice period, but with three choices of 10, 20 and 30 days. This will give us a more realistic picture for the final rollout."

"Interesting idea. Thanks. Drew?"

"I admit that the killings really shocked me and shook some of my confidence, but then I thought back to the Focus Groups. The stories we heard from them about how they wished their mother or father had known about their death so that they would have also known. No one wants to believe a loved one is going to die. But the Notice wakes them up to reality, so they can say their goodbyes and ensure there are none of those missed opportunities that eat away at the survivors forever. I also agree with Patsy on the Notice pre-sets."

"Thanks. Liz?"

"Keep it in. It's legal and it appears to be valuable."

"Succinct and to the point. What a surprise." Smiles all round. "Maria, you were also involved earlier. Your thoughts?"

"I will have to admit to a personal bias. My mom died suddenly, and I didn't get a chance to say goodbye. And as Drew said, we all heard similar stories with our Focus Groups. So, I see the value of the Notice. Obviously, I wish there were no collateral issues associated with our product, but since my function is charged with managing the public's perception of the VT2, that is my concern. What happens if the killings become a story before the IPO? Could that adversely affect the launch and future of VitalTech? That's my question and it should be everyone else's, too. And I'm OK with the expanded Notice presets."

"Thanks, Maria. You raise an excellent point. Don, I think we know your view on the Notice, but what about Maria's concern?"

"We all agree that the VT2 is light years ahead of the competition. But how long will that last? One year, two? I can almost guarantee that it won't be three until someone else develops a Notice-type alert. And when they do, we would have to unwrap ours – which we'd had all along – but in a competitive, reactionary environment, dramatically reducing our current sales projections. Also, if we launch without it, we may not be seen as such a major step up, and people won't swap their Fitbits, Garmins and whatever else they are using, especially at a premium price. And I'm 100% behind the expanded Notice periods.

"One more point," Don continued. "If you go back to what Patsy said earlier, gun sales are going up - by over 10% a year, in fact. The NRA is even offering discounts to senior citizens and they're approaching a million more sales. My point is this. Nobody cares about the danger of guns and gun deaths. Gun sales don't drop after mass killings, and the outrage is very short lived. I'd almost wager a bet that if a big story broke, it would help us."

Vijay replied with a concerned look. "Not a comforting thought, but hard to argue with. But that reminds me. When we finish the beta test discussion, Maria will present a process that she has developed, with input from Liz, to make sure that inquiries from the public, distributors, legal and law enforcement are handled efficiently and effectively. Users might be immune to gun death stories, but investors aren't immune to shoddy management.

"Who's next ... Wade? You've been pretty quiet. Want to – sorry – wade into the discussion about the notice?" Make-believe groans rose from the group at Vijay's poor pun and the mood lightened a bit.

"I say let's do it. And I agree with Don that the activation of the Notice with a doctor's registration adds a degree of complexity, and I'm shooting for 7 sigma defect levels."

"I thought 6 sigma was the highest," asked Vijay, half seriously.

"So far. But you should know that the tiffin carriers in India do better than 6 sigma."

"Whoa," Maria blurted out. "6, 7 sigma and tiffins. I thought I was doing pretty well with all the manufacturing jargon you throw around, Wade. Supply chains, productivity levels, just-in-time and even the alphabet soups like OEE, WIP, TQM, but what is sigma and tiffins?"

Wade, who loved talking about manufacturing, replied with the enthusiasm of a kid with his favorite toy, "6 sigma means that you consistently manufacture your products with no more than 3.4 defective ones out of a million; in other words, 99.9997% of all attempts are perfect. 7 sigma would eliminate the 3 defective ones. That's our target."

"And tiffins?"

"Ahh. Vijay or Ganesh could probably explain it better, but since you ask, all across India, millions of workers leave home for work, bright and early, to cover the distances that many have to go. As they are leaving, their wives or in some cases, mothers, begin to make up their lunch, and by our standards, these lunches are complex: Rice and two or even three dishes, plus their chapatis or other bread. They pack them into stacking tin containers, called tiffins, kinda like those camping kits you see. Then, the tiffin carriers come round the houses, collect the tiffins, and deliver them to the right people, almost all the time. If you've ever seen the chaos of Mumbai, that level of performance is amazing. Not sure how many meals are delivered but in Mumbai, I read it was over 200,000 per day. FedEx and Harvard Business School have studied them."

"Why don't they eat at restaurants near where they work?"

"Don't know. Vijay, Ganesh?"

Ganesh answered, "Eating meals out would be too expensive for most and sandwiches haven't taken over yet. Plus, food is very important, and everyone prefers to eat home cooking, with exactly the right spice combinations. Thinking about it is making me hungry. Let's move on!"

"Ganesh, what do you think about the Notice?" Vijay asked.

"Keep it."

"Are you just saying that because you're hungry?"

"Yes."

They all laughed, and Vijay said, "OK. I've had my doubts, but it's agreed to keep it in. Drew, please take us through the beta test details."

Drew explained the test participant configuration, age groups and other details. As discussed earlier, younger groups would be added, and each group would have a 50/50 gun/no gun composition. They would keep the same requirements regarding no clinical depression and no imminently fatal illnesses; and Patsy and her team would draft instructions to the referring doctors to watch for signs of depression and anger. The automatic notification to doctors of a patient's Final Notice that they uploaded during the alpha test would be kept, but the 911 notifications would remain suppressed.

The meeting was adjourned, and while there was general agreement and enthusiasm, it was obvious that the murders weighed on the group.

Vijay felt comfortable with how the meeting had gone. His colleagues were upbeat and optimistic, and despite the heaviness of the shootings, he finally felt good, too. One ingredient in his feel-good frame of mind was this afternoon's scheduled meeting with KKL, giving him a chance to see Jennifer again. And she was staying overnight, too. They had both been so busy, it had been two weeks since they'd been together. He had an hour and a half before the meeting, so he changed into his running gear and hit the pavement.

* * *

Vijay was back and showered and at his desk at 1:45 PM, in time to gulp down the blueberry protein supplement smoothie that Maureen had waiting for him. Thank God for smoothies and supplements, he thought, as he devoured both the smoothie and a full email inbox. At exactly 2:00 PM, Maureen announced his visitors, J. Edward Konig and Jennifer Andrews.

Vijay was ambivalent about J. Edward. He guessed him to be in his mid- fifties, but he was off by about 10 years, due to J. Edward's physical condition, or rather lack thereof. He wasn't a tall man and he was carrying 20-30 extra pounds. But despite his lethargy, J. Edward was enthusiastic in his backing of VitalTech and Vijay appreciated that. He also seemed confident and Vijay had to hope that this confidence was based on reality, because the financial world was all new to Vijay. KKL was successful, so Vijay assumed he knew what he was talking about.

Jennifer was often the bridge between Vijay and J. Edward. She could sense when Vijay was nervous about something, possibly an aggressive move suggested by J. Edward, and she would intervene and broker a compromise. She was very level-headed and very smart.

As he greeted them, he was struck, once again, by her beauty and hoped that the meeting and the rest of the day would quickly melt away, so they could be together in a much different way than the client relationship charade they were about to begin.

"J. Edward, Jennifer, thank you for making the trip up. It's good to see you both again. You remember Don, Liz, Maria and Ganesh? I've asked them to join us."

After the hellos, handshakes and settling in, Maureen came in to get requests for coffee and tea. Bottles of water and juices were on a sideboard. There were no soft drinks, thanks to Vijay's dual role of doctor and health enthusiast.

Almost immediately, J. Edward asked about the Final Notice option. "As you can all imagine, I was horrified to hear about the murders of innocent people by the test participants after receiving their Final Notices. Our country and guns have a long, strong and complicated relationship, and I was relieved when Vijay told me that the FBI felt there was no basis that would implicate VitalTech with the murders. And that being the case, I hope that you all are standing strong in your conviction about the benefits of the Notice feature."

Vijay was concerned that J. Edward was going to continue with his sales pitch, so he broke in. "You'll be pleased to hear that our Team unanimously agreed to continue with the Notice, with three small additions. To better understand the role of guns, we'll set up the test group on a 50/50 basis, guns and no guns. We'll also prepare a detailed briefing sheet for the conferring doctors, advising them to particularly watch for signs of depression and anger when the Final Notice is received. And for the post-beta test roll out, we'll strongly encourage registration of the user's doctor, so that they can become more active in the relationship. Finally, we'll be allowing users to set the Notice period to 10, 20 or 30 days.

We've also set up a detailed public relations flow process so that we handle calls from the public, clinicians, law enforcement, distributors, etc., efficiently and consistently. What we don't want is a screw-up that leads to a story breaking about the murders."

"That's great Vijay," J. Edward replied, looking at Don. "How does your marketing guru feel about that? Everyone's counting on you to sell a million of these things ... in the first month!"

There were chuckles from all and Don replied, "Keeping it in is the right move. The Focus Groups said as much, despite the grim reality."

J. Edward smiled and said, "Hmm, that might be a better name for it than Final Notice: 'The Grim Reality.' "

Following appreciative laughter amongst the group, J. Edward continued, "Hell, when Richard Branson was starting up Virgin Airlines, he wanted to call First Class and Economy, Upper Class and Lower Class." More laughter. "He got his way with Upper Class. Planning in advance for handling inquiries is a good idea but what are your contingencies for public relations issues? What if a story does break? We have some good connections with the media and if we know quickly enough, we may be able to quash it."

Before Maria could respond, Don jumped in and repeated his comment from the morning session. "Sorry to barge in but going back to your comment about our relationship with guns, I said this morning that if word got out about a watch that's causing people to kill others, I believe it would help, rather than hurt us."

"Why do you think that?" J Edward asked.

"First of all, everyone has pondered the question, 'If you knew, for sure, that you only had X days to live, what would you do?' Second, we're talking about people with guns, and they are different than people without guns, and not just because they have a gun. They have a gun because they know that there is a chance they may have to shoot someone. They may hope it never happens, but it could, and they have accepted that they can do it. Most of them have never shot at anyone but I know that everyone has at least someone that they might like to take out, if they could do so with impunity. A politician, boss, bully, etc. I couldn't afford the ammunition to take care of all the politicians I'd like to send to their graves before I climb into mine."

Smiles, chuckles and acknowledgement filled the room.

"And the final reason is that it would be a huge, unique and compelling story that would feed those fantasies. It would go viral and everyone in the world would hear about it within a week."

Vijay was concerned. "So, what you are also saying is that, by feeding their fantasies, there may be an even better chance that people with guns will act in this way when they get their Notice."

Two people in the room heard the apprehension and warning in Vijay's comment and one of them, Don, replied, "Oh I don't think it would change the odds."

The other person, J. Edward, shifted the conversation, "How many are you planning in the first beta test group, Vijay?"

"100 for the first wave, followed two weeks later by another 100 per week until we get to 500. We'll then add a final 500 to finish out the tests."

"And production?"

"That's looking good. We're even getting a grant from the Indian government."

"Yes, so I've heard. That's good news. Ganesh, how are the units pricing out?"

"Almost too good to be true. Better than planned. I was talking with your analysts the other day and even if we hit some serious snags, it might dent our margin forecast, but profits would still be way above normal expectations. We've discussed a $199 basic model price. At a volume of 500,000 in year one, our lowest, worst case forecast gross income would be 100 million, and obviously double that if we hit your million-unit notional target. Our estimated gross margin for the low-end volume range is in the 65-68 percent range."

"Notional? I'm betting the bank on it. We'll be talking with René at Credit Suisse in the next day or so to get an update on the current IPO climate and preliminary forecasts. Hopefully you'll be able to nail down final costs, so we can start to compress the forecast range.

"Let me ask a question. What if this thing really did take off, even faster than any of us thought? We're the only game in town at the moment, but if we stumble with fulfillment, we create openings and opportunities for others. It may sound crazy, but what if my 'notion' way underestimates demand? What if it's 1.5 million? Two million? Three? Or five?"

J. Edward was an optimist but not a stupid one, so when he came up with something like this, it wasn't just complete nonsense, and it gave everyone pause for thought.

Don, who was probably the biggest optimist in the room, said, "Wade seemed pretty confident in his production capability today."

But Vijay put it into perspective, "Yes, but we weren't talking about numbers like these. Let me talk with Wade and ask him what it would take – time and money – to reach those levels. It's a good idea to think about those possibilities so we can react more quickly. I'll get back to you with our thoughts."

They discussed a number of points and said their goodbyes. Vijay and Jennifer were free to confirm their dinner reservation publicly; after all, she was the Account Manager and was simply entertaining the client. They didn't, however, discuss their sleeping arrangements.

As everyone left, Maria stayed behind to see Vijay. "I've got a strange feeling about this. Do you think Don and J. Edward are plotting something?"

"Like what?"

"J. Edward seemed very interested in Don's scenario about the effect of a breaking story. And he steered us away when Don elaborated."

"You mean that he thinks it would work in our favor?"

"Yes. Even to the questions about our ability to handle huge volumes."

Vijay admitted to himself that he was probably gazing at and thinking about Jennifer more than he realized. "I'll talk with Don and make sure he doesn't go rogue on us."
"What about J. Edward?"

"I'll talk with him, too, but he had a point. We need to have a strategy to cope if something does come out. Have you thought about it?"

"I'm just finishing up a number of draft responses to deal with a variety of scenarios. I'll send them to you when I go back to my office."

"OK. I probably won't get a chance to look at them until tomorrow morning, so no rush. Thanks. Have a good evening." Because he knew that he would.

* * *

CHAPTER 14 – FOR THE BENEFIT OF SCIENCE

Austin, Texas. Dr. Madison Manatta was a climate scientist who had contributed to the scientific understanding of climate change by pioneering techniques to find patterns in past changes. He had been working with the Institute for Environmental Science in Austin. As a scientist, he dealt with... well, science: facts and information supported by recognized tools and techniques, using verified data, trends, observations and other evidence. Recently, he published a comprehensive report that proved, beyond any study to date, that climate change was real and, in fact, accelerating.

Invitations poured in from around the country and internationally, asking him to speak; and Dr. Manatta was suddenly very popular everywhere, except with people who made their money through oil and/or gas ... and particularly with two of the wealthiest people around, the Couch brothers. The brothers eschewed publicity and generally kept under the radar, spawning instead a myriad of organizations to help fight renewable energy ... attempts to contain exploration of oil and gas ... and pretty much anything that was based on scientific views. To fight their battles, the Couches funneled billions of dollars into their organizations and politicians. The Competitive Energy Institute (CEI) was one of those organizations, and Texas House Representative, Lamont Dumble, was their politician.

Nobody knows exactly how the marching orders were issued, but the Competitive Energy Institute issued a lot of negative releases about the validity of Manatta's research. The CEI information was based on "experts" who were being paid by the Couches. In the well-orchestrated attack, the press releases – using snippets of information from Manatta's work, out of context – came fast and furiously. And then, as part of phase two, Congressman Dumble - who had taken millions from the Couches in political contributions along with a whole lot more from other oil and gas interests – began to file enormous Freedom of Information Act demands for all of Manatta's emails, data collection, information from other collaborating scientists, and anything else they could think of. They then used selected pieces of information, again out of context, to suggest misconduct and even launch a civil investigation into Dr. Manatta's use of taxpayer money.

Others chimed in. U.S. Representative, Tea Party Rep. Joe Barton (R-TX), shared his belief that scientific evidence of climate change is "absolute nonsense." His basis of that has not yet been revealed. But it was lifelong lawyer and politician Dumble who 'knew' about climate change better than anyone. "We now know that prominent scientists were so determined to advance the idea of human-made global warming that they worked together to hide contradictory temperature data." That quote landed him in court and the data was proven, even to skeptics, to be true and complete.

Even when their accusations were found frivolous, without merit and empty, they weren't deterred, and the propaganda continued. And, given their enormous influence, it wasn't long before funding for Manatta's program was withdrawn, and all that remained was an unemployed climate scientist with a black cloud over his reputation.

A fortuitously scheduled speech in Austin, however, gave Dr. Manatta a means of redemption of sorts. Following his humiliation and being pushed out of his life's work, other research scientists and grant-based academics expressed concern about their futures and questioned aloud if the Institute for Environmental Sciences or other scientific research programs were viable places to continue their research. The Administrator of the Institute was concerned and asked Dumble, seen as the main perpetrator, if he would speak to them and address their concerns. Upon hearing of this, Manatta asked to formally present a question to Dumble during the speech, and Dumble agreed. He was quite sure that he could ride roughshod over the disgraced scientist, boosting his own ego in front of all these people on government handouts. Friends of Manatta warned him that Dumble would attack him mercilessly, but he persisted ... because he had his own plan.

As fate would have it, not long after Manatta was forced to pack up his office, banished from his profession, and made to be content with receiving hundreds of supportive emails and calls from fellow scientists around the world, he received his Final Notice. Unbeknownst to Dumble however (amongst many other things), was that Manatta was among the 61 people in the alpha test group of the VT2 who had access to guns ... quite a number of them, in fact. Following his death, Manatta's physician expressed surprise that his patient's condition had deteriorated so quickly; but then, he wasn't the one who was dragged through hearings, forced to listen to false accusations from 'scientists' who undermined his work with completely bogus data and assumptions, and literally destroyed his legacy.

It was all so easy. Manatta chose his Sig Sauer P938 Extreme to accompany him to the speech, given its very compact size. He was a little concerned with security, but he needn't have worried. He was listed as a special guest and was not even checked. His other concern was his proximity to Dumble. But as it turned out, Dumble invited him onto the platform and even introduced him. "Gentlemen" (even though there was a decent number of women scientists present) … "Many of you know Dr. Manatta and have heard about his abrupt departure from the IES. Dr. Manatta and a number of his colleagues colluded with each other to politicize data and studies relating to climate change and as a result, the Institute had no choice but to shut down the program. In the interest of fairness, I have invited Dr. Manatta to give you his version of the story. It will differ, of course, and you will not hear any substantiation to back up his version. Dr. Manatta."

Manatta stepped to the mic and, keeping his eye on Dumble so he didn't wander off, said, "I am very thankful to you for giving me this opportunity tonight. You and your co-conspirators have successfully set this country, no, the world, on a course that will truly hasten our demise through a complete set of lies and misinformation. You have not only ruined my life, but those of generations to come. And so, for the benefit of science … "

Even Dumble picked up that ominous note and his eyes widened as Manatta pulled his P938 from his jacket and began to empty 5 of his 7-shot clip into Dumble's body … slowly, one shot at a time, watching the blood flow out along with Dumble's life. He dispassionately observed the changing look in Dumble's eyes as his journey from the first intended wound through the penultimate wound unfolded, his expression changing with each shot, from incredulousness to shock and then increasing degrees of fear and pain.

After an initial gasp from the audience– virtually sucking all the oxygen from the room – an icy silence descended. (The attendees would agree unanimously that "sucking all the oxygen out of the room" was a scientific impossibility; however, more than one of them pondered whether or not there had been a brief drop in atmospheric pressure.) Dumble slowly sank, first to his knees and then – as Manatta drilled shot number six into the center of his forehead – fell forward, smashing his face to the floor with great force. Manatta looked out at the audience who were strangely calm – before emptying the last round into his own temple. Only then erupted cries of "Oh no!" ... "Oh my God!" ... and other cries of grief.

But when questioned by police, the attendees remained noticeably quiet ... answering with scientific detachment. What they saw were two deaths. Fact. One removed a threat to their careers and all they stood for. Fact. The other removed a revered colleague. Fact.

* * *

Quincy, Massachusetts. VitalTech's technology captured data indicating that Dr. Manatta's death was not consistent with the expected algorithmic results, therefore flagging the incident. But given the late hour on the east coast, nobody would see it until morning.

* * *

Kansas City, Missouri. Due to the high-profile nature of Lamont Dumble, however, Zoe Brouet did pick up the shooting from news bulletins and quickly matched it to the list that Vijay had just provided. Personally, she felt that some higher form of justice might have just been carried out. Professionally, however, she knew that a crime had just been committed and she was pretty sure she knew the why ... if not the exact trigger ... that caused it. She contacted the Austin FBI office to have someone collect the VT2 and smartphone.

CHAPTER 15 – MILES AND QASIM

Pasadena, California. Trudi was attending a song circle at the Pepper Tree Gallery. About a dozen people were there, and all of them were about her age. The chairs were arranged in a circle and the musicians had their guitars, banjos and fiddles sitting in their stands. The gallery was small, and it was a pleasant venue with the walls lined with local, original art.

She had been working on an anti-gun song and wanted to share it in the safety of supportive, fellow singer-songwriters. They loved it. Loved her melody and lyrics, and offered a number of good critiques and ideas, as well. But more than anything, she realized that she wasn't the only one who felt that the NRA had gone too far. Trudi was having more fun than she'd had in a long time.

Back at home, Vince was surfing the internet when a notification from his LA Times app popped up on his screen reading, "Congressman Lamont Dumble has been shot during an address in Austin, Texas. It was reported that Dr. Madison Manatta, a renowned climate scientist, shot and killed Dumble before taking his own life. For more ... "

Vince eagerly clicked for more information and in a nano-second he was looking at a news article: ***"Murder-Suicide Over Climate?***

"Dr. Madison Manatta, the world's leading climate scientist shot and killed Congressman Lamont Dumble (R-TX) at an address in Austin, Texas this evening. Congressman Dumble is Chairman of the House Committee on Science, Space and Technology and is widely known for his disbelief and attacks on the legitimacy of climate change as well as his close relationship with the oil industry.

"Congressman Dumble, along with BrightFahrt News and the House Science Committee, had attacked Manatta's groundbreaking research, hacked his email to gain access to cooperating scientists' information and memos, and then used excerpts out of context to smear Manatta with false allegations of misusing taxpayer money. Their claims were all proven false but, behind the scenes, Manatta's grants were withdrawn and he was forced to leave his post at the Institute for Environmental Science.

"At this point there is no additional information and police are questioning the 250-plus witnesses who attended the event."

Vince wondered if there was a geriatric aspect, which led him to look up Dr. Manatta's bio, but his hunch was disappointing. Manatta was 68 and that seemed too young to fit into the same mold as the Tucson and Joplin killers. Hell, Manatta was younger than Vince. Besides, there appeared to be a motive that was far more compelling than an old, unhappy guy in a retirement home or killing a store cashier over an argument.

He was suddenly alerted by Miles' whimpering that it was time to let him out for his evening 'business.' In fact, it was beyond that time but surfing the internet had a way of helping you lose track. He opened the door for Miles, but the warm breeze beckoned him. Realizing that he had been sitting for hours, he decided to take Miles for a short walk, so they could both stretch their legs.

He scrawled a note to Trudi, grabbed Miles' leash, and stood out on the back porch, breathing in the warm air, perfumed by the nearby flowering orange trees in his and the neighbors' yards. Miles returned and Vince clipped on the leash, delighting Miles, who was always ready to have a walk.

Down the street and around the corner there was a patch of vacant land, due to the layout of the houses, which belonged to the city and was always in a state of overgrowth. As Vince and Miles passed the area, they heard some voices and then suddenly, they heard a vicious growl and Vince felt the leash jerk wildly. It was quite dark, but it looked like Miles and a wild animal of some sort were fighting. It smelled like a skunk but was much larger and stronger than he presumed a skunk would be. Vince screamed and tried, fruitlessly, to pull Miles away. He reached down along the leash to grab Miles' collar for a stronger grip when he felt his hand and wrist gripped by the very strong jaws of a pit bull. Two dark figures approached and one of them yelled, "Rambo. Stop!" The jaws loosened but the growling continued. A car started to drive past but then stopped when the driver saw the unusual activity. He reversed and then nosed the car in to their direction with the lights illuminating the area.

Vince quickly took in the scene and saw Miles lying motionless on the sidewalk, two scruffy men, one of whom held Rambo by his collar, and his own hand, which was covered in blood and hurt like hell. The driver of the car shouted, "Are you hurt?" Vince looked at his hand again and replied, "Yes," but looking at Miles again he screamed, "Miles!!!!" And he fell to his knees to hold and comfort his furry friend. The driver pulled out his phone and called 911 and when he started to explain the situation, the two men mumbled something to each other and started to leave. The driver said into the phone, "Hold on," and then to the two men in accented English, "You must wait for the police."

One of the guys yelled, "Get the fuck out of my country!" as they melted into the darkness. The driver finished his call with 911 and knelt down to assist Vince. Miles was still breathing but bleeding badly around his neck. They were deciding what the best action plan was when they heard the sirens. A police car with two officers arrived first, followed by the paramedics, moments later.

As soon as they were told about the men and dog, one of the officers jumped back into his car and went to look for them. The other one started taking down details of what happened – names, addresses, etc. The Good Samaritan driver's name was Qasim Melho, an Uber driver on his way home. Both Qasim's and Vince's description of the two men were vague, as it was dark, and a lot was happening. White, mid 20's to early 30's, mostly black and/or brown clothes, loose fitting. One wore a baseball cap, the other a wool knit cap. That was about it. They knew the dog's name and that it was dark brown/black and medium size.

The paramedics were concerned about Vince's injuries and wanted to get him to a hospital without delay, but Vince – and the paramedics agreed – was also concerned about Miles, and they couldn't take Miles to Huntington Hospital ER, which was the closest. One of the paramedics suggested, given the late hour, to take him to AEC, the Animal Emergency Clinic on East Foothill Boulevard. Qasim said that he would take Miles to the AEC and let Vince go with the paramedics to have his hand looked at asap. So, Qasim and the paramedics loaded Miles into the back seat of Qasim's car with an improvised bandage around his neck to help stem the bleeding, and everyone sped off, leaving only the remaining policeman, who was looking around the area where the two men and their dog had been.

Vince asked one of the paramedics to help him get his phone out to call Trudi. Trudi had just walked in the door and saw his note. Vince explained what had happened and that Miles was being taken to the AEC on East Foothill by Qasim, an Uber driver who had saved them. He suggested that she go to the AEC and meet Qasim there in case questions were asked about payment, responsibility, etc. She could relieve Qasim if he was still there, and if he was, to please get his contact details. He owed Qasim a huge debt of gratitude.

The paramedics radio was squawking non-stop, and one of the paramedics told Vince that there had been an accident involving a tour bus and that the Huntington ER was overrun so they were diverting to St. Luke's. When they arrived, Vince wondered how much worse Huntington could be, as St. Luke's seemed like a war zone, too, filled with many of the bus accident victims. It seemed to take forever before he eventually saw a doctor who seemed to be barely successful in managing the chaos of the ER, barking orders to younger doctors taking care of the less injured bus passengers. It was only the pretty strong anesthetic they gave him that reduced his anxiety and put him out while they worked on his hand. A couple of hours later, Vince came around and another young doctor told him that there was no permanent damage to his tendons and ligaments, but he needed 35 stitches, internal and external. He would be in a lot of pain for a while and would need some physical therapy when the healing was underway.

Getting the relatively good news, his thoughts returned to Miles and he asked to make a call. The doctor told him that he would need to wait until he was moved from the OR to another area, which should be within minutes. She also told Vince that he could go home at that time. So, minutes later when he was moved, he anxiously asked a nurse to help him call Trudi's cell.

Trudi answered and asked how he was at the same time he was asking her how Miles was. Having heard that Vince was OK, Trudi said, "I wish I could say the same about Miles. He's still being operated on and the vet said it didn't look good. His jugular was torn, but fortunately not completely. A little bit more and he wouldn't have made it to the hospital. He lost a lot of blood and some of his organs started to shut down. We'll just have to wait and see."

"Do you know how much longer?" Vince tried to wipe away the tears, but he only had the one hand, so they just streamed down his face.

"No. The doctor said he would come out and tell me how it went and then he would need some recovery time to see if he would make it."

"OK." choking back tears, "Why don't you come get me after the Vet gives you an update. Then, depending on what he says … " Vince broke down and sobbed for a bit. Recovering a little, he said, "we can go home."

"OK, sweetheart. Hang in there. I'll be with you as soon as I can."

About an hour later, Vince felt Trudi gently shake his arm, the good one, and he woke up.

"How is he?" he asked, fearing her response.

"The doctor said he was one stubborn mutt and while he wasn't 100% out of the woods yet, the prognosis was good, although he may not bark anymore."

Vince and Trudi looked at each other and burst out laughing followed by full on crying. Vince said, "I want to hug that little guy so much, but I must admit that I won't miss that bark in the mornings."

They returned to the AEC and the night shift doctor told them that Miles was doing well, all things considered, but that they should go home, get some rest and return in the morning.

Trudi drove them home and Vince started to give her a recap of what happened, but he suddenly stopped. "Did you see Qasim?"

"I did, and what a nice man. He was prepared to stay there until one of us relieved him. I got his phone number and told him we would call tomorrow ... or now, it's today. We talked for a little while waiting to see what was happening. He's a Syrian refugee. One of the first, I guess, as he's been here about two years."

"I was very lucky he happened by. Very lucky ... " and then he asked, "How was your song circle?" Trudi loved that he thought of that, after all he had been through but before she could tell him, he had dozed off, as the medication intended. She drove the rest of the way home in silence, her brain whirling, and by the time she arrived, she thought again about Vince's desire to get a gun. But this time, she came to quite a different conclusion.

* * *

CHAPTER 16 – CLIENT RELATIONSHIP

Quincy, Massachusetts. The text said '4 seasons, rm 840 xx.' Vijay's humble roots were pretty close to the surface and his initial thought was why stay in a hotel when they'd be spending the night together anyway. But he knew that Jennifer did not want J. Edward or anyone else at KKL to know the depth of her "client relationship" with Vijay. So a hotel bill and a restaurant receipt would be required. And that even ruled out a cozy room service meal. But with the time approaching, he felt his pulse rate quicken.

Rechecking the text to make sure that the room he was standing outside of, 840, was correct, he knocked. Then, because the knocking sounded puny against the probably fireproofed, security door, he spotted a doorbell and pressed, just as the door opened.

"You're not impatient, are you?" she teased.

He stepped into the room and showed her, taking her in his arms and planting a long and passionate kiss. It was actually a series of kisses, with very little dialogue for a very long time. When they eventually untangled their warm and naked bodies, Vijay finally spoke a normal sentence. "I've missed you."

"You made that obvious," she teased again. "I've missed you too. Whoever said talk is cheap was right. So was the person who said 'absence makes the heart grow fonder.' "

They lingered for a while, holding each other and catching up emotionally. Jennifer noticed it was getting dark and suddenly realized that the late hour, and the pleasurable physical exercise, had unleashed another appetite. "Why don't we make ourselves look like we haven't been making love for an hour and get something to eat?"

"You won't have to twist my arm."

"Wow. You are pretty easy today." She smiled.

"I'll always be easy when it comes to making love with you and food. But tomorrow morning, it won't be so easy keeping up with me on the streets," he quipped.

"We'll see," she said as she headed to the bathroom.

Vijay enjoyed watching her naked body glide away. "Need any help in the shower?"

"Now that you mention it, there is a place on my back I can't reach." Vijay's 'help' almost caused them to miss the last serving time at the hotel restaurant.

Only after ordering their healthy meals – with requests to omit this and serve that on the side, substitute this for that, etc. – did they discuss the earlier meeting at VitalTech and any business. Not exactly a model business development approach, but then, neither was their relationship.

"You were very quiet at the meeting today. How do you think it went?"

"There was a lot to absorb and I was in listening/learning mode. Sounds like it's all going well and that's exciting. How about you?"

"I'm not sure I was able to focus 100%. There was this drop-dead gorgeous blonde there that I wanted desperately to get into bed with."

"And how did that go?"

"Pretty well."

"Just, 'pretty well?' "

"OK. Amazing, fantastic. How's that?"

"Better."

"As you can see, I'm still struggling with my focus, but I thought it went well. Maria shared a concern with me afterwards, however. She felt uneasy after Don expressed his view that a leaked story about the killings might spur interest in the VT2 ... and that J. Edward reacted to that possibility in a way that suggested he might want to help that happen."

Jennifer thought a bit. "I can see his point," she said, "but I also see the risk. What about a few focus groups to gauge reaction? Perhaps groups with sub-sets of gun owners, non-gun owners, and different age groups. In that way, if it proves that Don's hunch is right, we won't lose out on the opportunity. If it proves him wrong, both Don and J. Edward will see the proof."

"Gorgeous and smart. A lethal combination."

"And I intend to use them to my advantage with a certain client who possesses those same characteristics."

Their food arrived and for two very different but equally intense hungers, they ate quickly and returned to room 840. Despite a short night of sleep, and 'one for the road' when they woke up, they were out of the hotel at 6:00 for a planned ten- mile run. Ten miles for Jennifer and Vijay was about an hour or less, but they were in no hurry. They enjoyed each other on many levels. Back at the hotel they took one last advantage of the large walk-in, rainfall shower before saying their goodbyes. Jennifer wanted to attend one or more of the focus groups, which pleased Vijay, who promised to give her dates as soon as they were set up.

* * *

The next morning, when Drew Pierson arrived at his office, there was a file on his desk marked 'URGENT!'. It contained a single-page, alpha test user profile: a print-out showing vital signs with a telltale precipitous drop, an 'FN' in large caps, and a copy of a press release, "Politician and Scientist Dead." Drew scanned the first two documents and then, seeing the third, knew that this wouldn't be a routine day. He called Maria and then Vijay, getting Maureen, who said Vijay hadn't arrived yet.

When Vijay arrived at his office, uncharacteristically late, he greeted Maureen, who knew why he was late and why he was wearing a big smile. He asked her to get Drew and Maria to discuss Jennifer's Focus Group idea and she said they had already called for him and needed to see him. He didn't react with concern, just, "OK, good. Tell them I'm here now."

When they arrived, however, he knew immediately from their faces and demeanor that something important, and not good, had happened.

"What's happened?" he asked.

Drew explained that an alpha test user, Dr. Madison Manatta, had received his Final Notice, killed Congressman Dumble, and then committed suicide.

"On the list we sent Agent Brouet, was he listed as having gun access?"

"Yes," confirmed Drew.

Vijay knew then that Brouet would already know about this incident, or certainly would very shortly. He had intended to write to Zoe, but now that didn't seem adequate. He was also seriously concerned that this very high-profile murder-suicide might make the Focus Groups academic and make public to the world, the unplanned consequence of the VT2. He explained Jennifer's suggestion of Focus Groups to Maria and Drew and added his worry that this new event might outstrip any effort to control the news.

Maria suggested, however, that they do just that. "With the beta test about to start, why not come out with our release first to control the story? In that way the first news they hear about the VT2 will be positive with respect to the VT2's features. We can also address the unfortunate side effects in our own words and detail our efforts to monitor and control them with the help of participating doctors in the future. That shows that we are responsible and are trying to do something about it."

Drew and Vijay liked the idea and Maria said she would draft something straight away. Vijay suggested that she get Don's input, too, and that he would like to invite Agent Brouet back to discuss, in person, their plans for the beta test. He suggested that the meeting be relatively soon to forestall any releases by the FBI – giving Maria time to get her release out to the press. Maria and Drew were happy with that and Vijay asked Maureen to arrange a meeting with Zoe.

When they left, Vijay called Jennifer, hoping she hadn't boarded her flight yet. She answered, "Miss me already?"

"I do, but that's not why I'm calling. Do you have a minute?"

"Sure. My flight doesn't board for 20 minutes and I got here early because someone woke me up early."

Vijay smiling, "Are you complaining?"

"No! What's up?"

Vijay brought Jennifer up to speed on the Manatta-Dumble episode, recapping his meeting with Drew and Maria and their concerns that keeping this under wraps was probably not an option any more. Jennifer agreed and they decided that nothing would be gained with the Focus Groups.

She asked, "Shall I tell J. Edward?"

Vijay hesitated. "I guess so. Make sure you tell him that we'll be coming out with a press release momentarily. That might dissuade him from leaking it in case he finds out through another channel."

"OK. I'll tell him when I get back to the office. And by the way, I loved being with you again. I've missed you, or did I already tell you that?"

"You did, but you can't say it too many times. I've missed you, too."

Vijay heard the airport announcement in the background. "That's me. They're calling my flight. Gotta go. I love you."

"I love you, too!"

He sat there for a few minutes transitioning from the joy and deep feelings he had for Jennifer to the situation at hand. What would he say to Zoe Brouet? He wasn't sure, so he asked Maureen to see if Brouet could come to Quincy on Tuesday. He and the team would have a plan by then.

* * *

Austin, Texas. Agent Zoe Brouet was one of the few passengers on American Airlines flight 1561 who waited, as requested, until the seatbelt sign was off before unfastening her seatbelt and switching on her cell phone. She extricated herself from the uncomfortable MD80 seat, asking herself again if she was foolish for saving the FBI $125 by flying on American, not her favorite airline. As she walked up the jetway into Austin-Bergstrom International airport, her phone chimed, telling her she had a message.

Retrieving the message, she wasn't surprised to hear Maureen's voice. She was definitely going to visit VitalTech again.

Moving away from the stream of deplaning passengers, she called the number Maureen had left. Maureen answered immediately, and seeing the 816 area code, said, "Hello, Zoe.

Thanks for returning my call. Are you in Kansas City, or some other exotic place?"

"Austin, Texas, actually."

"Ahh. Well that is a bit more exotic. Vijay wondered if you could come to Quincy on Tuesday. Can you do that?"

"Let me look," fumbling with the phone. "Sure, is early afternoon OK? I can be there by two."

Maureen looked at her desktop Outlook calendar. "Great. So, it's a date. See you Tuesday at 2:00 PM?"

"Great. Bye for now."

As Zoe entered the baggage claim area, she spotted her colleague immediately – just as most species of animals recognize each other – even though they'd never met. The Bureau recruitment team had a formula for what they were looking for and they stick pretty close to it, she thought. She also wondered if that was a good idea. Troy Wilkins spotted her at about the same time, but he had intel to look for a short, good-looking woman with honey-toned skin.

"Special Agent Brouet?" Zoe outranked Troy so formality was required.

"It's Zoe. Hi Troy. Thanks for meeting me. Are we going to Manatta's place?"

"Yes. I'm parked right outside. One of the perks of being in the Bureau."

"There are others?" And they both laughed.

They drove to Manatta's apartment and Troy filled her in on what they had found. Once inside, she took in Manatta's four handguns. In addition to the Sig Sauer used at the shooting, there was a Ruger LC9, a Glock 26 and a huge Desert Eagle 50 caliber handgun.

Zoe's eyes widened, "I see why he chose the Sig Sauer. The others would be easier to spot, especially the Desert Eagle. Can you believe that? And this guy was a mild-mannered scientist," Zoe said, shaking her head. "Anything else of interest?"

"We have the VT2 watch and an iPhone which has the VT2 App. The app showed that a Final Notice was received four days before the murder."

Nothing much of consequence was found amongst Manatta's possessions. Divorced many years ago and with no children – not atypical of someone who lived, breathed and slept with their passion – Manatta was distraught over his humiliation, as verified in innumerable emails to colleagues.

Zoe suspected that he would have at least committed suicide if this opportunity hadn't presented itself. But the VT2 pattern was there. For some people, the Notice was clearly an opportunity for revenge with impunity.

Zoe's issue was what to do about it. You can't stop a doctor from telling a patient that he or she will die, so it seemed reasonable that you couldn't stop someone from getting a watch that will break the bad news.

Having collected the few facts, Zoe returned to Kansas City with more questions than when she left. She had a meeting with Regional Director Hawke tomorrow, which she wasn't looking forward to, and not just because it was Saturday.

She thought back to her first meeting with Vijay when he reopened the emotional wound she'd been nursing. She was happy with her decision to join the FBI, although she deeply lamented the rift it caused between herself and her father. Yes, there was danger attached to the job, but she was a big girl now and could take care of herself. And while she understood his deeper concern, she still felt that he was being irrational. When her mother was a child living in Tunisia, their family had suffered greatly at the hands of the police. Zoe could remember her father getting angry whenever he was reminded of those times. To have his daughter join the police was too much for him. And yet part of Zoe's motivation for joining the Bureau was to play a role in making law enforcement responsible. She wanted to be an ally of the majority of people who are on the right side of the law. But she never got to have that conversation with him.

* * *

Pasadena, California. The pain medication Vince was taking worked well and he actually had a sound night's sleep, so it took him a while to shake the cobwebs off. And then the emotional pain returned, hard. "Poor Miles," he thought, "having that beast of a dog almost rip his throat out, literally. I hope he's OK and will be OK." Trudi stirred beside him.

"Good morning," he said.

"How did you sleep? How's the hand?"

"Very well and OK, although we need to go to the ER again for them to have a look to see if they agree."

Trudi sat up, "I'll go make us some coffee. Do you want anything to eat?"

Vince also sat up, swinging his legs out of bed to the floor. "No thanks. Let's just have a cup and get going. I want to see how Miles is."

"OK," said Trudi, putting her robe on. "I'll put the coffee on and then call the AEC."

Trudi was just hanging up the phone when Vince walked into the kitchen, literally holding his breath. "They said he had a good night and is doing nicely, although they want to keep him another day."

"Whew! Can we see him?"

"Yes. We'll go right after we get your hand looked at."

* * *

The ER was much calmer than the night before and the doctor on duty seemed pleased with the night shift's work, telling Vince to keep taking the pain medication as needed for sleep or pain and the antibiotics as prescribed until the pills were finished. He also advised him to see his doctor in a day or two to discuss physical therapy and monitor his progress. Both Vince and Trudi were relieved, but they were really just focused on seeing Miles.

On the way to the AEC, Vince confessed, "I just can't get the sound of that dog attacking Miles out of my head. Poor little guy just goes around being nice and friendly with every dog and person he meets. I hope the vet is right when he said that he's OK, but I wonder if the trauma will affect him? Maybe less friendly and trusting?"

"It wouldn't surprise me, but he's gone 10 years without being attacked, so if he has a problem, hopefully it will pass."

"I certainly won't take him out late at night anymore. It was so nice out, but I feel really guilty because I did it for me. Because I was sitting for so long."

"You couldn't know. It's not like you took him into the woods where wild animals lurked. And by the way, I think it's time to discuss a gun."

Vince looked at her in surprise, wondering about the depth of this change as they pulled into the AEC parking lot.

When they got inside, Miles seemed very happy to see them, but it was apparent that the little "big dog with very short legs" had won over the staff, putting Miles at risk of being spoiled. The staff all beamed at him when they walked by, giving him those little scratches between the ears that he liked. And someone had loosely wrapped some white gauzy material around his neck to cover the bandages, in a way that made it look like a stylish scarf. He was one cool-looking dog, and Vince decided right then that he would get him one of those red western bandanas to cover up the big shaved swath on the lower side of his neck.

Miles was still in a bassinette type gurney, strapped in with an IV tube dripping into a front leg. He had lost a lot of blood and the vets wanted to keep him close by for another day. Vince and Trudi stayed a while, talking to him in soothing tones and scratching his head. Miles appreciated the effort but didn't understand a word they said.

On their way home, Detective Lucker from the Pasadena Police called to see if he and his partner could stop by. Vince asked if they found the guys and was disappointed when Lucker said no. They agreed to meet at 11:00 AM.

* * *

After Vince and Trudi's early start and busy morning, which was not over yet, they both suddenly realized they were famished. Trudi set about whipping up some omelets before the police arrived: egg whites only for Vince, with non-dairy cream cheese and spinach, and the same for herself but with the whole egg. She didn't need to avoid the cholesterol, but she liked the tofu cream cheese, and it was a way of supporting Vince's dietary requirement.

Over brunch she reminded Vince to make an appointment with Dr. Parker, to look at his hand and get a physical therapist referral. He said he would, and at almost the same time the doorbell rang.

Detective Lucker and his partner Detective Reed seemed too young to be detectives, but Vince realized, that was just a sign of growing old. He led them into the living room and Trudi asked if they wanted a coffee or water. The savory smell from breakfast lingered throughout the house and the detectives were probably hungrier than thirsty. They declined, perhaps hoping to move the interview along more quickly so they could grab lunch.

They asked about Vince's hand and Miles' condition and seemed genuinely pleased to hear that it was going well.

While they had a number of corroborating reports that fit the description of the two men and the dog, they hadn't located them yet. The police at the scene had collected evidence that suggested recent meth usage, but no usable fingerprints were found. From the other descriptions, the dog was probably a pit bull, a breed that can become very aggressive, especially to other dogs. It's what they were originally bred for.

Detective Lucker asked, "If we find guys that match this description, could you identify them in a line-up?"

Vince thought for a moment, recalling police movies of line- ups where the people were all of similar height, coloring and clothing and he realized, "No. I don't think I could."

Knowing looks passed between the two detectives and Lucker said, "Without that, we wouldn't have a case."

"But if they had a pit bull, too?"

"Circumstantial but weak. Did they say anything?"

Vince thought for a long time and said, "Yes. One of them shouted 'Rambo, stop."

"That's good, if we can find all three of them and ID that Rambo is their dog's name. Would you recognize the guy's voice?"

Vince thought and said, "Yes. I think so." And then he remembered that they swore at Qasim and the hate in their voice was etched in his memory. He filled the detectives in on the words of hate directed at Qasim and they hungrily took notes.

Lucker added, "We'll be meeting with Qasim this afternoon so hopefully we can get a bit more information. But obviously, we need to catch them before we can do anything."

"Qasim saved Miles' life and possibly my hand. He could have driven by and avoided the hassle, but he didn't. I plan to go see him in person and thank him."

"You're right. He did the right thing and we will thank him too. But I'd appreciate it if you didn't talk with him or see him until after we do. It avoids anyone trying to entertain doubts of collusion if a trial ensues."

"When are you seeing him?"

"At 1:00."

"No problem."

Trudi had been sitting there quietly, listening to the conversation and the small chance of ever bringing the guys and dog to justice. "If Vince had been carrying a gun last night, could he have legally used it?"

Vince was more surprised than the detectives, and Lucker answered, "It depends on a number of factors. Can I ask, do you have a gun?"

"Not yet," Trudi answered.

"If he had a gun and fulfilled his legal requirements, I think – and this is my opinion – he could have legally shot the dog in self-defense."

Trudi persisted, "What about the guys?"

"Not unless it was self-defense and remember, it would be the word of the two of them against one, unless Qasim was on the scene and testified on Vince's behalf."

Trudi wasn't happy with the answer but said no more and thanked Detective Lucker.

The detectives told Vince they would keep him appraised if they found the men, and for Vince to get in touch if he remembered anything else. He saw them out and returned to see what was up with Trudi.

Vince hadn't seen the fiercely protective passion building within Trudi after her husband and dog were attacked. For her, the game had changed. It was war.

* * *

CHAPTER 17 – PLANS & A PRESS RELEASE

Quincy, Massachusetts. Maria handed the draft press release to Vijay.

FOR IMMEDIATE RELEASE

Timed For Success: Revolutionary VitalTech Watch Launches Second Phase of Testing Your Health

Quincy, Massachusetts. Having completed a very successful initial test of its revolutionary VT2 – the watch that tells time while it watches your vital signs – VitalTech has announced a national roll-out via a comprehensive beta test.

Following exceptionally positive feedback from test participants and doctors, Dr. Vijay Patel, VitalTech's CEO and Founder, praised the device, his team, and the participants for an extremely smooth trial run. "I want to thank everyone involved for their cooperation and diligence in making this an unusually efficient process."

The VT2 stands out from any other wearable sport/health device on the market due to its very advanced and sophisticated diagnostic capabilities. Dr. Malcomb Caldwell of Harvard Medical School holds the device's abilities in very high esteem. "To call it a sport watch or health watch or any kind of watch is a major understatement," he said. "It is an extremely advanced diagnostic tool that makes many current laboratory tests unnecessary."

Dr. Patel elaborated on this praise. "As a physician, mathematician, scientist and health enthusiast, I have been driven to discover more sophisticated and helpful data to guide our habits, as well as interface between patients and physicians. The VT2 represents hundreds of man-years of research and has achieved my initial goals in that respect.

"It is important to note that this device transcends anything on the market, and in fact, it possesses capabilities that are not even available in some laboratories. As such, the information it generates must be used responsibly and in conjunction with a physician.

"All VT2's in our beta test will be issued through licensed physicians who will assist us in screening out users for whom the device may prove inappropriate or dangerous. While our unique, optional 'notice of impending death' feature – or Final Notice – has already helped many users to settle their affairs and achieve emotional closure with loved ones during our initial test, it is not without risk. A small number of patients have reacted to the optional 'notice of impending death feature' by carrying out crimes against others."

For more information about the VT2 and beta test enrollment, visit our website at www.vitaltech.com or contact us directly at (617) 471-4344.

CONTACT:
Contact Person: Maria Moon
Company Name: VitalTech LLC

Voice Phone Number: (617) 471-4344
Email Address: mmoon@ vitaltech.com
Website URL: www.vitaltech.com

"Nice job, Maria. That addresses the issue and you've nuanced it nicely. I expect that when some reporters start digging, especially with the Manatta-Dumble story, the headline will be quite different. Like 'KILLER WATCH LAUNCH.' " Neither Maria nor Vijay could keep from smiling.

"Do you know how we're doing with the distribution of the first batch?" Vijay asked.

"Are you kidding? Drew and Wade had them out the door the day after we agreed to the plan! We used an expanded list and we already have over a hundred new users lined up."

"Great!" Vijay continued, "I've asked Zoe Brouet, the FBI agent, to come out on Tuesday. I'd like you here and I'll get Liz and Drew as well. I have a feeling that this meeting will be different than the last one."

Maria, holding the release, "OK. So, is this good to go?"

"Yes. Get it out asap. And thanks, Maria."

* * *

Boston, Massachusetts. It was early evening and Matt Harper was sitting at his desk at The Boston Globe reading the VitalTech press release. He read a dozen of these a day but because it was local, and the headline grabbed him, he devoured every word. He was a techie and a health enthusiast, so the article pulled him in, but when he got to the part about a number of patients reacting to the impending death notice by committing crimes, he was almost foaming at the mouth. He picked up the phone and called Maria Moon's number, 471-4344, listed on the release, and got her voicemail. Matt was a successful reporter in part because he was resourceful. He left a brief message and then called 471-4300 for the VitalTech automated switchboard, telling him to enter the four-digit extension or first three letters of the last name of the person he was trying to reach.

Unprotected by Maureen, who had gone home for the day, Vijay picked up his phone. Matt introduced himself, adding that he was with The Boston Globe, a name that carried some weight, especially in the Boston area and especially to a start-up company wanting to get noticed. Matt explained that he was calling about the press release and flattered Vijay on the successful field trials and plans for the beta test roll-out. Then he got down to the real reason for his call. The crimes.

"I was intrigued by your comment about crimes being committed by a segment of the test users. Can you tell me more about that?"

Vijay immediately sensed that he was on thin ice and he didn't know exactly how to handle that question. Any answer would lead to more questions and if the Globe ran something, would that be good or bad? So he punted.

"Have you spoken with Maria Moon yet?"

Matt was honest, "I tried, but just got her voicemail. Look, Dr. Patel, I'd like to help you generate excitement and a market for the VT2, but I need more information. I'd be happy to meet with Ms. Moon and you to discuss it further."

Sensing an out, or at least having the comfort of Maria being with him, Vijay replied, "OK. I'm not sure of Maria's schedule next week, but we can call you back on Monday morning to set a meeting. What's your number?"

Matt gave him his number and pushed, "Can you tell me what kind of crimes have been committed?"

"No. I'm sorry. You'll have to wait until next week."

"OK, Thanks. I look forward to your call."

Vijay dialed Maria's cell, "Sorry to call so late but I just got a call from The Boston Globe. Matt Harper? He was digging into the crime aspect. I told him we'd call back on Monday to arrange a meeting. I thought it would be good to get The Globe on our side."

Maria agreed and asked if Vijay thought that Matt was satisfied with that. Vijay thought so and they decided to leave it until Monday.

* * *

Matt Harper sat there thinking. He didn't want to wait until Monday. He began typing into Google, Nexis-Lexis, and a number of other search engines, looking for a link between VitalTech and crime. Nothing. "If it's in the FBI domain, I may not see anything," he thought. He started searching for investigations by the FBI, and there were a lot of them. But then twenty-something pages down the list he saw, "FBI Investigates Cashier Murder in Joplin, MO." There wasn't much, just that the killer, Quentin Moore entered a convenience store and shot and killed the cashier on duty. Why would the FBI investigate that? He looked up Quentin Moore in the on-line phone directory. It was an hour earlier in Missouri, and not too late, so he dialed.

Sharon Moore answered and Matt, on a hunch, told her that he was following up some stories about how technology sometimes conspired with human nature to lead people to do things out of their normal character. He verified that she was the widow of Quentin and asked if Quentin was one of the VitalTech test users. She wasn't sure but told him that the FBI took Quentin's sport watch and iPhone away for analysis. VitalTech didn't sound familiar to her but the watch was a VT2 brand. She remembered the name. Matt pumped her for additional information and she was very open and forthcoming, telling him everything she had told Zoe Brouet. He thanked her and then tried to put the pieces together.

This was just one example, but what if, after receiving their Final Notice, people who wanted revenge got it … with impunity, knowing that their days were seriously numbered? How many were there? One or two wasn't much of a story, but at least he had a hold card for his meeting at VitalTech next week.

* * *

Pasadena, California. Trudi and Vince brought Miles home, making everybody very happy, although the staff at the AEC would miss him. Miles' bandages would need to remain for some time. However, an even greater discomfort for Miles, not to mention embarrassment, was the big plastic cone he needed to wear, preventing him from using his paws to remove the bandages.

Vince's bandaged hand made life awkward for him, too, especially with his laptop, but the pain was manageable; and so, with not much to do, he dozed off frequently. Trudi wasted no time taking over some of the surfing duties on her iPad, which she loved. She walked into the kitchen with it and said, excitedly, "There's a gun show at Ontario this weekend. Are you up for it?"

One part of Vince wasn't interested in doing much of anything – that was mostly a result of the pain pills that hadn't yet left his system. Another part of Vince wanted to say, "Hell, yes!" He compromised. "Sure. What day is it?"

"Today and tomorrow," chirped Trudi. "$14 each."

"OK. Let's do tomorrow. Can we bring Miles?"

Trudi looked at the iPad, "No. No pets. But he'll be OK on his own for a few hours. It's a little over an hour on the 210 and there shouldn't be much traffic on Sunday. I'm kinda curious, but we don't need to stay long. And I wouldn't buy a gun without Rueben's input, anyway."

"I agree. I'm off to Dr. Parker's now."

"Oh right. Are you OK to drive?"

"Yes. I'll be fine."

* * *

Vince had been going to Dr. Cyrus Parker for as long as he could remember. He told Parker about the dog attack and

Dr. Parker thought that the hand looked OK. He asked Vince if there was any pain, and Vince said that there was very little. A little itching. He became agitated during his explanation and was obviously angry. He also seemed a little more distant and edgy to Parker.

Always thorough, the doctor asked Vince about blood test results and if they gave him an injection. Vince said yes and explained that samples were taken at the ER. He had also been told that Parker would get them. Parker said he hadn't yet and would follow up.

Parker was an old school GP who was skeptical of fads and new trends except for technology. He wasn't an expert, but having lived a very long part of his life simply, he appreciated the way technology – like smart phones, computers, applications, Bluetooth, wi-fi, etc. – affected people's lives. That appreciation had always been a common interest that he and Vince shared and talked about in the few non-clinical moments they had together. So, it was natural that he mentioned a new watch/health monitor that he had just received for placement with a patient. It was undergoing final testing and he offered one to Vince, who needed no arm-twisting to accept. Parker told him that this thing was predicted to take off like iPhones did at first.

Vince was thrilled and they both chuckled about the Final Notice feature. Given Vince's age and current state of health, they activated it for the 30-day notice. Dr. Parker really got Vince's attention, however, when he passed on the information from VitalTech that some users in the earlier test had killed people after receiving their Notices. Vince wondered if the senior's home killings, the store clerk in Missouri, or even the scientist shootings were among these events. Dr. Parker was unable to answer that question but as they discussed it, they agreed it was possible. For Vince, it was fascinating to think that he might be sharing the same technology that had triggered those deaths. As Dr. Parker was completing the forms, he realized that he needed one additional piece of information from Vince, and asked, "Do you own a gun?"

Vince answered "No," and for no particular reason failed to mention that he had plans to look at one tomorrow. Dr. Parker probed a bit more into his general state of mind, cognizant that Vince was angry. He asked specifically how the incident with the dog had affected him. Vince told him that he was angry that people could get away with that degree of irresponsibility with little or no risk of punishment. He explained that even if they found them, chances were, they wouldn't be charged with anything.

They wrapped up the appointment and when Vince left, Dr. Parker completed his paperwork, which included a brief questionnaire. He was worried about Vince. On the questionnaire he indicated that Vince did not own a gun, was moderately agitated and in answer to a question asking for the physician's view of the likelihood that Vince would use a gun in anger, he entered 3 out of 5.

* * *

Trudi was out when Vince arrived home, so he sat down with his laptop and looked up VitalTech and Googled the company along with shooting, killing, guns and other combinations. He saw the press release on the VitalTech site with the mention of crimes being committed. And there were a number of newspaper articles, but they weren't related to

187

VitalTech. He looked at the app and the more detailed desktop version and could see that the app had begun to build up his baseline data. The VT2 information had advised that it could take up to 24 hours to build a full profile.

* * *

CHAPTER 18 – THE GUN SHOW & NEW FRIENDS

Pasadena, California. It was a beautiful Sunday morning, and after their coffee and toast, they fed Miles and let him stay outside. About an hour and fifteen minutes later they pulled into the Ontario Convention Center parking lot, paid their $5 parking fee and wondered why they shouldn't get a discount, as their Prius took up half the space as the massive 4x4's, Humvees and pick-up trucks that seemed to make up 90% of the vehicles. They took extra care to note where they parked because their car was completely hidden by the behemoth, gas-guzzling pieces of steel all around them.

As they walked to the ticket windows amidst the growing crowd, they felt out of place, despite having dressed down to jeans and hiking boots. The crowd was mostly middle aged with some younger people, along with a few senior citizens, some in wheelchairs. A number of families with young kids or dads with kids also made up the attendees. Even before they got to the ticket windows, there was a large NRA display, selling chances to win a gun and/or join. Peppered in between the displays were political signs denouncing various anti-gun or pro-gun-safety politicians. Some were in poor taste.

They bought their tickets and had their hands stamped in case they wanted to leave and return and followed along with the mass of humanity. Given the nature of the show and signs that "respectfully" asked people not to bring loaded weapons into the show, they were pleased to see the semblance of security for backpacks and purses, although it wasn't terribly thorough. Enough to catch a large machine gun or rocket launcher, perhaps.

A number of people were carrying folding luggage carts and once past the ticket booths they saw why. Wholesale ammunition tents and displays were set up with what seemed like enough ammunition for a world war! And people were stacking up cases of ammunition on their carts to bring back to their trucks. Obviously, there was no limit, or if there was, it must be a lifetime supply.

Inside the hall there were hundreds of displays, from Bibles to bullets, beef jerky to body armor, political T-shirts – mostly denigrating anti-gun/pro gun-safety politicians or touting their right-wing heroes. There were swords, knives, gun safes, spare clips, hunting apparel, flashlights, boxes and bags of ammunition and lots of guns ... rifles, shotguns, gun kits (to get around the assault rifle ban in California) and handguns. The Army could have shopped here and not needed much else, except perhaps a tank or two. They stopped at a handgun vendor and looked at the range and prices. Vince overheard a couple of rough-looking customers at the booth and one asked the other something, in what sounded like Russian, about a particular gun that was small in size. His friend answered in English, "But it will kill," followed by something (possibly a repeat) in the foreign language.

The handguns were all laid out on large flat tables, tethered to the table with wire cables, long enough to allow freedom of handling. They tried holding a number of guns to see how they felt in their hands and were surprised by the weight of some. They also considered prices, discovering an amazingly wide range, and decided that $500 would be their target price. Some felt comfortable to one of them but not the other, and a few felt good to both. Vince couldn't help but notice that when Trudi picked up a gun, she seemed to change and looked every bit as formidable as the female police and government agents he'd seen on TV. He wondered if he looked as good.

One gun that they both liked, for the feel and weight, was a Glock 19. Vince had heard the name Glock but didn't know in what context. He asked the vendor, "If we wanted to buy a gun today, how would that work, given the 10-day waiting time in California?"

"Do you have your Handgun Safety Certificate?" the vendor asked.

"Not yet," Vince replied.

"You can go over to the far corner of the hall and take the test, get the certificate and then come back to buy the gun. I'll give you a receipt and you can pick it up at the Glendale Gun Store in 10 days."

"OK. We haven't really studied for the test." Trudi added.

The vendor replied, "You shouldn't have any trouble with it. Do you have any questions about these guns?"

Vince really didn't want to engage in a sales conversation and said, "Not at the moment. Thanks."

They walked in the direction the vendor pointed to and saw the display for the HSC test. There were also options for concealed carry permits. Vince told the heavy-set woman behind the tables that they each wanted to take the test. The woman explained, "That will be $50 for both. I'll give you the tests and you can use this area," pointing to the end of the table near the wall, "to fill them out. No colluding," she said with a smile. Vince and Trudi took their test forms and shuffled down to the end of the tables. They had read all the material and discussed it but still, they were both a bit nervous. Not that anyone they knew would know if they failed, but really, how embarrassing would that be!

When they scanned down the list of questions, they smiled at each other.

1. A safe practice when handling a gun is to rest your finger on the outside of the trigger guard or along the side of the gun until you are ready to shoot. True/False

2. To "know your target, its surroundings and beyond," you must consider that if the bullet misses or completely passes through the target, it could strike a person or object. True/False

3. Drinking alcohol while handling firearms is safe if your blood alcohol level remains below the legal limit. True/False

4. Which of the following safety points should you remember when handling a gun?
   a. Never shoot a gun in celebration.
   b. Do not fire at water, flat or hard surfaces.
   c. Wear ear and eye protection when shooting a gun.
   d. All of the above.

5. Safety Rule Number Two is keep the gun pointed:
   a. To the north.
   b. In the safest possible direction.
   c. Up.
   d. Down.

As the vendor said, they wouldn't have much trouble. The test lady seemed impressed with their scores and they each received their very own HSC.

They browsed around a bit more and Vince took Trudi by the arm and turned her around to face a stall selling walking canes, the kind that look like most old timers' canes, except these had Taser tips! They laughed out loud and immediately wondered if two or three friends of theirs who used canes had theirs armed with Tasers.

After a while the show was just more of the same and they headed to the food and beverage area to get a coffee. It felt good to sit down and they realized that they been there for an hour and a half. So, they finished their coffees, navigated their way past the 4x4's, pickups and Humvees, found their Prius, and went home to Miles.

* * *

On their way home, Vince suddenly decided to call Qasim. As Trudi drove, Vince awkwardly held the phone in his bandaged right hand and poked at the keys to pull up Qasim Melho's details and number. Qasim answered on the second ring and seemed pleased that it was Vince. He asked how he and Miles were doing and was happy that they were both "on the mend." Vince then realized that he hadn't really thought through why he was calling Qasim, other than to thank him, again, for rescuing them. But he asked very spontaneously (and perhaps because he had nothing else to say) if Qasim would like to come over to their house this afternoon or tomorrow. Vince saw Trudi glance at him sideways and there was a moment's hesitation, and Vince added, "Are you married?"

Qasim replied, "Yes, I am. And we have a young son, who is two."

"Why don't you all come over? Are you free this afternoon or tomorrow?"

Qasim asked Vince to hold on a minute and Vince could hear muffled talking in the background, and then, "Yes, we would like to. I am working today and tomorrow until 2:00 PM. Could it be 3:00 tomorrow?"

"Perfect," said Vince, looking at Trudi, hopefully, who was concentrating on the road as she pushed the speed limit by what she thought was a legal 5 mph over it. Vince gave Qasim his address and they said their goodbyes.

Trudi smiled and said, "Well it's a good thing we have nothing on tomorrow. I'll get an assortment of cookies or maybe bake some."

194

"Thanks."

"Thanks? He saved you and Miles, so he's my hero, too."

"I know Qasim is an immigrant, but I don't know anything about his customs or anything about him."

"Well, we're about to find out."

* * *

The next day, at 3:00 PM sharp, the car that doubled as Qasim's Uber parked in front of Vince and Trudi's. Qasim, dressed in tan chinos and a short-sleeve shirt, his wife, who wore loose fitting trousers, a long-sleeve blouse and a stylish shawl, and their son, in shorts and a Disneyland T-shirt, emerged. Vince and Trudi greeted them at the door and welcomed them in. Qasim's wife, Rasha, presented Trudi with a traditional Syrian cheesecake called Halawet Jeben. When Trudi tried to pronounce the Syrian name, Rasha smiled warmly and said, "Syrian cheesecake is fine." It looked and smelled divine and with its golden flaky top, resembled no other cheesecake she had seen. Jack, their son, was introduced. He was sweet and shy.

As they were sitting down, Qasim asked after Miles and wondered if Jack could see him.

"He's been asking since I told them we were coming over if he could see Miles. I tried to describe him but perhaps not well."

Vince said, "Sure. Come on Jack, help me get him."

Jack looked excited and eagerly jumped up with Qasim on his heels.

As they went to fetch Miles, Trudi asked Rasha if Jack was born in the USA, hoping at the same time to elicit some clues about the Melhos.

Rasha's English was excellent, with only a hint of an accent. Perhaps reading Trudi's mind, she explained that they were from Aleppo. She had been a teacher of English and French and Qasim was a mechanical engineer with the Syrian Railroad. When the early signs of violence erupted during the outbreak of the civil war, they, as did many people, underestimated how it would escalate into the horrific war it became, so they stuck it out. Rasha was pregnant and fleeing the country wasn't an appealing thought. But then a grenade was thrown into her classroom and Rasha, in a reflexive reaction, threw herself on the closest child. That child lived but 13 others didn't, and Rasha's back was shredded with shrapnel. The doctors were able to get most of it out and the physical pain was gone, but she still set off metal detectors. She also lost her baby.

As soon as she was well enough to travel, they fled to Turkey, where an aunt and uncle of Rasha's lived. Even though these were still the early days of what was to become a mass exodus from Syria. Rasha's relatives confided to them that they weren't sure of Turkey's long-term stability either, and suggested that they try to immigrate to the USA. They took their advice and after almost two years, they were granted a visa. That was two years ago, and they were hopeful that in another three-to-four years, they would become US citizens. When Jack was born, they wanted an

American-sounding name and surprisingly, 'Jack' is also a popular Syrian name.

Trudi was mesmerized by Rasha's story and felt an enormous admiration for this soft-spoken but truly brave woman.

The four boys came back, with Miles at Jack's side. "Vince, Rasha has been telling me their amazing story of their escape from Aleppo to Turkey and finally, here. I can fill you in later but what they have gone through is incredible!"

"Well, I for one am thankful that you made it to the USA. We may not be a perfect country, but most of the time we are better than most places."

Qasim replied, "We've been very happy here. We do encounter the occasional person who doesn't know us and says bad things, but we don't take it personally. Or at least we try not to."

With Jack in the room, Vince decided not to get involved in one of his bare-it-all questions. Instead he said, "Miles has really taken to Jack. Maybe because he's closer to his size."

Trudi asked, "Would you like coffee or tea? And what would you like, Jack?"

Jack looked at his parents, who nodded OK, so he asked for milk.

Rasha added, "Tea for me, please."

Qasim nodded. "Same for me."

Vince asked for a coffee and said, hopefully, "And a piece of that amazing looking ... Syrian Cheesecake!", as they all laughed.

Trudi got up and Rasha asked if she could help. Trudi welcomed her.

Meanwhile, Jack was sitting on the floor with Miles, who was in a flat-out prone position, head in Jack's lap. The men looked down and smiled at the warm scene. It briefly raised Vince's nightmare of Miles being mauled by the pit bull but the thought quickly receded. Qasim may have had other, even more disturbing thoughts, as he reflected on how thankful he was that Jack was here and not back there. Vince asked Qasim if he'd spoken with the police. "Yes, I have, but I don't think I was much help."

Vince agreed. "Neither was I. I might be able to recognize the voice, but in the dark, even with your headlights, I didn't get a good look at them. I was more focused on Miles."

"I watch for them when I have fares around the area, but so far I haven't seen them. What happens next?"

"Not much can happen unless they find them. Even if they do, I'm not sure what charges they can bring. It may be what we call a 'slap on the wrist.' "

"I'm familiar with that saying. In the Middle East it's a 'slap on the nape of the neck.' Doesn't really cause pain but expresses displeasure."

"Exactly. I blame the men more than the dog, but my guess is that, if they are caught, the dog will get the major punishment. He would probably be put down. Killed."

"I have very little experience with dogs, but I think they are like children. Good parents reduce the chance of bad behavior."

"I agree." And changing the subject, Vince asked, "So, how long have you been driving for Uber, Qasim, and what's that like?"

"Almost two years now. I'm grateful for the opportunity, but it's hard work for what we make. The system is very clever, however, and I appreciate the science behind it all."

"What did you do in Syria?"

"I was a mechanical engineer for the Syrian National Railway, so I worked indoors, in offices and machine shops. This is better in some ways because I'm outside in the fresh air and I have a little more flexibility with my time. It also allows Rasha time to do some tutoring."

"What does she teach?"

"French for Americans and English for foreigners," Qasim said with a smile. "Seems funny, doesn't it?"

Vince, smiling too, reflected on this. "Yes. Sometimes the whole world seems strange."

Trudi and Rasha returned with trays of tea, coffee, and a glass of milk, along with the cake and some chocolate chip cookies that Trudi had baked. The milk and cookies were the first things that diverted Jack's attention from Miles. Even then, he didn't want to disturb Miles, so they placed some cookies on a napkin on the chair Jack was leaning against.

Trudi poured the teas and coffees while Rasha served up the cake. They made a great team.

Vince impatiently had his first bite of cheesecake and his eyes told the story, as his mouth was too busy. "This is absolutely amazing!" he said finally.

"Thank you!" His request for another piece was granted just moments later.

The afternoon idled by and the four strangers found a lot in common to talk about. Jack munched his cookies with one hand and stroked Miles' head and back with his other. All was good in Pasadena.

After heartfelt goodbyes, Vince and Trudi returned inside and they both felt the same way. Qasim and Rasha were genuine, warm, brave and intelligent people. They wanted to see them again and add them to their group of close friends.

Vince commented, "Amazing. Out of such a terrifying incident, something so good can emerge."

Trudi jested, "And I hope you're talking about more than the cheesecake!"

"Of course." What he was also thinking was what a great meal Alma's lamb followed by Rasha's cheesecake would make. But he would have to settle for leftovers tonight.

* * *

CHAPTER 19 – THE CIRCLE LINE

London, England. Nigel Holmes was sick. He knew that, which was one of the reasons why he flew back to the UK, where he could get treatment under the UK's National Health System. The reputation of the NHS may be tarnished because of long waiting lists – even for serious issues such as heart by-pass operations – due to years of bureaucratic neglect; almost annual strategic changes directed down from government at the behest of major consulting firms; and just the normal inefficiencies inherent in healthcare. But when you are treated, it's done by highly skilled clinicians using cutting-edge technology.

A British citizen, Nigel had worked for Lloyds of London for 30 years, including the last five years in New York. Nigel liked New York and it also provided a 3,500 mile buffer between him and his bat-shit crazy ex-wife. Nigel had an excellent health insurance package from Lloyds that covered the ridiculously expensive routine care he required in New York from time to time. But for serious issues, the Company wanted him back in the UK. He was fine with that and hoped that his ex wouldn't know he was there, which would have been easy except that he wanted to see his daughter and granddaughter. The first priority, however, was to get medical attention.

Nigel's visits to doctors in New York had been almost exclusively for annual checkups: blood tests, cardio workup, etc. During his last annual exam, however, the blood tests revealed a change and his doctor, Dr. Howard Brinkman, asked him to come back in a month's time for another checkup. He also registered him in a test group for a sport/health watch trial that appeared particularly effective in ongoing blood diagnosis. Two weeks later, he received the watch and instructions for setting up the app. And at his follow-up exam, two weeks after that, his doctor told him about the ongoing changes that the watch, a VT2, was picking up. It was prompting him to refer Nigel to a specialist for more tests.

Nigel explained Lloyds' policy – that he would be returning to the UK for further tests and treatment. If that seemed extravagant, bear in mind that Lloyds knows how to calculate risks and costs: the flight and company flat costs paled in comparison with US healthcare costs. Nigel inquired about returning the VT2 but the doctor told him to keep it and just update the app to show his new doctor's details. He said the VT2 could do as good a job as extensive testing, and in real time. Nigel was amused by one question the doctor asked, which seemed to come out of the blue: "Do you have, or have access to, a gun or guns?" The answer was 'No' in New York and a capital 'NO' in the UK, where simply owning a gun is generally a crime.

Back in London, Nigel had no problem getting an appointment with his GP – general practitioner and gatekeeper to any specialist. Seeing the specialist was a different story, even with the Lloyds private insurance option. He didn't have a six- month wait like some, but even the three weeks seemed excessive. Still, he was able to see his daughter, Penny, and meet his five-year-old granddaughter,

Emily, for the first time, on one unusually sunny Manchester day. That single day ever so slightly helped him to deal with perhaps his biggest regret in life, that of being separated from them for so long, a situation engineered by his ex-wife, who drove a wedge between father and daughter with all kinds of sordid stories after the divorce.

Nigel reflected about his return to London. The City had changed, or perhaps it was his recollection. There appeared to be a rougher element woven into the longwearing fabric of the City with its well-dressed bankers and office staff. Lloyds had provided Nigel with a nice, but small, fully equipped company flat in the City of London, very busy and congested by day but quiet at night. He did enjoy watching British television – the comedies, dramas and even the news. Real news. He was still puzzled how top-level politicians could spew lies out with impunity in the US, at least on some channels. And who needs a thousand channels?

It was while watching a David Attenborough re-run about the mating habits of foxes one evening that his VT2 buzzed continuously. The screen read "Final Notice." He recalled Dr. Brinkman mentioning this function but he never thought it would happen. Was it really happening or was it a malfunction? His phone rang, which was unusual in itself, and when he answered, it was his New York doctor.

"Dr. Brinkman?"

"Yes, Nigel. I just received your Final Notice alert. You were supposed to enter your new doctor's details into the app."

"I know. Sorry, but I was going to enter my specialist's details when I see him. Could this be a false alarm?"

"Anything is possible, but you need to call your doctor as soon as possible, first thing in the morning, and have him fast track an appointment. Have him call me if he has questions. In fact, here's my direct line."

After hanging up, Nigel sat there in total disbelief. Perhaps it's a fault with the system. That happens all the time with technology. He fell asleep on the sofa wondering if it was all a dream. A very bad dream.

* * *

In the morning he accepted that it wasn't a dream, but he still held out hope that there was a technical issue. He called his GP and explained the urgency to the practice manager as suggested by his New York doctor's call yesterday evening. He didn't get into the VT2 alert with her, and after being put on hold for a couple of minutes, she came back on the line with an appointment for 2:30 PM that afternoon with a specialist on Harley Street, Mr. Trevor Sedgwick. Nigel almost smiled at the British labels calling doctors "doctors" until they reach a specialist level, where they become "mister" again. But he was in no mood to smile.

He spent the rest of the morning thinking about what needed to be done, if it was, indeed, true. He had kept his will and insurance beneficiary information in a current state so all of that was in order, and he would need to brief Penny, and hopefully see her and Emily again. The thought of that pained him greatly however, and he was unsure if he should or not.

At 1:45 PM he set out for the short walk to the Tower Hill Tube station for the 10-minute journey on the Circle Line to Great Portland Street station. The doors of the train opened, and the exiting passengers came out as always; but as he entered the car, he was pushed hard against the edge of the door by a couple of skinheads sporting an array of tattoos. Their behavior was not only unusual in Nigel's experience, even by New York standards, but it was very atypical of normal British Underground, or Tube, etiquette.

Inside the car, the two thugs stood directly in front of two young business types, glaring at them until they vacated their seats, so the thugs could sit, even though, as the train left the station, there were two women standing, as well as one man much older than Nigel. He looked at the two skinheads as hard as he dared to see if it could magically make them give up their seats for the women. All that earned him was their menacing glare in return, plus an equally evil, "Wot are ya staring at, ya hapless old geezer?" Nigel quickly looked away and if you'd have asked him, he'd have to admit, he was scared.

At the Great Portland Street stop, the two thugs got up and literally pushed people out of their way, laughing as they went. Nigel, still shaken, made his way to Harley Street to see Mr. Sedgwick, feeling older and frail. He wondered if just that ugly experience could make him feel this way.

Trevor Sedgwick specialized in internal medicine. He was about 50 years old and exuded abundant gravitas and confidence. Nigel explained the urgency, as forecast by the Final Notice received by his VT2. Hearing that, and without knowing any real history, Sedgwick was skeptical of the device's ability to predict death, raising Nigel's hopes, but when Sedgwick reviewed Nigel's files, and especially when he compared them with the VT2 App's history since the last results, he became concerned about his condition. Hearing that Dr. Brinkman had invited his call, and given the five-hour time difference, Sedgwick decided to call Brinkman, as it was still morning in New York.

Doctors are scientists and are trained and conditioned to use facts as the basis for decision making ... despite the fact that in the USA, pharmaceutical companies use attractive former college cheerleaders as representatives, trips to exotic destinations, or other incentives to make the facts a little less... well, factual. As a practicing physician in the UK, however, Sedgwick had never been seduced by those distractions, so he was open to what Dr. Brinkman had to say.

Sedgwick listened to Brinkman's opinion of Nigel's medical issue, a rare and aggressive condition, interjecting questions, and also, with even greater interest and more questions, Brinkman's assessment of the VT2. He was impressed, especially considering the correlation between Nigel's vital signs on the VT2 app and Brinkman's recent lab tests and analysis. When he finished the call, he appeared more somber.

Nigel had been listening to and looking at Sedgwick intensely during the phone call, trying to assess the opinions being formed. As Sedgwick was gathering his thoughts and writing down a few notes, Nigel's anxiety grew to a point that he asked, "What is your opinion?"

Sedgwick replied, using the words Nigel feared: "I'm afraid it's not good. The notice that your watch provided is consistent with your condition. I'm sorry, but it's highly unlikely that the forecast is inaccurate. I would like to have you admitted to King's College or London Bridge Hospital today, if possible. Both are good although, depending on your insurance, London Bridge might be more comfortable."

There was something about the way Sedgwick said 'comfortable' that bothered Nigel. "Comfortable?" he asked.

"Yes, I'm afraid that your watch is correct and perhaps all that either facility can do is make you comfortable. Another choice is Royal Trinity Hospice."

There it was. Nigel had a very short time. "Could I possibly delay it by a day or two?"

"The blood disorder you have is extremely aggressive and also rare, so we have very little data to predict how much time you have. Both Dr. Brinkman and I agreed, however, that the one- week notice is probably accurate; but it could be a day or two in either direction. What we do know is that your physical condition will deteriorate rapidly and it's quite possible that in a day or two, you will need to be in a care facility. I suggested a hospital because they could gather additional data about your disorder."

"OK. This is all a shock, as you can imagine. Can I call you tomorrow to make the arrangements?"

"Of course. But don't leave it too long. You'll be much better off in care, wherever you decide."

Nigel wasn't even sure he had the strength to stand up, but he did and once outside in the crisp afternoon air, he rallied a bit. His mind lost in thought, he walked automatically to the Great Portland Street tube station, put his return ticket into the turnstile and proceeded to the Circle Line platform. It was moderately busy with mostly a single row of travelers strung out along the platform. The electronic sign showed a train arriving in two minutes.

Tube-riding Londoners have perfected the art of staying in their own space as a form of self-protection. Morning and evening commuters often have no choice but to ride crammed against each other. To actually look at and 'see' the person you're crammed up against is discouraged – therefore headphones keeping voices out and eyes straight ahead, reading the same advertisements on the walls for the hundredth time – is the accepted norm.

Despite this practiced art of cocooning, Nigel suddenly realized that the person in the first row, just to his right, was one of the thugs from his earlier journey. Nigel's first thought was to move way down the platform; but then, he stopped. He felt the growing rush of air that the trains create as they hurtle through the tubes beneath the city. That rush seemed to buoy him as he heard the train approach. It would race into the station at great speed, just a couple of feet from the waiting passengers, and then quickly brake so that all cars gave access to the platform. With no specific plan in mind, he slowly shifted to the right so that he was directly behind the thug as the train entered the station at about 30-40 mph.

The train stopped, and Nigel followed the skinhead through the open doors, watching him as he pushed a woman out of the way to take the last remaining seat. Nigel might explain what happened next as an "out-of-body experience" as he walked up to the thug and with a voice that resonated with authority and lack of fear, said, "Get the fuck out of that seat and allow this woman to sit." The skinhead looked at Nigel, and even his pasty white complexion paled as he gulped and rose from his seat, skulking off down the car. Nigel's altered state returned to normal when his normally "blind," "deaf" and well-behaved fellow passengers burst into cheers and applause.

Nigel called Penny that evening for a teary good-bye and he shared his solicitor's contact details. The next day he called Mr. Sedgwick and asked them to make arrangements for him to be admitted to King's College Hospital. After all, he was born there, and this would complete the circle, which happened five days later.

* * *

CHAPTER 20 – TWO MEETINGS

Quincy, Massachusetts. Maria and Vijay met on Monday morning and discussed the call from Matt Harper. The Boston Globe was an important paper and both Vijay and Maria wanted it on their side as they neared their IPO. But how much to reveal and how would the Globe treat it?

The press release clearly stated that some users had committed crimes against others after receiving their Notice. It wasn't a stretch to assume that the crimes were murders, so they decided to be honest with Matt and answer his questions, without giving him more than he asked for. Vijay asked Maria to call Matt and arrange a meeting. He would like to attend. She called Vijay back a few minutes later, telling him that she had Matt on hold, and that he couldn't do it today but could tomorrow. Vijay said that they could give him an hour at 1:00 PM tomorrow.

* * *

Pasadena, California. Vince and Trudi took Miles to see their vet, Dr. Lisa Putnam. She was horrified to hear about the attack but thankful and relieved that both Miles and Vince were on the mend. Miles liked Dr. Putnam, despite the indignities she had carried out on him over the years. That was a long time ago, but the little peanut butter dog biscuits were fresher in his memory and absolutely current in his nostrils. She removed his cone, giving him false hope and a piece of peanut butter biscuit, perhaps as an apology, as she carefully unwrapped his bandages. The wound looked OK, but Dr. Putnam stressed the importance of keeping the cone on so that Miles couldn't hurt himself. She prescribed a course of Clavamox for five days, twice a day, and then she would see Miles again. She showed them how to change his bandages and look for excessive amounts of blood or fluid, in which case they should bring him back immediately. And then, sadly for Miles, the cone was replaced.

When they returned home, there was a message from Dr. Parker's office. Vince needed to go into the Pacific Diagnostic lab on 2135 Colorado Blvd to have another blood test done. The samples taken at the hospital appear to have been lost. He made a mental note to go in tomorrow.

* * *

Quincy, Massachusetts. Matt arrived 20 minutes early for his one o'clock meeting but it was clear that the meeting would start at 1:00, so he spent the time thinking about his meeting strategy. He knew that the Final Notice triggered aggressive action in some people, and he knew of one such case – Quentin Moore. The press release indicated more than one, but how many? And what were the details? That would be the interesting part, especially since the FBI was involved. So much sexier than the police.

At 1:00 PM sharp, Maureen answered her phone, said "OK," and came over to get him. She led him up the industrial stairs and then into Vijay's office before disappearing.

Vijay greeted him warmly and introduced Maria Moon. "How can we help you, Matt?"

Matt explained that he had read their press release with great interest, generated by both the technical nature of the watch as well as the comment about crimes being committed after receiving the Notice. He started off with the technology. "How long has the VT2 program been in development, and do you mind if I take notes?"

"No problem with the notes. Almost three years now. A combination of my medical, mathematical and athletic interests, it's actually been ready for a long time but we've been testing it extensively and it keeps passing the tests." Vijay proudly replied.

Matt finished a brief note. "How does it work in practice with its smartphone interface?"

Vijay began explaining on a high level, but Matt wanted additional information and his questions displayed a surprising knowledge of technology and medicine, prompting Vijay to ask, "You seem to have a much better than average grasp of medicine. How did that come about?"

Matt replied, somewhat sheepishly, "I started out in pre-med, wanting to be a doctor, but as the costs mounted up, I opted for journalism, with all its many facets – good and bad."

Vijay understood. "I know what you mean. That's probably what inspired me to invent something. After more than ten years of college, I felt that I was challenging the national debt for largest deficit honors."

Matt chuckled but pressed on to get to what he really wanted to talk about, "Tell me about the Final Notice with respect to the timing. When is a Notice received?"

Vijay's warning antennae buzzed a bit and he glanced at Maria as he replied, "The Notice has been found to be extremely accurate up to 30 days. Our beta test will have a user choice of 10, 20 or 30 days. Interestingly, while we have found a few instances of death occurring before the Notice period, it has never been later."

Matt took another step. "I guess unnatural deaths would be included in that group."

"Yes, and undue stress or depression can cause a heart attack or stroke at any time."

"What can you tell me about the crimes mentioned in the press release?"

Maria answered, "In a few cases, users who had access to guns, and who received their Notice, have reacted aggressively and killed people."

"How many times has that happened?"

Maria stuck with their game plan. "There have been three that clearly seem to be a combination of the Notice and anger."

Matt sensed some waffling, "And are there others that are less clear?"

"One other. It was an unwitnessed shooting in Texas where the shooter, through a combination of an angry confrontation, alcohol and guns, committed a crime at the same time as receiving his Notice. Also bear in mind that there were 100 users in the alpha test."

"Do you know how many had access to guns?" "Yes. About 60."

"Are these killings concerning you as you move forward with your testing and ultimate launch?"

Vijay took the lead again. "Absolutely. We even considered removing it but all of our focus groups rated it as their favorite feature. During our alpha test, the devices were issued by physicians who were instructed to screen out those people who are clinically depressed or, in their view, may not handle the Notice well. Our beta test will put added emphasis on these restrictions and include even more clinician instruction."

Matt went for his prize, "Have the killings attracted law enforcement attention?"

Vijay and Maria looked at each other, and as agreed, Vijay replied honestly, "In most cases we have been contacted by investigating police asking about the watch or the app." He hesitated a second and added, "And we have been working with the FBI to help them develop a plan to deal with these events. They recognize that what someone decides to do when they know they are dying is up to that individual, whether they get their "Notice" from their doctor or their watch."

Matt understood but asked, "Is it normal for the FBI to become involved in something like this?"

Maria and Vijay looked at each other and realized that they hadn't discussed this question and although Zoe had told them, they didn't think it was their call to reveal it. Maria responded, "Good question. I don't know. Maybe because it involved multiple jurisdictions?"

Matt accepted this but asked, "Who from the FBI have you been talking with?"

Maria spoke again. "I think we'll need to have them call you. I don't want to step out of bounds on this. That OK?"

Matt expected this and said "Sure. I'm guessing that you won't want to or be able to give me details on the users committing crimes."

Maria confirms, "No. That would really be out of bounds, but perhaps the FBI will."

Vijay's phone buzzed and after answering, he stood up saying, "Matt, I'm sorry, my two o'clock is here. We squeezed you in but time's up."

"No problem. I appreciate your time and help. I may have some follow-up on questions. Maria, OK if I call you?"

"Sure, you have my number. Also, my job is to stay ahead of anything in the media about us, so if you write anything, I'd appreciate a heads up. I'm happy to fact check anything you write, so you're not spewing fake news, too," she said with a smile.

Matt laughed and said, "It's a deal. Thank you both very much for your help."

Maria and Vijay looked at each other, pleased with themselves. They had stuck with their plan. Now they waited to see what the FBI had in store for them.

As Matt descended the stairs, he couldn't help but notice the attractive young woman, sensibly dressed, with sensible shoes, waiting in the lobby. He pretended to get his papers in order and button his coat deliberately as Maureen went over to the young woman and said, "Agent Brouet, Vijay can see you now."

"Agent Brouet," Matt forced himself to remember until he got to his car and wrote it down.

* * *

Zoe liked Vijay, felt that he was being honest with her and wanted to do the right thing. She hoped that he would understand the issue of a warrant, and after the "hello's" and "how are you's," she got right to the point. "After the Manatta-Dumble incident, my boss had a warrant issued to ensure we get the required data for the beta test users. I told him that you would volunteer the information unless there was a legal issue and that you had provided it for the alpha test users, but he didn't want to take any chances. I hope it hasn't or won't create problems for you when news of the warrant gets into the public domain. It takes a couple of days."

Vijay understood and explained their actions and gave her an update. "After the high-profile murder-suicide, we decided to be proactive and issued this press release." Zoe quickly read the release. "Matt Harper, the reporter from The Boston Globe, picked up on the crimes comment and, being local, he pursued it. He asked for details of the crimes and we declined as we did when he asked who at the FBI was handling this. Here's his card. We said we'd pass it on."

"When does enrollment for the beta test begin?" Zoe asked as she took out her notepad.

"It already has. We've sent out information packs to an expanded group of physicians. There are an initial 100 participants waiting to be confirmed this week, another 100, two weeks later, and then 100 each week until we reach 500. If all looks good, we'll issue another 500."

Zoe had been writing this down and then she looked up and said, "I'm trying to figure out how I'll be able to keep ahead of this."

Vijay interjected, "Only 50% will have gun access."

Zoe smiled. "That makes it only a little easier but still … when will we get advised of the Final Notice?"

"We can program it in so you receive it in real time. Also, the users can now opt for a 10, 20 or 30-day notice. That might help you prioritize urgency."

Zoe thought, "Yes, it should." Then aloud she asked, "What about doctors? By law they are required to inform law enforcement of any threats or conditions that might make a crime likely. What is the procedure now?"

"Doctors get copied on Final Notices in real time, just as you will. You will have the doctor's contact details and could send them a note to advise you asap if they perceive any behavior that might be dangerous. In fact, we can communicate with them again, as they issue the VT2s. What details would you like on the contact request?"

"I'll set up a new hotline email that will ring sirens when a message is received. You'll have it by the end of the day."

Maria asked, "Just so we're in the loop, will you be contacting Matt Harper? I'm certain he'll call me if he doesn't hear from you. And were we right about not releasing details of the shootings?"

"Yes, on both counts. I might direct him to local law enforcement locations about the shootings, as long as they are no longer under investigation. If he can pry the info out of them, it's fine with me." She thought for a few seconds and added, "We're really sailing into uncharted waters as you add significant numbers to your user base. I'm not sure what else we can do. Any ideas?"

"Not off the top of my head," replied Vijay. "Unfortunately, the VT2 can't analyze mental states. At least not yet. And so far, for what it's worth, there haven't been any shootings by women."

"How many women with access to guns did you have in the alpha group?"

Vijay looked at a paper on his desk and replied, "Ten. Not a big sample."

Zoe asked, "Are you going to supply us with the same information when you do the full post-beta test rollout?"

Vijay had been avoiding this moment. "I don't think we can, even if we wanted to; and selling a product that comes with a warning that 'this information will be shared with the FBI' will not exactly boost our sales. You can't get this information now from people buying guns. Even having a doctor wired in will be optional, although it will be highly recommended. And depending on who's in charge politically, people may or may not have a doctor to involve."

"I understand, but what if we get a warrant?"

"We'd have to fight it."

"And I understand that, too. I'm not sure how we could justify it, given that we don't even know who buys a gun – even the information you give us regarding gun access will be incomplete because some states don't allow doctors to ask their patients. OK, let's leave it for the time being. You've been very helpful and cooperative, and I really appreciate that. I'll send you a hotline e-mail address shortly and I look forward to receiving the beta test enrollee information soon. Anything else I should know?"

"Maria?" Vijay asked.

"I think that covers it. You'll deal with Matt Harper?"

"Yes."

"What if we get additional inquiries? "

"Hmm. Hopefully there won't be many but go ahead and give them my office number. I'll brief someone with the information I'm comfortable releasing."

"OK. Thanks for your understanding, Zoe. We'll be in touch if anything new develops."

"Thanks, Vijay, Maria."

* * *

There were nine messages on Maria's desk when she returned to her office: seven from newspapers and two from TV news networks. Things were about to heat up. She wasn't sure if this was the tip of the iceberg but decided to prepare an FAQ briefing sheet that covered the same points discussed in their meeting with Matt. Vijay agreed.

* * *

Maria's phone continued to ring and, as a courtesy – as well as to dig a bit – she called Matt Harper. Matt was pleased to get the call and Maria explained that the release was getting a lot of attention and wanted to give Matt a heads up in case he was sitting on the story for some reason.

Matt told her that Special Agent Brouet had called him, and that she shared with him some high-level details of two cases that were closed: Quentin Moore and John Mason. She had explained that the other two were still being investigated.

Matt asked, "By the 'other two,' I'm presuming she meant the third one which may or not have been triggered by the Final Notice. What was the fourth one?"

Maria realized that Matt was digging again and she needed to steer him back to her agenda, "Come on, Matt, you have all of the information that is in the public domain at this point. In your opinion, does that constitute a story that someone would run with?"

Matt sensed the pushback but was interested in what Maria was saying. "What are you getting at?"

"My concern and fear is that we will soon see a number of stories with guesses and stretches of imagination that could be harmful to our beta launch."

"You may be right. Tell you what, if you promise to keep me updated, whenever information becomes newly available, like the fourth incident, maybe a half step ahead of the pack, I will release a story that might help other publications print responsible stories."

"That's a deal. Will you run your piece by me first?" "Sure. I'm sending it to you now."

Maria exclaimed, "So you were already going public? And you tricked me into promising to give you a jump on your competition!" But she was smiling at his mild treachery.

Matt laughed and said, "Well, I was about to press 'Send' to give you a heads up when you rang. I'm on your side. Friends?"

"Yes. Let me read your article and I'll get back with you. And thanks." Still smiling, she opened the file that Matt had sent.

Smartest Watch on the Market Measures Health & Answers a Big Question

Quincy, MA. *VitalTech LLC is releasing its revolutionary new health monitor, disguised as a watch, in a limited nationwide beta test. And if you want to try out the VT2, you'd better get an appointment with your doctor asap to grab one of these amazing devices.*

The VT2 is like having an ongoing blood test, without the needles and lab visits, and the level of sophistication of the automatic analysis is unprecedented. The VT2 is so sensitive and analytically accurate that it can detect an irreversible decline in your health and predict your death, answering the age-old question, "If you knew, for sure, that you were going to die in 10, 20 or 30 days, what would you do?"

Of course, the answer to that will vary tremendously from person to person; but for some, as VitalTech has found out, it means getting revenge with impunity; and for those with guns, it might include killing.

VT2s will be available beginning April 10th from a licensed physician. The beta test price is $150 and includes the watch and the associated app. Beta test users will get to keep their watches, which will be upgraded with additional software if the tests reveal any required patches. The final version is expected to sell for $200-$250.

More information can be found at www.vitaltech/ vt2.com.

Maria considered the news story and felt it set the right tone, establishing interest while dealing with the negatives, as well. She replied to Matt that it was good and fine with her.

* * *

CHAPTER 21 – THE GUN

Pasadena, California. Both Vince and Miles had continued to make good progress. Miles' wound was looking good and a very smart red bandana now covered the shaved area of his neck as well as the light bandage over the still obvious stitches, which would dissolve in time. He now had a new harness to use for walks instead of his old collar, and he seemed happy, content and displayed no signs of emotional baggage, even when they approached other dogs on their walks. Of course, the cone had been removed so he had every reason to be happy.

Vince's bandages had been removed, too, and except for the redness, persistent soreness, and itching around the bite marks, it seemed that his hand was pretty much back to normal. Where Vince and Miles differed was in their minds. Vince was not relaxed when out with Miles, even in the daytime. In fact, he avoided walking in the dark. It wasn't fear that had hold of Vince, although he wasn't entirely unafraid. Never far from his consciousness was the attack that he and Miles had endured. And that, in turn, evoked memories of the incident in the mall parking lot, which although minor in comparison, made Vince wonder how much everyday life had changed. He was indignant that there were people out there who were so callous, cruel and ... immoral. Vince was no babe in the woods and he hadn't been living in a cave, but this was the first time he had ever experienced, first hand, a really brutal physical attack with potentially really serious injuries, or worse. Ominously, too, Vince thought that if he had a gun with him that night, he would have used it without another thought. And so, as soon as he had 100% mobility of his hand, he suggested to Trudi that it was time to call Rueben and get a gun. She agreed.

Vince called Rueben and told him that he and Trudi had their Safety Certificates and were ready to pull the trigger and buy a gun. (He didn't actually use those words. Rueben would have groaned.) They agreed to go the following morning – being retired had its advantages – and Rueben suggested Turner's Outdoorsman on Arroyo Parkway in Pasadena. Trudi and Vince would pick him up at 10:00.

In the meantime, Trudi had volunteered to watch Jack for a few hours while Rasha looked for more permanent child care, so she grabbed her guitar and headed out, hoping to get in some more practice for tomorrow's song circle. So much had happened since last week that she couldn't believe how fast the time had flown by.

Vince did some last minute on-line gun research and took a nap. He was awakened by his cell phone ringing. It was Dr. Parker's office inquiring about his blood tests, as Pacific Diagnostics didn't have a record of a recent test. Vince had forgotten all about it and apologized, promising to go tomorrow.

* * *

The next day Vince and Trudi picked Rueben up to help them become, as Rueben put it, "responsible gun owners."

Rueben had never been in a Prius before and was impressed with the ride and quietness.

Vince added, "And don't forget about the 50-plus miles per gallon. What do you get in that big pickup of yours?"

"About half that but it keeps me from being laughed at when I go to the station."

"You're retired. You don't go there often, do you?"

"No. I do the occasional training gig. Pays me a few bucks and I get to see old friends and perhaps make a positive impact on the newer recruits."

Rueben asked them again about their willingness to use a gun if they had to and Vince answered yes, very quickly. Trudi followed with her yes, adding that she hoped she never had to.

Turner's Outdoorsman was like the gun show plus fishing, but despite the size of the store, all the action was in the gun section, and this wasn't even the weekend. As they walked to the handgun section, Vince told Rueben that they had looked at some guns and they liked the look and feel of a Glock. Rueben was impressed and agreed that the Glock was an excellent gun. He explained that many of his colleagues used Glocks, primarily because they were dependable. The last thing you needed is a cool looking gun that jammed. They used to be made only in Austria but then some were assembled in Georgia and now some are manufactured in Georgia, as well.

They looked at the Glocks and after both Vince and Trudi handled the different models, they decided on a Glock 19, 9mm, for $519. It was relatively light and small. The young woman serving them, Bethany, added that it had a mild recoil as well. Vince asked if they could get the NRA discount and Bethany answered, "Yes," as long as they were seniors. She also suggested buying a special NRA one-year membership for $30, instead of the usual $40, and they would each get a free NRA duffel bag. They declined the NRA membership and produced their HSCs and driver's licenses (flattered that they would be asked to prove their senior status). They completed all the paperwork and Bethany explained that in 10 days they could return to get their gun.

Bethany asked about ammunition and they both looked at Rueben for a suggestion. He confirmed that they still wanted to get shooting range training and recommended that they bring their own ammunition. Rueben felt that the absolute minimum for shooting practice was 50 rounds and suggested that 200 rounds of 124gr FMJ 9mm Ammo by M.B.I. was a good choice. M.B.I. remanufactured ammo using previously-fired brass cartridges. Recycling the cartridges made good sense and both the police and military used remanufactured ammo. 200 rounds at $44.00 was a good buy, too. The 200 rounds would give them enough for very basic training with extra for later use.

As they were walking out with their bag of ammo, Vince surprised Rueben by asking about a good holster.

"You know that you can't carry this gun around with you?" Rueben asked.

Vince hesitated for just a second too long and said, "I know. It was just to keep it clean and covered."

Rueben made the point that a small gun vault with biometric, or fingerprint, access was the best idea. They started at just under $200. Coded ones were about half that, but he didn't recommend them because when the pressure was on, remembering a code might not be easy. In either case, he suggested shopping online for the best price and selection. They also discussed shooting range training and Rueben gave them some ideas on good training ranges, adding, however, that he would rather not be involved with their training. As friends, he didn't want the responsibility of being the one who taught them. He explained, "If this was for hunting, that would be different. But this is about protecting yourself and I don't want to take that responsibility in case you make a mistake, or something goes wrong. The ranges I suggested are pros."

Vince and Trudi understood, and they made their way home after making one of the most sobering purchases of their lives, but with only a small package of ammo to show for it. They dropped Rueben off, thanking him sincerely, and drove home. It was all rather anti-climactic. Trudi put together a quick salad for their lunch and then dashed out to look after Jack and perhaps have some time with Rasha for a cup of tea when she returned.

Vince went online again, researching gun vaults, and although the biometric ones were indeed twice the price of the coded ones, he could see the downside of having to remember your code, perhaps in the dark, and under extreme pressure. He selected a couple on Amazon and saved them to discuss with Trudi later on. While he was on the site, he also looked up "holsters," and one of the choices that came up was "holsters for concealed carry." He browsed through these, making a number of notes as he went along. He tired again and took a nap.

* * *

Rasha handed off Jack's supervision to Trudi as she left to check out a day care center. Trudi enjoyed watching Jack and Jack enjoyed hearing Trudi play and sing. Rasha returned within an hour, triumphantly announcing that she liked the day care center and Jack could start immediately. Rasha had recently been hired as a French tutor by a private school in Glendale and she worked there for three hours a day, three days a week. Trudi and Qasim had been taking shifts watching Jack, but the day care center would take Jack for five hours on each of those days, giving Rasha some breathing room between the lessons and dropping him off/picking him up.

The job was perfect. The school had students from varied backgrounds including African American, Latinos, Asians and a sizeable mix of students of Middle Eastern origin.

The Melhos were doing well and they had been following the recovery of Vince and Miles with great interest and concern. Trudi and Rasha had really hit it off. Rasha loved Trudi's stories about American life through her music, although, as she explained to Trudi, much of it was universal. On the other hand, in this mutually supportive relationship, Trudi admired Rasha's strength and calmness, and found her background and history intriguing.

Over a cup of tea, Rasha told Trudi that Vince had asked Qasim to enlist the support of his fellow Uber drivers in watching for the two men with the pit bull, but so far, no one had seen them. The drivers covered a wide area, so hopefully someone would see them sooner or later. Trudi was surprised and a little concerned with this and hoped that Vince wasn't planning to take the law into his own hands.

She expressed her gratitude however and changing the subject, asked if they'd like to meet some of their friends, the Khans and the Martinezes. She was sure that Rasha would like Alma and Doris.

Rasha said they would love to and they even had a baby sitter for Jack now, as a woman at the day care center offered her services after hours. They didn't have any evening engagements at the moment but Qasim normally worked three nights a week – Saturday, Sunday and Monday. However, he could usually trade with other drivers. Trudi said she would check with the Khans and Martinezes and let her know. Rasha asked the question that Vince would have hoped she would: "Can I bring anything?"

Trudi quickly replied, "Syrian cheesecake?"

* * *

Trudi went home, excited about her idea to get together with the Khans, Martinezes and Melhos. Vince had just woken up from his nap. Trudi was carrying her guitar and Vince realized that he'd never heard how her song circle had gone. Trudi gave him a quick recap and said she was planning to attend again, that evening. She asked how his hand was and he said better, although it itched and perhaps it was the stress and ordeal, but he was easily tired out. Trudi also gave him an update of her chat with Rasha and asked about his idea of enlisting the Uber drivers to look for the two men and a dog. He deflected any concerns about him turning vigilante and simply told her that it seemed like a good idea to get extra eyes out there. She accepted that and told him of her idea to get everyone together. He liked the idea, especially the part about the cheesecake. He told Trudi about the gun vaults and she told him to get the one he liked best. He didn't tell her about the holsters.

Trudi got ahold of Alma, who said they were pretty open for the next couple of weeks. She then called Doris and they agreed on a week from Saturday and she confirmed it all 'round. Trudi was really happy to have something so positive to look forward to. The ordeal with Vince and Miles had worn heavily on her. Vince saw the date as the day he could collect their gun.

* * *

Trudi had gotten a couple of "Beast Burgers" for dinner, the futuristic vegan burger that actually bled like the real thing. As Vince bit into his, he realized that he had once again forgotten his blood test! He made himself a big note and the next morning he went to the lab where they seemed to want to drain him dry, filling a number of little vials. He hoped Dr. Parker would be pleased.

* * *

CHAPTER 22 – TWO TESTS

Quincy, Massachusetts. Many doctors hadn't even gotten around to looking at the VT2 package they had received before their office staff started receiving calls for appointments and questions about the VT2's availability. Maria's hunch and Matt's lead had paid off. When Matt's story broke, other newspapers, wire services, television networks and cable news picked it up, all across the country. Most had followed Matt's tone, if not hype, although there were a few cable news and internet news sites that chose to go the alt-fact way. The worst was BrightFahrt, the neo-nazi site, which ran an editorial by Gyro Spirulinas, "Killer Watch to Level the Playing Field," where he urged his equally nutcase right-wing followers to kill liberals when they received their Final Notices. That was even too far for a couple of conservative lawmakers!

Vijay called an urgent meeting with his team to discuss increasing the beta test user base so as not to alienate doctors besieged with requests. Wade had been able to push out enough units to increase the first wave to 500, which were scooped up immediately. Drew had sent messages to all the doctors on their distribution list not to accept any new VT2 - related appointments, but the requests had come in so quickly that there were about 2,500 people who had already booked appointments to get their VT2s. In addition, many doctors had backlogs of people wanting appointments, but they had been refused after receiving Drew's notice. Based on the estimated numbers, they would need another five to ten thousand to cover this demand.

Drew and Patsy were concerned about keeping up with those volumes insofar as test analyses were concerned. They were still in the early stages of hiring additional staff to cope with the rollout volumes. Don and Ganesh were concerned about a suggestion that discount vouchers be issued to those with appointments who would not be getting a beta test watch, thus diluting income. Maria was concerned about staying on top of the large number of press articles. And Liz was concerned that without a controlled rollout and ramp-up, new issues could become really big issues if they weren't caught and fixed early on. The only person not worried was Wade. He was confident that he could handle the increased demand. Bring it on!

And all of that was Vijay's concern, as was the risk of poor customer and aftercare service.

They had a good discussion and avoided simply going for volume. It was a good problem to have and they began to make some decisions. The first was that they would keep the beta test to 1,000 users, as originally planned. That would allow Patsy and Drew to control the data analysis of the test results as well as containing unforeseen problems to the thousand-user base. It would also ensure that Zoe didn't freak out, although Vijay would call her to tell her that they were accelerating the test roll-out.

To assuage the 2,000 people on the waiting list who would not get their watch during the beta test, VitalTech would issue a 50% discount coupon which could be redeemed at whatever the final price was set for when the full rollout began. They felt that was a compelling offer and would take some heat off the doctors. They would also issue up to 5,000 $25-off vouchers against the full retail price for doctors to distribute to patients who were not able to even get an appointment. Finally, Maria got approval to hire a PR assistant and a full- time secretary.

Drew, feeling relieved, raised the point that throughout the alpha test, the device and app had performed so well that very little software adjustments and zero hardware adjustments had been required. So, if this continued to be the case, the transition from beta test to final rollout could be very short, allowing them to still capitalize on the initial demand.

More satisfying than any other aspect of the discussion was the tangible evidence that they had a winner. Although the team had always been confident about their product, knowing what consumers will buy always carried a risk. They also realized that in addition to managing the beta test, they really needed to gear up for the full rollout.

Vijay thanked the team and called Jennifer to give her an update. She had told Vijay earlier that J. Edward was thrilled with the early demand but that he also appreciated that the growth needed to be controlled.

In the first five minutes of their call, Vijay updated her on their decisions, and Jennifer felt they had done the right thing. She would pass the news along to J. Edward. They spent the next 20 minutes talking about the two of them and when they could see each other again. Vijay wanted to stay close to base, so she decided that their client relationship needed some maintenance and told him she would see him very soon. That news, plus the positive actions from the team meeting, put Vijay in top spirits!

* * *

Pasadena, California. Vince and Trudi were still drinking their morning coffee when Dr. Parker's call came in. All he said was I received your blood tests and I need to see you asap. Vince asked why, and Parker flatly said, "Just get here asap."

Vince was concerned but simply told Trudi that it was Dr. Parker and he wanted to see Vince. Trudi was concerned but Vince more or less convinced her that it couldn't be serious. He gave her a kiss on the cheek and said he'd be back soon.

When Vince arrived at Dr. Parker's, the receptionist told him to have a seat and that he'd be next. When Vince was sent in, Parker looked at Vince's hand again. Vince had been scratching it and there were superficial scabs and even some freshly dried blood. Parker asked about the scratching and Vince told him that the area around the wound itched intensely. Parker asked if he had headaches, felt generally weak or had other flu like symptoms. Vince said definitely yes to the headaches but didn't think he had a fever. Parker stroked an electronic thermometer across his forehead and said, "99.8." He asked Vince if he felt any anxiety, agitation or confusion. Vince reflected on his behavior and realized that yes, a little of all of that.

Parker looked closely at the blood tests again with the large red note scrawled across the front page, "Urgent screening for Rabies required."

"The lab called me this morning about these results and we need to carry out some additional tests immediately."

"For what?"

"Rabies. The tests had anomalies that raised some questions. There haven't been reports of rabies in dogs in southern California for years. Bats occasionally and increasingly in skunks, which makes it possible for transmission to dogs."

Vince blinked with recognition and said, "Skunks. The night that Miles and I were attacked, the dog smelled like a skunk."

Parker looked as if he had been diagnosed with rabies. He was white. "Shit! We need to get you into the ER asap to have those tests done."

Parker whispered. "Vince, if not caught in time, rabies is usually fatal."

"Do you think it's too late?"

"I don't know. Let's get you to the ER first and let them run the tests. Are you OK to drive over to the Huntington on your own?"

"I think so. But why didn't they give me a rabies shot that night at the ER?"

"You told me that they had given you an injection!"

"They did, but I don't know what it was for. I was half out of it at the time. The place was like a war zone. Total chaos. Thinking back, it's not surprising that they could have missed the call. The doctors and nurses were being pulled left and right attending injured people. Did they just miss it?"

"I don't know. Let me call Huntington right now and see what they did."

"I was treated at St. Luke's, not Huntington."

Parker buzzed his secretary and asked her to call St. Luke's ER and find out what treatment Vince had received.

Parker explained, "It's not an automatic treatment action if it's a dog bite in what's considered a safe area, although I would say it should have been considered since the dog that bit you was not available for examination."

Parker asked if the police had made any progress finding the guys and their dog and Vince asked additional questions about rabies. Parker's phone buzzed, and he picked up, listened, and told Vince that they had only given him an antibiotic shot so he needed to go to Huntington asap.

Parker called ahead to give the ER a heads up and make sure they had the rabies vaccine and he encouraged Vince to think positively. At least they knew what it was and modern medicine could work miracles; and Vince, looking for any supporting evidence that his optimism was realistic, anchored on the thought that he hadn't received his Final Notice. When he arrived at the ER, the doctor on duty, Dr.

Malindra, explained to him that several tests were necessary to diagnose rabies in humans. They took samples of Vince's saliva, serum, spinal fluid, and skin biopsies of hair follicles at the nape of the neck. When they were finished, they suggested he go home and rest and they would call as soon as the samples were analyzed.

Vince drove home thinking about how and what he would tell Trudi. He was strangely composed, for some reason. In part, it might have been the shock of knowing that he might soon die. Another reason might be that he now had an even stronger moral case to find the two guys and dog. He called Qasim using his hands-free phone. Qasim said he would remind everyone again.

When he returned home, Trudi met him at the door, wanting to know what Dr. Parker needed so urgently and what took him so long? His composure started to dissipate but he led her into the living room and sat her down on the couch. Taking a deep breath and sitting next to her, he said, "I may have contracted rabies."

"From that dog that attacked you and Miles?" It was more of a statement than a question.

He explained that he had gone to Huntington where they took a number of samples for testing, and they would call him. His laptop was on the coffee table and he opened it, saying, "Let's look up rabies and see what we're dealing with." He entered, "rabies in humans" and received a number of hits with very similar information:

"Signs and symptoms in humans

"The average incubation period (time from infection to time of development of symptoms) in humans is 30-60 days, but it may range from less than 10 days to several years."

They thought back about when he was bitten. "It was one week ago yesterday, so that's 8 days," said Vince.

He read on: "The first symptoms of rabies may be very similar to those of the flu, including general weakness or discomfort, fever, or headache. These symptoms may last for days."

Trudi asked if he had any of that and Vince confirmed the headaches and the fever that Dr. Parker discovered.

Looking at his laptop again, Vince read: "There may be also discomfort or a prickling or itching sensation at the site of bite, progressing within days to symptoms of cerebral dysfunction, anxiety, confusion, and agitation."

"Well, I've had the itching and low levels of agitation."

"As the disease progresses, the person may experience delirium, abnormal behavior, hallucinations, and insomnia."

"A little insomnia, which has made me sleepy during the day. Grouchy? Or more grouchy?"

Trudi almost smiled. "A little."

As they read the last paragraph, "The acute period of the disease typically ends after 2 to 10 days. Once clinical signs of rabies appear, the disease is nearly always fatal, and treatment is typically supportive. Once a person begins to exhibit signs of the disease, survival is rare," Trudi gasped, and tears welled up, causing Vince more pain than the thought of his death. Their grief was almost unbearable.

He took her in his arms and said, "Let's not jump the gun. The tests aren't back yet."

Still holding Trudi, Vince continued, rather than let a heavy silence weigh down too hard, "When that dog attacked Miles and me, he smelled strongly of skunk, and Dr. Parker mentioned that there had been an increase of rabidity in skunks, so maybe the dog had been bitten by one. Miles has rabies protection, but I don't."

"Why don't they give people rabies shots along with measles, mumps, polio, etc.?"

"I don't know. I don't think it's that easy nor is it usually necessary. The big question is why they didn't give me something or say something that night?"

For the moment, there was nothing they could do except wait for the call from Huntington, so Vince, who had another headache, went to lie down. Trudi said she'd wake him when the call came. It came about an hour later and it wasn't what either of them wanted to hear. Vince had tested positive for rabies. They wanted him back as soon as possible to begin treatments. Trudi had taken the call and she asked if that meant he would be OK? Dr. Malindra hesitated a second and said, "Mrs. Fuller, I will be very honest with you. His chances are not very good, but there is a chance."

Trudi woke Vince up, passed along the news and said, "Let's go get you a chance!"

They sped off to Huntington with Trudi at the wheel, and checked into the ER asking to see Dr. Malindra. He came out to get them a few minutes later and brought them into a small examination room. He explained the procedure without repeating his view of Vince's chances of beating the rabies virus. They would first give him a local shot to numb the hand, and then inject human rabies immune globulin in a number of locations around the wound. In his opinion this should have been done the night of the attack. The dose was commensurate with his weight and if they couldn't inject the full dose in the wound area, they would inject the balance in his upper arm. They would then inject the first in a series of four shots of rabies vaccine. Additional shots would be administered three days later, seven days later and 14 days later.

Vince mentioned the internet article about the long-shot odds of beating rabies once contracted and Dr. Malindra said, "Let's get you weighed and dosed up and continue the process with success in mind. You're alive so we have an advantage."

Following the procedure that Dr. Malindra had outlined, Vince truly felt like a pin cushion as they went out to their car.

* * *

Mobile, Alabama. The 'Women for a Better Future for our Children' (WBFC) group were mostly liberal and mostly Democrats and Independents. They were black, white, and other colors; Christians, Jews, Muslims and atheists; straight and gay. They usually met and interacted as a supportive group, focused on their own specific situations, and rarely were they militant. But this was one of those times.

Alabama Senator Alan Gehrhardt was holding a Town Hall meeting to rally support for yet another of his far-right objectives – getting rid of the Alabama Department of Education and allowing the private sector to run it. This idea might have been conceived on account of Alabama's education ranking of 49th in the nation. Or perhaps it was the result of Senator Gehrhardt's attending Alabama schools, which would also give him an excuse for authoring Alabama Senate Bill 24. SB24 repealed Alabama's statute that required a permit to have a concealed handgun on your person or in a vehicle. The bill allowed everyone who was previously denied a lawful permit to now be able to conceal a handgun … anywhere. That sounds crazy, even for Alabama, and most of the law enforcement leaders in the state and even a few fellow Republican lawmakers decried the bill. But SB24 squeaked by and Gehrhardt was on a roll … bank rolled, no doubt, by the NRA.

The WBFC knew that if Gehrhardt was successful with the abolition of Alabama's Department of Education, there might not ever be a future, let alone a better one, for their children. So, they decided to attend the Town Hall meeting and make their voices heard.

On the far right extreme of the alt-right universe, a loosely formed group of men was also planning to attend the meeting. These were men who, if not actual members of the KKK, neo-Nazi, white supremacist, racist, bigot, and misogynist camps, were certainly aligned with their beliefs; and they came to support their hero, Senator Gehrhardt.

It was difficult to say why any of these low-functioning morons were interested in Alabama's education future, as they certainly had not derived any benefit from it; but perhaps it was to exercise their gun-toting rights under SB24.

This event, with its cast of characters, was exactly the type of event that Sheriff Don Blakely had highlighted in his unsuccessful efforts to stop SB24. As he put it, "Alabama law currently prohibits weapons at organized protests. A repeal of the current law by the passing of SB24 will allow handguns to be present at both peaceful and non-peaceful protests. This is especially troublesome and dangerous for protests that espouse or evoke hatred. Although the First Amendment protects protests, these gatherings will now be attended by persons possessing a handgun hidden from the view of law enforcement. SB24 will also allow persons with a past history of violent behavior to do so, as well." And oh, was he right!

Fifteen members of the WBFC joined the well-attended "Town Hall" meeting at the East Mobile High School gymnasium. They carried with them neatly hand-lettered signs reading "Our Children are our Future," "Our Children Deserve a Better Future," and "Our Children's Education IS NOT FOR SALE!" – pretty moderate slogans by any standards. The WBFC members were not alone in being against the Senator's plan. In fact, a large majority of the crowd was there to speak out and protest against him, believing that education run by the private sector might make education better for the wealthy, but worse for everyone else.

Gehrhardt began the session by spewing a bunch of "alternative facts," also known as lies, and the audience called him out with that label. A procession of attendees used a pair of mics to put questions to the Senator, who not so deftly dodged their intent, followed by more chants of "LIES!" A young and obviously passionate young woman, Tiffany Clayton, a member of the WBFC, refused to accept Gehrhardt's dodge of her question and persisted, demanding an answer. This led to some of the Senator's supporters shouting her down, which led to shouts from the other side, which led to pushing and punching. Security personnel rushed in to break things up and then, a shot rang out, followed by more, followed by a stampede to exit the gym.

When it was over, three people were wounded – not seriously – from gunshots; eight others required medical attention as a result of the stampede; and one was shot dead. The outcome was not nearly as bad as it could have been, especially as the dead victim, Lance Cartwright, was one of the gun-toting Gehrhardt supporters, who was armed and out on parole. His gun also matched shots hitting two of the three wounded. Neither the murder weapon nor the shooter, whose shot killed Cartwright, was found.

As it turned out, this event was a minor prelude for something much bigger.

* * *

CHAPTER 23 – SENATOR JOHN MC ADAM

Washington, DC. US Senator John McAdam had been in office for almost 30 years and had just been re-elected to another six-year term. The Alabama Senator was a moderate Republican who deeply regretted the direction his party had taken. He was a fiscal conservative but socially liberal. He wasn't as conservative and inflexible as the Tea Party was, nor was he as liberal as most of the Democrats on the "other side of the aisle." But he truly cared about the difficulties that many people faced to achieve a comfortable life – a life where hard, honest work was available, where they could get quality healthcare for themselves and their families, send their children to good schools and at least junior college. He wished his party was more tolerant and less bigoted and he also realized that he had become part of the problem.

When first elected, he sincerely believed that he was elected to represent his constituents. He abhorred the thought of taking outside money that would need to be repaid by voting and acting in the interest of his benefactors, instead of the people who elected him. He disliked the pork barrel tactics and was often a lone voice against the addition of questionable addendums to otherwise good bills. The older senators tried talking with him and explaining the way things worked, but he was not easily swayed. McAdam worked hard for his constituents, shuttling between DC and various cities in Alabama to listen to the people.

When his first term was nearing completion, he campaigned on the same platform he had the first time: "I will work hard, day and night, to fight for what you want and what is in your best interests." He was stung a bit that another GOP candidate had joined the race to challenge him. It wasn't the competition that bothered him. It was the support for the other candidate from the Republican Party and the significant funding from the steel industry and others. In addition, the word in the Senate was that McAdam was not a team player. He won his seat again, although by a slim margin, and it was a far more pragmatic John McAdam that began a new term.

Still, the GOP's guiding principles at the time were not impossible to live with. Ronald Reagan was the first President he served under, followed by George H.W. Bush, Bill Clinton, George W. Bush and Barack Obama. The Reagan and H.W. Bush years were his best and even when Bill Clinton was in office, Congress was still doing the job they were elected to do: move the country forward through good legislation, healthy and rigorous debate, and compromises that made sense for everyone; at least in Clinton's first term.

His next two elections were easier, with the first being unopposed and the second election contested by a younger candidate, who had the passion to serve and was sincere in his efforts. Accepting money from donors who would want to call in the debt one day had become normal, as had turning a somewhat blind eye toward many of the pork addendums, unless they were completely out of line.

But it was during the George W. Bush years that it all changed. McAdam could see that the new President was being manipulated by a few people who brought in a completely unethical – even by congressional standards – approach. Bold-face lying became OK and the "kinder and gentler" America that W's dad espoused rapidly began to disappear, as the Tea Party wing gained control. His big regret, however, was that he had stopped fighting. He watched many old guard Republicans and Democrats being swept away by the far right, thanks to Citizens United and/or the NRA's money. So, he played it safe.

Now, however, things were getting completely out of hand. Freedoms were not just being squeezed, they were being stripped. He felt all alone on the "Hill", perhaps because the others were not speaking out either, or perhaps because he really was out of step with the GOP.

When Alabama State Senator Alan Gehrhardt introduced and shepherded through AL SB24, he was enraged and embarrassed that his state could pass such an irresponsible bill. It was one thing to have a fringe bill introduced, but when it passed, that was an indictment against everyone in the party in power, even at the US Senate level. When he brought it up with his fellow US Senators, they dismissed it on the basis that it was a State bill, and those guys at the State level were a flakey group. The minor leagues. But he wasn't buying it.

Even before this affront to his intelligence, McAdam had decided that this term would be his last. He was 80 years old, and would be 86 when his term was up, and that was enough. He was lucky not to have any health issues, although it seemed like he was tired all the time. As he reflected on his tenure in the Senate, he knew that he had strayed far from the path that he envisaged when he began: too many compromises for the wrong reasons, too often voting the party line when he disagreed, and too much turning blind eyes. The recent shooting in Mobile was proof that he was right and that all of his fellow Senators who chuckled about it were wrong, but that wasn't going to burnish his legacy. What about his own conscience? Was there still time to overcome his mistakes of the past 30 years? His answer to these questions was a decision to change his "don't make waves" behavior that had guided him for much of his career. Politically, he had nothing to lose, so he would try to fight for what he believed in for the next six years.

He prepared a list of the issues he felt most strongly about, and he knew that even if he got some modest support from his fellow GOP colleagues, which was doubtful, success in righting any of these wrongs was very much a long shot. His list included:
-Getting money out of politics
-Setting term limits for Senators and Representatives
-Breaking the NRA's hold on the party
-Ensuring that healthcare was maintained – at least at the current level
-Ensuring freedom of speech
-Safeguarding voting rights

He spoke with a few of his colleagues about his "new" ideas. Their reactions ranged from muted to outright hostility. He received a fair hearing from two women senators, who were usually more moderate in their beliefs, but he knew that these potential allies were looked upon as novelties, with thinking way outside of the GOP mainstream. Obviously, he would get more attention from the Democrats, but that would be of little practical help.

He decided to go public with one of his ideas and see if that would help garner support from colleagues and the electorate. And to ensure he got the press coverage he wanted, he chose as his first topic: freedom of speech.

John McAdam had chosen his first topic well. The current Administration was flagrantly undermining and curtailing freedom of speech through a concerted effort by everyone at the White House to denigrate as incorrect, false or outright lies, any news that was critical of the Administration. As a result, The New York Times, The Washington Post and CNN, amongst others, were banned from White House briefings; and some that weren't banned stayed away in solidarity.

The public was upset, the Democrats were upset, but no one from the GOP seemed to care at all. McAdam knew that voicing concern would be breaking ranks and frowned upon, but he was about to find out just how much.

He made contact with a correspondent he knew at The Washington Post and given the rarity of GOP dissent on the assault on freedom of speech, a prominent article appeared the next day citing a lone Republican voicing concern. McAdam was quoted as saying, "We must have a free, even adversarial press if we want to preserve our democracy. Authoritarian leaders understand that the first step in demolishing liberties is to destroy the free and independent press."

Even before leaving for the Senate the next morning, his phone was ringing nonstop, mostly from reporters at other papers and the TV networks. Within the course of an hour he was booked to appear on MSNBC, CNN, and even Fox News. He had also given a dozen newspapers the same quote as he had given The Washington Post, along with additional comments in answer to their questions. One that many asked was whether he felt the current President was becoming or trying to become a dictator. His response to that was, "I'm not saying that. What I'm saying is that it's up to everyone, in and out of government, to ensure that it can never happen."

While those calls and attention were exciting, and he felt that he was finally saying what he thought, the other calls he received – from his Senate colleagues and White House staff – ranged from disappointment to outright threats. It was therefore with some trepidation that he made his way to the "Hill" for the day's session. When he arrived, it was as though one side of the chamber could plainly see that he was carrying the plague while the other side thought he was the Messiah. Even the two GOP women sympathizers knew better than to acknowledge him. As the session came to order, the most despised Senator in the Chamber, by either party, Todd Creud of Florida, was given the floor, where he lashed out at McAdam for breaking ranks and dishonoring the President. McAdam actually thought for a moment that, given the speaker, it might help him, as unpopular as Creud was, but the cheers and thunderous applause from the GOP ranks dashed any hopes of that. Even the Democrats, sensing the mood, kept low.

McAdam rose to reply, and he was acknowledged by the Leader, who may have hoped that he would recant. A few boos sounded out but they were called to order and McAdam replied, "I have been a member of this body for almost 30 years and I have watched with dismay as our party has become more intolerant, more mean spirited ..." – the boos began again but McAdam had a booming voice and raised his volume enough to be heard – "more destructive and more interested in scoring points than representing our constituents. You ... we, are an embarrassment to this country. It is not how our founders intended our government to function and they, too, would be embarrassed. But I, even if I am alone, will no longer sell myself to the highest bidder, turn a blind eye to the self-serving bills, and obstruct good legislation simply because it came from the other side of the aisle." And with that, he walked out to a deafening chorus of boos and headed for Union Station to catch a train to New York and his first round of television appearances.

If the Republicans thought they just had a loose cannon with McAdam's Freedom of the Press issue, they were wrong, as they found out during his appearance on Morning Joe. Joe Scarborough and Mika Brzezinski thought they had a good show with a prominent Republican Senator standing up for the First Amendment, which really shouldn't have been news at all, but as he was the only one speaking out, it was news. What they hadn't counted on was the depth of the Senator's transformation. No one had ever passed through the Senate and publicly trashed the process and his colleagues before. So, after asking him their leading question about his stand on the Freedom of the Press issue, they sat there calmly absorbing what he had said to The Washington Post, asking some additional questions; but as they began to wrap up, McAdam added, "And this is just the tip of the iceberg" and he rattled off his list. Joe quickly realized the opportunity and called for a quick break, "We'll be back in a moment with Senator John McAdam and his views on what is wrong with the Republican Senate."

During the break, they quickly rearranged the balance of the program before they returned to the Senator for his bare-all, tell-it-like-it-is critique with what needs to be fixed. Joe and Mika were seasoned political hacks and they milked his additional five points for the remainder of the show so well that the gasps from the Senate could almost be heard in New York. McAdam's performance and potential were witnessed by Rachel Maddow, also at MSNBC ... John Berman, CNN ... and Bret Baier, Fox News ... who all made adjustments to their own shows to ensure they could reap the full potential. Their marketing departments quickly blanketed their networks with promotional advertising to generate viewership for what they perceived to be major news events.

Meanwhile, McAdam's voicemail box quickly filled up, his phone was bleeping madly with text messages, and the emails and Tweets were, as they say, "trending." He had the phone numbers of most of his Senate colleagues stored on his phone, so he could easily identify whom the messages were from; and after listening to a few that he half-hoped would be constructive, he deleted the rest. The others were from other television stations, newspapers, other media outlets and constituents. He listened to one from a constituent and it was very positive. Then another, and then more, and all but a couple were extremely positive and encouraging. If he had harbored any doubts about his recent course of action, this feedback erased it.

McAdam basked in the media spotlight, and while speaking his mind and speaking from his heart, he won the many battles with increasingly aggressive anchors and panel members who sought to discredit him. His exposure and national attention rivaled that of the top Presidential contenders during the last election. Alone, in his hotel room, however, his heart welled up with longing and deep regret that his wife of 55 years, Anne, wasn't alive to see his about-face change. He knew that she had been disappointed that he didn't fight against the wrongs and fight for the rights, but she would never criticize nor second-guess him. He missed her, and these last two years without her had been harder than he liked to admit. And he was tired. Very tired.

When he returned to the Senate, he anticipated a hostile reception and he wasn't disappointed. He was a leper, but he didn't care. He knew what he was doing, and it was the right thing to do, finally. Right from the outset of the session, the sharks were out, calling for censure, even Expulsion. Expulsion from the Senate was unlikely as that would require a number of Democrats to vote Aye, and he didn't think that would happen. Censure required only a simple majority and the GOP had that. It would take a while without the complete agreement of enough members and any motion would have to go to committee. With a one-week recess looming, nothing much would happen before then. So, McAdam pretended to listen to the virulent accusations, smiling often at the hypocrisy of the speakers.

Meanwhile, the media was having a field day, feeding activists across the country, who rallied behind McAdam's six-point list. Most of the points had already been central to activists' rallying cries, but one began to emerge as the most popular, and this was the one that the incumbents feared the most: Setting Term Limits. Shortly before the recess, McAdam received an unannounced visitor, Senator Lawrence Grant, from Mississippi. Senator Grant, like McAdam, had been in the Senate for decades and for the most part, they thought along the same lines. McAdam hoped that the visit was one of support, even if only moral, but he was wrong.

Grant had been co-opted by a group of Senators to talk with McAdam as a last gasp effort to get him to see reason and halt, if not reverse, the damage he was doing. They knew that the issues would become even more prominent if the Senate acted to censure McAdam, although a majority wanted to do at least that. Grant was one of the most reasonable voices in the Senate, but he didn't cut McAdam any slack and told him that even if McAdam didn't speak out any more, a motion for censure would come out of Committee. He needed to recant and make an apology. He could cite exhaustion or give some other reason for his irrational remarks. His colleagues might even consider his call for action on the erosion of Freedom of the Press, although Grant told him frankly, that consideration was all he would get.

McAdam listened during the brief visit and Grant pleaded with him to reconsider his position. He asked, or more accurately, told him to think about it; and added that a few Senators would like to meet with him in Montgomery next week during the recess, so they could strategize the best way forward when the Senate reconvened. McAdam smiled inwardly as he knew that recently, many Senators wanted to avoid going to their home bases, as activists and even former supporters were clamoring for Town Hall meetings, so they could rebuke their Senators. So, a detour to Montgomery would give them a good excuse. McAdam remained gracious and said he would think about it and they were welcome to come to his home in Montgomery, although he warned Grant not to hold out much hope. McAdam left it that Grant would contact him with two to three possible dates and times for the visit.

After the meeting, McAdam began to feel a bit of remorse at the cost of his actions. He had lost a number of friends and he was, indeed, hurting a number of people that he liked. Just then, a call came in to his office phone from a constituent that buoyed his conviction that he was doing the right thing. But try as he might to feel good, he was just too tired. He needed a break.

* * *

Pasadena, California. As Vince returned from a short morning walk with Miles, Trudi was in the kitchen with a cup of coffee and the mail. "Guess what? We've won a trip to the NRA headquarters in Virginia!" she said, rolling her eyes.

Vince gave her a kiss on the cheek and poured himself a cup of coffee. "How did that happen?"

"When we got our discounted gun, we were entered into a drawing. It's to celebrate their millionth Senior Discount sale."

"Wonderful," matching her eye roll. "When is it?"

"Early next month."

Hearing that, Vince hoped that Trudi didn't see that he thought it might be too late. Not that he was at all interested in going.

Vince had all but been given a death sentence, even if his VT2 hadn't buzzed yet. His arm was still a little sore from his second rabies shot and he was angry, wanted revenge, and soon he would have a gun to do the job. He called Qasim again to see if anyone had seen the suspects and to tell Qasim that the dog may have died. Qasim asked why he thought that and Vince gave him a very loose version of the truth that the doctors had detected some possible rabies presence and had started him on a preventative course of the rabies vaccine.

Qasim was alarmed by that news but Vince downplayed the seriousness and assured him that everything was under control. Somewhat mollified, Qasim commented that without the dog, finding two guys with vague descriptions, who may even have changed their clothes, just got much more difficult. But Vince was not about to give up. He was becoming obsessed.

* * *

CHAPTER 24 – THE BAD, THE WORSE & THE UGLY

Montgomery, Alabama. McAdam caught a Delta flight at 3:00 PM via Atlanta to get him into Montgomery at 5:45 PM. From there, it was just a short taxi ride to "The Retreat," McAdam's beloved neoclassical revival home in Montgomery's Garden District, with its massive oaks draped in Spanish moss ... the home that he and Anne had tastefully restored and enjoyed for almost 50 years. As had been the case for the past two years, McAdam's arrival at The Retreat brought him both joy and a sense of emptiness.

The house smelled of the furniture polish that Mrs. Mays used, and he knew she must have been there earlier that day to air out the house, dust, and make it ready for his arrival – ensuring that he had fresh orange juice, plenty of coffee, English muffins and peanut butter for breakfast. Mattie Mays had been their housekeeper at The Retreat for almost 20 years and he guessed that she missed Anne almost as much as he did. As the years passed and the children left home, the required cleaning diminished and he reckoned that she and Anne did more sipping tea and chatting than cleaning; but he also knew that the two had formed a bond, and with him away so much, he was happy for that. He looked forward to seeing Mattie again – although he always called her Mrs. Mays – and he knew she'd drop by late morning, tomorrow.

He had a glass or two of wine and some peanuts, his favorite evening repast and looked forward to a good night's sleep; but as tired as he was, he didn't sleep well. Some of it was due to his concerns about the new path he was taking, but mostly it was the excitement about the new path. For the first time in a very long time, he was enthusiastic about his work. He wasn't looking forward to seeing Grant and the promised GOP "committee" that would be urging and threatening him to change direction. And he wasn't looking forward to seeing Doc Turner, either, but that was because Turner was a bleeding- h e a r t liberal, who always dispensed his political advice along with the medicine. He made a note to call Thomas and Rebecca, his son and daughter. Thomas worked in Silicon Valley at a company whose name he could never remember – partly because his son changed jobs a lot, and partly because the companies all had names that were not real words and were so new that he had never heard of them. Thomas had explained that frequent job changes were routine in the tech world and seen as a good thing. Rebecca, on the other hand, was a doctor in Massachusetts and, like Doc Turner, didn't agree with his politics. She had, however, emailed him shortly after his interview on MSNBC, saying she was really proud of his views. She also asked what happened to bring about the change.

After his favorite breakfast of fresh orange juice, strong black coffee, and a well-done English muffin loaded with crunchy peanut butter, he took a stroll around the grounds of The Retreat. Gus, his gardener, had also been there recently and everything looked its springtime best. Anne loved her gardens and spent as much time as she could, caring for her plants until she could no longer care for herself. His eyes watered a bit as he thought of her, on her knees, weeding and trimming, her wide brimmed straw hat shielding her fair skin from the sun. He decided to call Rebecca and put his mind back on a positive track.

As he had hoped, Rebecca was in, having chosen to take a Saturday off, and she sounded happy to hear from him. She immediately picked up the question from her email and wanted to understand what made him change his views on so many issues. She was too young to know that her dad had once been an independent thinker, instead of the "toe the party line" conservative she had come to know. McAdam was honest with her, something that had always been a characteristic of the family's dealings with each other. The kids were honest with him and Anne, and with each other; and he and Anne did their best to be honest with Thomas and Rebecca. He admitted that over the years, as the party had drifted further to the right, he had gone with the tide and followed. It had been easier that way, but in the end, it had gone too far.

Rebecca commented, "This would have made Mom so happy." She hadn't intended it to hurt her father, but it was like a knife in the gut.

"What do you mean?" he said, almost gasping.

Rebecca realized by his tone of voice that she had made a mistake. She and her mom had discussed politics, and specifically her father's politics, many times. Her mother always defended her husband, saying that although he didn't agree with a lot of the party's direction, he worked behind the scenes to change it, bowing to the majority only if changing anything was impossible.

"Just that you're taking a stand on these important issues."

"Because I never did before?"

Rebecca was desperate to avoid hurting her father. She was proud of what he was doing, even if it was late in the game. "I didn't mean that. Mom was always proud of you and knew that you did what you could and what you knew was right. I just meant that you really put it out there with those six great points."

McAdam was mollified a bit, and pleased that Rebecca wasn't just doing a high-level bullshit job on him. She knew what he was standing for.

"OK, thanks. Not sure what I'll be able to change, if anything, but it's actually been exciting to give it a go. Tiring, too."

Rebecca switched into the other side of the dynamic duo role of Loving Daughter - Doctor. "Are you feeling alright?"

"I'm OK. Just tired. I'm seeing Doc Turner on Monday and he'll tell me how much time I'll have to complete my agenda, and no doubt, he'll prioritize it for me."

Rebecca laughed. She knew Doc Turner. In fact, he was the one who inspired her to be a doctor. She remembered the day he asked her if she wanted to listen to her heart with his stethoscope. She said yes and from that day on, being a doctor was all she ever wanted to do; and listening to her heart was something that always came naturally, co-existing with the dictates of her scientist's brain.

"Tell him I said hello. In fact, I just thought of something. There's a company here in the Boston area that is testing a new watch/health monitor. It has the capability to monitor your blood. Ask Doc Turner to get you signed up for one, and if he has a problem getting one, tell him to call me. I know some of the manufacturer's people and maybe we can pull some strings for a distinguished Senator."

"What's it called?"

Rebecca clicked away on a computer and replied, "VT2."

They finished up their call and overall, it made McAdam happy. He always felt that Anne would have liked him to be more independent in his thinking and more liberal, but she never specifically said as much. Rebecca had tried to cover her slip-up but it was really not a surprise; it was just the truth.

* * *

Pasadena, California. Vince had picked up the story about McAdam as he trawled through the web looking at gun incidents. He saw the Mobile shooting and McAdam's response to it, thinking that there was finally one Republican who was not afraid to speak out. He was still amazed that out of the almost 300 GOP US Senators and Representatives, there was still only one.

He now had three of his four rabies shots and nothing changed. He still had the headaches, fever and was irritable. And he was becoming more anxious about getting justice before it was too late.

Trudi had, independently, come across McAdam too, while surfing online, reading about the WBFC shooting incident. Her dislike of the NRA had turned to hatred. These tragedies were all so easily avoidable!

* * *

Montgomery, Alabama. McAdam waited until the West Coast hour was more sociable and called Thomas. Thomas was pretty much apolitical, and McAdam didn't even know what party he backed. They just never talked about it. All was well with him and as McAdam didn't even know what to ask about his work, the call was short, but warm.

As expected, Mrs. Mays dropped by just before noon. She, too, had seen McAdam on TV. CNN, in her case. She was happy about his stand on healthcare and voting rights and she didn't ask why he was changing. She was just happy that he was. She and her family relied on healthcare insurance and she also hoped she would live to see the day that she, her family, and friends, could go to the polls with only the excitement of casting a ballot, instead of wondering if there would be something wrong with their ID, or police intimidation; something that white people have never seen or felt. McAdam wondered if she was aware of his newly adopted positions because they had a long-term relationship or if, in fact, the message really was resonating across a wider circle.

So, he asked, "Are your friends and family aware of what I've been saying?"

"Yes sir, Senator. You better believe they are. You keep talking like that and you'll win really big, next election." McAdam smiled and thanked Mattie. He didn't need to get into his decision not to run again. They talked a bit more and Mattie said she'd come by on Wednesday to check that everything was OK.

After Mattie left, McAdam's light breakfast was fading fast and he knew what to do about it. Sam's BBQ for lunch. He'd been going to Sam's for as long as he could remember and as varied and good as the food was in DC, Sam's was even better. He pulled into the parking lot, packed with pick-ups and cars, in front of an old run-down building with smoke pouring out of a crooked smokestack. The smell of deep wood smoke was all around. The young woman at the desk inside welcomed him with that typical southern charm that can't be replicated. He ordered the combo plate of smoked sausage on top of slow-cooked BBQ pork, with amazing baked beans, fries, and slaw like nowhere else.

Absolutely stuffed, but knowing that his appetite would return that evening, he stopped in at The Fresh Market on the way home and picked up some other food items, including a Shrimp Noodle Bowl. He had always liked to cook but never had the time, nor, it seemed, the ever-expanding list of necessary ingredients. The Bowls at Fresh Market were like a kit, which were easy to put together, and included all the ingredients. The shrimp one was his favorite.

His poor night's sleep and lunch at Sam's, no doubt, combined to make him very tired, so he took a nap and this time, slept well. That evening, after another stroll around The Retreat's gardens, he successfully executed the directions for putting together the Shrimp Noodle Bowl and he tuned in to Fox News, hearing the tail end of an interview with Todd "Todey" Creud, who called McAdam a traitor and un-American. He sure has a fitting name, McAdam mused. He realized, however, that even if it hadn't come from the generally despised Creud, he didn't care. He was over that hump of indecision and second- guessing. His course of action was clear, and nothing would stop him from trying to make an improvement in the status quo.

He switched off the TV, poured himself another glass of cabernet sauvignon, and opened a book that Rebecca had given him for Christmas, "Breakfast of Champions" by Kurt Vonnegut, for the first time. Before going to bed – after finishing his wine and a substantial part of the book – he checked his e-mail messages. Amongst the many was one from Senator Grant.

"John: Are you free to meet with some of our colleagues on Wednesday, 1:00 PM? There will be 3 attendees: Tim Wooley, Chick Lawnley and Todey Creud. (Sorry about the last one.) I won't be able to attend. They will be arriving on Tuesday and are staying at the Renaissance Hotel. They'll depart on Thursday in case you need more time to discuss things. Also, would it be possible to meet at The Retreat? It will be more private and less likely to attract attention. Please let me know asap. Lawrence"

Talk about the bad, the worse and the ugly! And that was just Creud! McAdam reviewed the list. Tim Wooley from Kansas was a hard-line whacko. He received almost a million dollars from a pro-Israel organization and he was a defense industry darling, getting mega bucks from them. He was one of the Senators who sent a letter to Iran ... thinks the problem with Guantanamo is too many empty beds ... calls food stamp recipients addicts ... and is against equal pay for women, and protection for women from violence.

Chick Lawnley of Indiana was even older than McAdam and made him (well, his former self) look like a rebel by comparison, with his ass-kissing ways. He made a fortune from industry, and this trip away from his constituency was just what he needed. They were after his scalp.

And Todd "Todey" Creud was the most despised Senator in a poll amongst Senators. He was such a far-right fundamentalist "Christian" that he actually wanted American laws to be based on Christianity. And if you're black, God help you (even if you are Christian!). He had a reputation when he was a prosecutor to be unreasonably eager to punish, even when there was no evidence. He was just plain nasty.

A further note on Todey: He got his nickname as a kid because he liked playing with toads, perhaps because they never laughed at him or called him names. He even seemed to embrace the name, and one of his unusual behaviors was to squeeze his pet toads so that they peed on his hands. Then he would chase the other kids around to rub his toad piss hands on them. Sadly, for Todey, in addition to not being very bright, he was also a very slow runner, so he never actually got to anoint anyone with toad piss. He kept using the name though, even when he first ran for office, and it might have been the smartest thing he ever did because he did have a toad-like face; so when people saw him, the name and face formed a strong image and bond of recognition. Whether that's true or not is uncertain, but in the absence of any other logical explanation as to why people voted for him, it will have to do. As for his unusual last name, speculation was that his family must have changed it when they immigrated from their home planet.

These three lovely guys weren't coming to discuss. They were coming to demand, threaten and execute. And that was the reason behind selecting these three: intimidation. But McAdam was beyond that.

* * *

Pasadena, California. Trudi was tired and decided to go to bed, but Vince had taken a long nap and was still wide-awake.

He did some web surfing and when he was pretty sure Trudi was asleep, he grabbed a jacket and went outside with Miles.

He knew that Miles would quite happily nose around the yard and then wait to be let in. As Vince hadn't been taking him out in the evening, Miles probably never thought about his master going out the gate instead of back into the house.

Vince walked to the attack area, but no one was there. He began to walk aimlessly, trying to come to terms with his situation, the unfairness of it all, and poor Trudi, who will have to pick up the pieces. He returned to the house with no answers and very little hope. Miles was his one consolation, as he wagged his stub of a tail and happily led the way into the house.

* * *

CHAPTER 25 – AN APPOINTMENT & A SHOOTING

Montgomery, Alabama. It had been a while since McAdam had seen Doctor Angus Turner. He had good intentions but never seemed to get around to it. Turner looked a little older to McAdam, and if asked, Turner would have said the same about him. He too had seen some of the media coverage of his current patient and he was pleased, at least with this aspect of his condition. Turner joked with him a bit about it taking so long and that now he'd have to work harder to keep McAdam alive, so he could right some wrongs. They had known each other a long time. Doc Turner had helped bring Thomas and Rebecca into the world and he was with the Senator and Anne as she departed.

To Turner's question about his health, McAdam replied that he felt OK, just very tired most of the time.

Turner asked, "You do remember how old you are, don't ya?"

"Yes, I know, but I feel like I've aged a lot in the last month or so. I should feel elated that I'm finally doing the right thing, but even when I'm feeling very good about what I'm doing, I'm still tired."

Doc Turner asked if he was getting enough quality sleep and McAdam confessed that he often didn't sleep well. Turner wrote a prescription for some blood tests to see if it showed anything abnormal. That reminded McAdam to ask about the VT2 and also to tell Turner that Rebecca said hello. A flash of recognition appeared on Turner's face and he excused himself, returning a few seconds later with a FedEx envelope. Opening the envelope, he said, "This just came in and it may have something to do with it." He pulled out a rectangular box with a paper wrapped around it. Turner looked at the paper and read,

"Dear Dr. Turner: Dr. Rebecca McAdam asked me to send you our VT2 watch/health monitor which is out for beta testing. It's for her father, Senator John McAdam. If you have any questions, don't hesitate to call me and when you see the Senator, tell him 'Thank you' for his recent stand on politics- as-usual.' Kind regards, Patsy Carter, Head of Clinical Affairs, VitalTech."

Neither Doc Turner nor McAdam were the least bit technical, but the instructions were pretty straightforward, and they were pretty sure they set it up correctly. Doc Turner looked at the questionnaire and asked, "Do you have a gun, John?" He noted down McAdam's responses: Yes, there was a gun in the house that he bought for Anne about 20 years ago. He was away a lot and it seemed a good idea. Turner reminded McAdam that he needed to fast for his blood test that he would arrange for 7:00 AM tomorrow and told him to call if he had any questions about the watch. When McAdam left, Turner completed the questionnaire, indicating that his general state of mind was "normal" and that the likelihood that he would use a gun for safety reasons was 3 out of 5. He wished it was all that simple to know what people would do in certain situations.

* * *

McAdam left Doc Turner's in good spirits. Two more intelligent people had endorsed his stand and Doc Turner didn't seem too concerned about his health. He'd get his blood tested in the morning and hopefully that might help identify a reason for his tiredness. Probably just iron deficiency. He'd experienced that a few times because of his "on the road" eating habits. Maybe he'd pick up a kale salad for lunch.

* * *

Pasadena, California. Vince was still brooding over his fate, his chances of survival, and his frustration about not finding the thugs. His phone rang, and it was Qasim. One of his driver colleagues had seen two men who loosely fit the description of the guys they were looking for, out near the Rose Bowl. They didn't see a dog; however, as discussed, there may not be a dog anymore. Qasim had called Inspector Lucker and given him the address, and Lucker had told him that he would pass it along to patrol cars in the area. Qasim had also told Lucker the news about rabies and that the dog may have died.

Vince wanted more details: time, exact location. Qasim told him it was within the last 20-30 minutes and it was near Rosemont Avenue & North Arroyo at "Entrance A." He didn't think Vince would go and, even if he did, Qasim didn't think anything would happen, as there was a good chance it wasn't those guys anyway.

Vince became agitated, struggling to make a decision on whether to go or not. He was confused, and his head was pounding, and he was tired, so he popped a couple of aspirin and lay down for a nap. Trudi was shaking him, shouting "Vince, Vince, wake up!" He came to and rolled over as Trudi was almost pulling him out of bed. She was very upset.

"What's the matter?" he asked her as he sat up.

"There's been a shooting at Rasha's school! It was just on the news."

Vince took a few deep breaths and cleared his head. He called Qasim's cell. Qasim was already on his way to the school from Azusa. He'd spoken with Rasha and she was OK but sounded hysterical. Vince told Qasim that he and Trudi could head over there right now and see if they could help and comfort her. Qasim was grateful and Vince and Trudi headed out.

When they arrived, there were police, ambulances, fire trucks and news satellite trucks all over the place. They had to park quite a distance away and then ran back toward the school. Not surprisingly, they were not allowed past the cordoned off area. They asked a policeman at the entrance of the sealed off area if they could attend to a friend of theirs in the school as her husband would not be able to get there for a while, but they were told that no one was being allowed in until the area was declared safe and the people inside could be processed for information. They asked if people were hurt or killed but the policeman said he was not at liberty to give out any information. Seeing a local news satellite truck with a reporter being filmed, they went over to see what they could find out. Vince called Qasim and gave him an update while Trudi got closer to the reporter and camera.

The reporter said that a single, white male had entered the school, killed the security guard and then entered the first classroom he came to, spraying bullets from an assault rifle. A woman, possibly a teacher, slammed the door shut and locked the killer in, preventing him from going any further. The killer, upon hearing the door slam, tried to open it and appears to have tried to shoot the lock out. A nearby patrol car had arrived and an officer fired through the classroom window, killing the shooter. There are no other details of casualties at this time nor is there any motive, although the school has a number of students from international, particularly Middle Eastern, backgrounds.

Trudi filled Vince in on what he missed, and they tried to think if there was anything they could do. Ambulances had been arriving and departing through a cordoned off area at the side of the building and by now, a crowd of anxious family, friends and others had gathered outside the school. They saw Qasim drive by, slowly, looking for a place to park. He disappeared around the corner and they waited for him to return. Qasim got the same answer from the officer at the entrance as they – and everyone else – had received, so they had to wait, although he was told that immediate family members would be admitted soon. Qasim had heard a pretty similar report on the news about the shooting, and he was one of the lucky ones because he had heard from Rasha and she was OK. Trudi asked Qasim if Jack needed to be picked up but Qasim had made arrangements on the way over.

Not long afterward, another officer with a bullhorn made an announcement that immediate family members would now be admitted. They were asked to show ID and specify who within the school they were related to. A civilian woman was standing there as well with a checklist to verify and keep tabs on who was entering. As Qasim lined up to enter the school to get Rasha, Trudi told him they would wait for them to come out.

After what seemed like hours (and it had been almost an hour), Rasha and Qasim emerged. He was holding her, and she was sobbing. When she saw Trudi, she threw her arms around her, sobbing all the while. Qasim went over to Vince and told him that a teacher and five students had been killed and a number wounded. He then said, it might have been much worse except that Rasha was walking down the hall to that very classroom, heard the shooting, slammed the door from the outside and locked it, preventing the shooter from leaving. A policeman shot the killer as he was attempting to shoot the lock out.

Rasha was a hero. The police and school officials had been very complimentary about her quick thinking, and the officer who shot the killer said that the shooter was in the act of shooting the door down and didn't see him at the window. It also allowed him to take extra care that no children were in the line of fire. But Rasha's heroic act was no consolation to her. She knew these children and she was on her way to teach them French. She also knew the teacher, Valerie Rice, whose classroom she was about to enter, and she knew that one teacher was dead. Although it hadn't been confirmed, it was logical that Valerie was the victim. To her, it was all too reminiscent of Syria. Rasha stopped sobbing and urgently grabbed Qasim to tell him that she wanted to get Jack and go home. They said their goodbyes and the Melho's departed.

Vince and Trudi drove home, and Vince kept thinking about the heroic role that Rasha had played. Trudi was shocked and filled with awe and anger. She also asked out loud the question that just hit her, "What if the shooter had arrived a few minutes later?" Rather than spark a conversation, they rode the rest of the way home in silence. When they got home, Vince went in and turned on the evening news. Trudi came in with two glasses of wine. They watched the local news channel and saw the same reporter they had seen earlier. His report now included a lot more detail:

"We have more details from the International School at Glendale shooting this afternoon. The shooter, Harland Wimpey, 28 years old, had ties with white supremacist groups. An initial search of his apartment turned up literature and rantings against immigrants and Muslims. The International School has a sizeable number of students from the Middle East. Wimpey also had a veritable arsenal of weapons and ammunition.

"One teacher and five children, aged between 8 and 10, have been killed. Their identities have not yet been released. A security guard was also killed and according to witnesses, Wimpey seemed to look for the guard first. After killing him, he entered the first classroom down the hall, shooting into the classroom as he entered. It appears that a part-time teacher, Rasha Melho, may have saved many more children by locking Wimpey into the classroom. Her action diverted his attention and during his effort to escape by shooting down the door, a Glendale police officer, responding to a 911 call, was able to gun Wimpey down.

"This appears to be a hate crime and begs some questions. Why, with California's relatively strict gun laws, can someone like Wimpey gain access to so many weapons, including banned assault rifles? Second, how effective is the strategy of having armed guards at schools? It certainly wasn't effective this time.

"We'll be back at 8 o'clock with more details."

Vince muted the TV and looked over at Trudi who was staring at the screen. She said, "I keep thinking about Rasha and what if ...?"

Vince nodded. "I know. And I keep thinking how she escaped Syria and spent all that time going through the vetting process, only to be thrown right back into it over here in the 'land of opportunity.' "

"How could anyone shoot children?"

"Because they're chicken-shit cowards. He has the perfect last name, doesn't he - Wimpy! I think terrorists should be called 'cowardists.' They prey on the innocent. Wherever they come from, they are cowards and that should be what they're called." Vince was angry and agitated and Trudi could see it.

"How about sushi for dinner? I'll get it and you can relax." But then she saw blood on his right hand. "What did you do to your hand?"

Vince looked at it and explained that it was the itching and he must have scratched it too hard. It was a reminder that the rabies was still active, and it was depressing. Depressing for both of them so the subject was dropped.

Trudi called in their order for their usual White Dragon rolls and seaweed salad at Ichima Sushi while Vince unmuted the TV. He was asleep when Trudi looked in on him on her way to Ichima. Vince woke up when he heard her return with their dinner and was surprised that he'd dozed off.

"I must have dozed off while you were gone."

Trudi laughed. "You were gone before I was gone."

"Hmm. It's been a stressful day."

"That it has!"

After dinner she called Rasha and got a busy signal. After a few more times she called Qasim's cell and he answered straight away, explaining that the media has been hounding Rasha for a statement and they finally took the phone off the hook. He handed his phone to Rasha. She told Trudi that she was having a hard time dealing with what happened. The school was closed tomorrow so Trudi asked if she could come over and stay with her, which would allow Qasim to work while she could help Rasha with Jack. Rasha welcomed her offer enthusiastically and they agreed that Trudi would come over at 10:00 and they could talk, have lunch and entertain Jack.

Vince was asleep before the 8 o'clock news so Trudi watched it alone. There wasn't much new. They gave the identity of the slain teacher, a 25-year-old woman (as Rasha had correctly surmised) and added that in addition to the five children killed, there were eight others wounded, none in critical condition. There were a number of witnesses interviewed who praised Rasha's actions and Trudi was bursting with pride at her friend's bravery and quick thinking.

Then the NRA spokesman, Dwayne LaPlant, was asked about the failure of the presence of a guard to prevent yet another school shooting: "The NRA has advocated armed guards as a way to stop these attacks, so what do you say about the failure today of that suggestion? Will you continue lobbying for armed guards at schools?"

"This wasn't a failure," retorted LaPlant. "In fact, the killing of the guard alerted school officials, who were able to call 911, even before the shooter began shooting the children. And our suggestion of armed guards was only part of what we recommended. We suggested that every teacher should be armed and trained. And until that happens, shooters will always go for the guards first."

The reporter, shaking her head in disbelief responded, "Guards, teachers, who else?"

"California should revisit its gun laws. Allow concealed carry and maybe shooters won't be able to carry out crimes so effortlessly. As you know, we have lobbied hard to initiate a countrywide concealed carry permit plan so that anyone's concealed carry license will be valid in all states. So, California won't have a choice."

"Good night, Mr. LaPlant. We're out of time," said the reporter, still in disbelief at what she'd just heard.

Trudi was also in disbelief and enraged! Not only did LaPlant not even acknowledge any sorrow for the victims, but he blatantly stood there and advocated that more people should have guns. She sat there hoping to doze off, but her anger and grief prevented it. She grieved for those children, for the parents of those children, for the families of the slain teacher and the guard, and for all those who lost someone they loved that day. And she grieved for Rasha, who had already been through more than anyone should endure, only to come to this country where she realized it wasn't much different than the chaos she left. And it was only then that she remembered her doctor's appointment earlier that day. Seemed like days ago. Was there a concerned look on the doctor's face when she said they would get back to her with her exam results?

* * *

CHAPTER 26 – TURNING POINTS

Montgomery, Alabama. McAdam had arrived at 7:00 AM for his blood test, having made sure he fasted from 7:00 PM the night before. His reward for the fasting and early start was a great cup of coffee and a world-class blueberry muffin at Café Louisa. The coffee was dark, strong and very round, and the blueberry muffin was still warm and chock full of big juicy blueberries.

He read the current issue of The Montgomery Advertiser and noted an overnight shooting at a craps game. The homicide rate was up over last year. Turning to the Editorial page, he smiled and was almost overcome with pride as the newspaper's Opinion piece that day was in support of his "Stand for Reason." The Advertiser had a long reputation for its social conscience, attacking the Ku Klux Klan and, in 2008, endorsing the presidential candidacy of Senator Barack Obama. Pointing out that our political process had strayed far from the vision of the Founding Fathers, especially in the last decade, the paper hailed McAdam as a beacon of hope to get our government working again, to represent the people of our country as opposed to political party dogma ... or worse yet, purely personal gain. McAdam squirmed a little bit reading parts of it, but he knew, or certainly rationalized, that his past improprieties were for re-elections, as opposed to personal gain.

As he finished his muffin and downed the last of his coffee, his watch started to vibrate, and his iPhone signaled a message: "Final Notice!" Assuming it to be related to the ineptness of Doc Turner and himself with the setup, he wasn't alarmed. He pressed a button on his watch and saw that it was 8:05 and Turner might be in. He called, and Turner answered, saying that he was just about to call him. He was equally confused and suggested that McAdam come in and they could call VitalTech and get it straightened out.

When McAdam arrived, Doc Turner had the VT2 out on his desk and was poring over the instructions. He had McAdam open his VT2 app on his iPhone and they checked the settings. Neither of them could see the problem so they took up Patsy Carter's offer and called her on Turner's office speakerphone. She was in and after some self-deprecating banter from Turner, on behalf of himself and McAdam regarding their technical skills, she asked for the serial number, talking them through the process of finding it. They could hear her tapping on a keyboard and then her acknowledgement at finding his account. Turner quipped that at least they had done that correctly and they all chuckled.

Sitting in her office, Patsy checked the setup and settings first, before looking at any clinical data. All seemed to be in order. She noted that the Final Notice function was set for 30 days and she opted for the tried and true software fix of changing a setting and then going back to the original. She changed it to 10 days and watched as the Final Notice was deleted. McAdam commented over the speakerphone that his VT2 buzzed and the "Final Notice" had disappeared. Both he and Turner breathed a sigh of relief. But then Patsy reset it for 20 days and they all watched with concern as the Final Notice re-appeared. McAdam and Turner asked what just happened as the VT2 buzzed again. Patsy asked them to hold on a bit longer as she needed to check something else.

'Something else' was the data that the VT2 was collecting. She could see that there was almost no history as the watch had just been set up yesterday; but the VT2 had been put through and passed many tests with just 24 hours of history. She asked if she could call back within a few minutes and hung up to look at the detailed data coming through. Like an autopilot system on a plane that senses minute changes in speed, altitude, winds and other conditions, much more acutely than a pilot can, the VT2 blood analysis sensed changes that are impossible to track unless someone's blood is being analyzed in real time, or at least hourly, using sophisticated algorithms. And what it was showing was that Senator John McAdam's blood analysis was on a downward trajectory that predicted his death in 20 days.

Patsy didn't like the position she had just been put into. She had decided to pursue a non-patient-facing career for a reason, and she loved the mix of technology and medicine that VitalTech offered. But she was now dealing with a real person, and that was different. She called Dr. Turner's office and asked to be put through to Dr. Turner, but not on the speakerphone. Turner answered and sensed from the receptionist's request that this might be a tough call. And it was.

Doc Turner was different, and he practiced medicine on a very personal level. Most of the time that was good, but as Doc Turner aged, so had many of his patients and the news he had for them, as he now had for John McAdam, was not good. In addition, the cause of McAdam's impending death had not even been diagnosed yet. Turner explained what Patsy Carter had told him in plain talk, but with a wealth of caring and empathy. He explained that while the technology behind the VT2 was sound, it was often unable to provide a specific diagnosis. The morning's blood test might answer that question but even then, it would be a snapshot in time and further tests may be required. Doc Turner said he would call the lab and get them to rush through the results and then they could discuss next steps.

McAdam asked, "Do you believe that the Final Notice is accurate and that I'll be dead in 20 days?"

"Based on what Doctor Carter told me, this thing has been infallible, so we have to treat it seriously. But let's see the blood tests first before we discuss the color of your headstone. Can you get in here tomorrow morning at 8? I should have the tests by then."

McAdam thought about tomorrow and his meeting in the afternoon was almost a worse thought than death. "Sure. See you at 8. And thanks."

* * *

Kansas City, Missouri. Special Agent Zoe Brouet had been reviewing the recent additions for the VT2 beta tests, which she had filtered by gun users. She was coping with the accelerated pace of the test ramp-up as her boss, Eric Hawke, had given her the resources to follow up with potential problems. As she was viewing the list, she saw a notification on her screen announcing a new Final Notice. When she clicked on it she almost gasped when she saw Senator John McAdam's name. She had been watching with interest the publicity that had been surrounding him recently and was impressed and curious about his breaking ranks. She also saw that she had received an earlier Notice for him today, then a removal, and then this new Notice. That hadn't happened before and rather than call VitalTech, she decided to call McAdam's listed physician, Dr. Angus Turner.

As she dialed, she clicked on McAdam's file and reviewed the short questionnaire that was completed for each beta test user. She was immediately put through to Dr. Turner. He explained the mixed-up signals and confirmed that he didn't see McAdam as a risk to carry out a crime as a result of receiving his Notice. If anything, he thought McAdam was more at risk of being killed than killing, given the waves he was making in Washington. He was only half joking. Zoe took it all in, accepted Turner's prognosis, and asked that he get in touch with her immediately if anything changed. Turner told her that he'd be seeing the Senator in the morning after his blood tests came back.

* * *

Pasadena, California. Rasha and Qasim finally accepted that the media would not go away until they had a chance to hail the hero in the International School shooting. Rasha phoned Trudi and asked for her help and support to get through it. Initially there were a relatively small number of publications, TV and on-line sites wanting to talk to her. Some wanted in- person video interviews, some were OK with telephone, and some with Skype. They wanted to interview a local heroine but what they didn't know was Rasha's whole story, and that would become a game changer.

As Rasha and Trudi discussed the upcoming interviews, it was clear that Rasha did not want Jack to be included in any of the coverage. Not his picture, not his name, not his age. She arranged for extra day care time and Trudi volunteered to take him and pick him up to minimize the chance of anyone seeing him. Rasha asked for Trudi's advice on how to handle the interviews and what to say and not say. Trudi gave her some advice, but she was not experienced in handling interviews either, although she had certainly seen and read many. If she had more experience, she might have realized that the press wasn't as interested in what was known about the shooting as much as what was inside Rasha's head, both during and after the shooting.

Trudi had just returned from dropping off Jack when the local TV station crew arrived for the first interview. Trudi recognized the reporter from the news program she had just watched. Her name was Cara Houston. She seemed very nice and did her best to put Rasha at ease, although that was a tall order. She explained how the interview would work and that it was not a live feed, so if at any time Rasha wanted to stop for a minute, it was OK. It was during this warm up period of making Rasha comfortable and getting to know each other that Ms. Houston learned about some of Rasha's background and recognized that this interview would be different than she had envisioned it. Also, that it would be longer. She excused herself and went outside to call the station to explain and to see if they could fit in a longer segment. It was approved.

The taping began, and Cara Houston led off by explaining that she was sitting with Rasha Melho who, with her quick thinking and action, saved countless lives in yesterday's school shooting. She decided to stick with this story line and then add on Rasha's background. Rasha explained that she had just arrived at the school and was walking down the hallway when she heard the shooting. It seemed to be coming from the classroom that she was en route to and she ran to it. As she cautiously looked through the open door, she could see Miss Rice, the slain teacher, and a number of students lying on the floor, and a man with his back to her shooting toward the windows, knocking out glass. The classroom door opened to the outside, and her first thought was to contain the shooter, so she slammed the door as hard as she could. She had been holding the classroom key in her hand in case Miss Rice had the door shut, so she quickly locked it and moved away from the door. She heard a number of shots and saw bullets coming through the door and then it just stopped.

Cara Houston asked, "You said you ran to the classroom? Why? Weren't you afraid?"

"Yes, of course, but they were my students. I know them, and they were in danger."

"And why would you need a key if the door was simply shut?"

"The doors have different settings. 'Normal' is for the door to open from the inside if the door is closed but remain locked from the outside. It's for safety. I needed to lock it to keep the man inside."

"Weren't you concerned about locking the man inside with the children?"

"Yes. So I slammed the door very loud, so he would know he was trapped, and hoped that he would stop what he was doing. After I slammed the door, all shooting was aimed at the door, as he tried to get out."

"Have you ever been in or seen a situation like that before?"

Rasha was surprised by the question, hesitated and then answered, "Yes."

"Where?"

"Aleppo in Syria."

"Why were you there and what was the situation?"

"My husband and I lived in Aleppo. I was a teacher and our school was attacked sometimes."

" 'Some times?' More than once?"

"Yes. Sometimes with guns. Sometimes with bombs. Sometimes with grenades," she said, as tears streamed down her cheeks.

Cara handed Rasha some tissues and asked if she needed a break. Rasha wiped her eyes and said she was OK to continue. The reporter asked some additional questions about their journey and immigration and finished up by asking Rasha about her feelings regarding her new life in the United States in light of this incident.

"I think this is a very good country. I think that shootings here are not normal like in Aleppo, but I do not like it that so many people here have guns. My husband drives a taxi and he sees people with guns. I read about other shootings. Why do people need guns? There are no rebels or

ISIS people. It makes me very sad. Children should not be shot at. Children should not live in fear. I saw that in Aleppo. It should not happen here."

Cara thanked Rasha and wrapped up. When they left, Rasha began to sob and Trudi held her. "You did a great job." All Rasha could say was, "Those children."

* * *

CHAPTER 27 – BAD NEWS, NEWS & A WALK IN THE DARK

Montgomery, Alabama. McAdam returned to The Retreat on autopilot. He couldn't remember the drive home. All he thought about was he had 20 days. What did he want to do? Or could it all still be a mistake or perhaps there was a cure for what he had that could stop the clock from ticking? He tried to fight the urge to sleep but his early morning start and now the stress were taking their toll, so he laid down for a nap. Four hours later he awoke, confused about where he was and wondering if all this dying in 20 days had been a dream. He was pretty sure it wasn't, but he looked at his VT2 app and it confirmed that a 20-day Final Notice had been received today. He went into his study, unlocked his desk and pulled out the file labeled "Will & Important Papers."

Three hours later he had re-read the important documents and made a note of actions required depending on the outcome of his discussion with Doc Turner tomorrow. And then, he suddenly realized he was very hungry. That blueberry muffin had been his sole sustenance today. He didn't feel like fixing anything and his instinctual pragmatism led him to conclude that eating healthily wasn't important. On the other hand, he didn't want to eat in a restaurant in case he ran into someone he knew, because he wouldn't be great company tonight. This combination of thoughts, desires and inputs led him to call Pepper Tree Steaks N' Wines. A Montgomery institution, Pepper Tree could be your favorite butcher, wine store, restaurant, or the best damn takeaway steakhouse around. It looked like a place you would never think to visit, let alone a place with amazing food, but perhaps that was part of its appeal. He called in and ordered a 16-ounce rib eye, rare, with extra rub, roasted sweet potatoes and grilled asparagus, so still kind of healthy. He also asked that their outstanding sommelier – and she was top drawer – pair it with the perfect red wine. Price no object.

Back at The Retreat, after picking up his dinner, he opened the wine to let it breathe a bit as he plated his food as patiently as possible, almost drooling as he did. He popped in a Nora Jones CD and sat down to finish his day as he began it, with a good meal. The 2012 "Hundred Acre Cabernet Sauvignon" was a great choice, and yes, he had said price was no object. He sprinted through the first few mouthfuls but then settled into a more leisurely pace, not knowing how many more times he would be able to enjoy a good meal, or anything else, for that matter. One glass over his normal two glasses, he felt sleepy again, despite his four-hour nap, and he trundled off to bed, not looking forward to tomorrow.

* * *

Pasadena, California. Vince returned from the physiotherapist just as Trudi finished getting dinner ready.

"Hi honey. How was your session?"

"Fine, hand feels pretty good. How did it go with Rasha?"

"She was great, but would you mind an early supper. I'm famished, and I can fill you in as we eat. I'd also like to catch the 6 o'clock news to see the interview."

"Sure. I'll just go wash up."

As they quickly ate their early supper, Trudi filled him in on her day with Rasha, but she didn't fill him in on the call she received from her doctor. Trudi thought he had enough on his plate right now. Leaving the kitchen cleanup until later, they sat down with their wine to watch the 6 o'clock local news.

The news anchor announced that a special, exclusive interview with Rasha Melho, yesterday's local hero at the International School shooting, would follow this evening's news. But shooting seemed to be the main topic, even before the segment on the school tragedy. The news anchor announced that the FBI was investigating the shooting in St. Louis, Missouri, of two Indian men (from India) by a white man who yelled, "Get out of my country," before opening fire. And another investigation in Washington State was underway where yet another Indian man was shot by a person who yelled, "Go back to where you belong!" before shooting him. The FBI was investigating both as hate crimes.

Trudi commented in a flat, deadpan tone, "Someone should be killing people like the ones doing this. We have immigrants like the Melhos and Khans who are everything and more that makes this country the envy of the world; and then we have these low-life assholes who think that because they are white and have lived here longer, they have some kind of exclusive rights."

Vince was a little surprised to hear Trudi speak so forcefully, but he agreed.

"You know, if I had been carrying a gun the night that Miles was attacked, I might have granted your wish. Those two pieces of shit are parasites and add nothing but misery to everyone's lives."

It was clear that Vince's experience and Trudi's friendship with Rasha had changed them. Maybe not as much as their rhetoric would suggest, but a shift, none the less. They continued their conversation until the segment with Rasha began.

Cara Houston, the reporter who conducted the interview, appeared live to introduce the segment. She added some personal details about Rasha that she had gleaned from their talk before the interview, as well as information from talking with others who knew Rasha. That included Trudi, who had filled in some facts about the Melhos' time in Aleppo and their departure.

Cara said, "We'll now run the interview I conducted earlier today with Rasha Melho, an amazing woman who saved many lives and who all of us should welcome to our community with open arms."

Following the interview with Rasha, Cara had also interviewed the school Administrator, the police officer who shot the shooter, and the parents of Valerie Rice, the teacher who was killed. The Administrator stated that everyone was in a state of shock and that counseling was being provided to both parents and students. She also questioned the value of armed guards who would simply become the initial targets for someone with the intent of shooting schoolchildren. And she sided with Rasha about the danger of having so many guns in the hands of civilians, adding that she would never work in a school where all the teachers were required to be armed. She finished with praise for Rasha, adding that while Mrs. Melho had only been with them for a short while, she was liked by everyone, and had already become a valuable member of the teaching team.

The Glendale Police Officer, Jeff Sykes, commented that as he approached the building, he could see shots coming through the windows from the classroom, but "until the gunman turned around to shoot through the door, I couldn't get a clear shot." Sykes said there is no doubt that the slamming door allowed him to take the shooter out, and that if the shooter had gone across the hall to another classroom, he would have had a much more difficult task of stopping him.

Finally, there was an emotional segment with Diana and Isaiah Rice, the parents of Valerie Rice, the teacher killed by the gunman. They said that all their daughter ever wanted to do was teach children. She had been teaching for just two years.

Vince switched off the TV. They were both upset. Vince even opened another bottle of wine. They were both very proud of their friends, the Melhos. Qasim stepped in to help Vince, and Rasha's quick and brave thinking saved countless lives at the school, and yet there were scum out there who would shout at them to go back to their country and maybe even shoot them. They talked for a while and Vince switched on the TV just before 8:00 PM and went to Fox News. After some typical liberal bashing and alternate facts, they introduced their friend, 'Duh-Wayne' LaPlant from the NRA to comment on the spate of recent shootings and in particular, the school shooting in Glendale.

"Thanks for having me back, Sean."

"Well, thank you for joining us Dwayne. We wanted your take on the school shooting in Glendale, California yesterday."

"Well, people are always sad when young children die, but this school was targeted because they were mostly foreign and from the Middle East. Even the teacher, who they hailed as a hero, is a Syrian refugee. And, by the way, Sean, our experts believe that what she did endangered the lives of those children by locking the killer in with them."

If Trudi had their gun in her hand, she would have shot the TV at that point.

"And Dwayne, what about the comments from the school Administrator ... that having the armed guard there proved ineffective, and that she wouldn't work in a school that armed all its teachers?"

"As we've said before, Sean, having one without the other is like a sandwich without the bread or bread without the meat. So, if she doesn't want to work there, she can find another job in a less safe school. Even in this school, the teacher in the classroom that was attacked, Miss Price, I believe, was negligent by having the door open."

"Thanks, Dwayne. Always good to have you on our show."

Vince threw the remote at the TV and then leaped up to turn it off manually. "He couldn't even get the dead teacher's name right! And he blames her for being negligent!"

He was shaking with rage. Trudi was only mildly concerned about his reaction because she was very upset, too. Vince had a headache and went up to take some aspirin and lie down, leaving Trudi, this time, to clean up the kitchen. Just as he closed the medicine cabinet, he felt his VT2 buzz and the screen read "Final Notice." He looked at his VT2 app on his iPhone and saw the expanded message: "Contact Doctor!" The fucking rabies was killing him. He had 30 days to live. No sense tracking Parker down at night. He'd call in the morning. But what about telling Trudi? He decided to wait.

As Trudi cleaned up, she thought of the irony that both she and Vince could be dead much sooner than they'd ever imagined. They had a good life, but with the exception of bringing Dave into the world, they'd changed nothing. And the world needed changing. She thought about the shooting at Rasha's school and the NRA's reaction, and their whole effort to arm the entire country, using reasons that defied logic and experience. More guns kill more people. It's that simple. And yet stopping the NRA wasn't that simple.

***

294

CHAPTER 28 – IMPROVEMENT FOR THE GOP

Montgomery, Alabama. Thanks to the wine, not wanting to face the day, or perhaps whatever was wrong with him, McAdam slept well and had to rush out the door to get to Doc Turner's by 8:00. The office didn't officially open until 8:30, but the door was unlocked, and Doc Turner's door was open. He called McAdam in when he heard him arrive.

"I'm just delving into your results now and from what I've seen, it's worrying. Seeing this adds credibility to the VT2 alert, and I'm just looking at a snapshot. The VT2 is analyzing nano-trends. What I don't know from either one is what is wrong with you, although the possibilities that derive from these scores are all bad news. So, let's do this. I want you to see Dr. Walsh, an internist, asap. As soon as Sally gets in, I'll have her call and arrange an appointment and call you. Any time you can't see her?"

"I have a meeting this afternoon at 1:00. That's all."

"OK. Unlikely she could squeeze you in today anyway. There's usually a line down the street to get in. Sally will call you as soon as she sets it up. I have to tell you though, John, I'm worried for you."

McAdam left Doc Turner's in semi-shock. He was having a hard time thinking straight and organizing his thoughts. He realized that not having coffee yet wasn't helping, so he dropped into Café Louisa again. After his steak dinner last night, he still wasn't hungry, so the aroma of freshly baked items didn't tempt him today. He ordered a large coffee to go and went home.

It was about 11:30 when Mattie Mays showed up, as promised. She worried about him like a mother, even though she was much younger. She asked if he'd had breakfast and when he said, yes, coffee, she just said, matter-of-factly, "I'll whip something up. It's not good for you to go without eating for so long." And she disappeared into the kitchen while he went to his study to think about how to handle the meeting today. His decision was to ignore the Final Notice until Dr. Walsh weighed in.

Mattie called him into the kitchen and made him sit down and eat his lunch in a civilized way. He told her he had some people coming to see him and she said she would make some tea and coffee and set it up and then disappear into the bedrooms to change the linen, do some ironing, and then come out and clean up when they left. McAdam agreed, actually liking the idea of someone else being around. He finished his lunch, shaved, changed clothes and got ready for what was not going to be an enjoyable experience.

The terrible trio arrived right at one o'clock. McAdam thought that this should be added to their list of positive accomplishments, as there weren't many others. They went through all the handshakes and "nice to see you" bullshit and McAdam led them into the living room and told them to make themselves comfortable. Right on cue, Mattie appeared to ask if they would like some tea, coffee or lemonade. McAdam used the calm before the storm to ask how things were going in their constituency, smiling inwardly as they squirmed with the reality. He doubted that they had heard of The Advertiser's endorsement of his positions on the "six points" needing change. But if they had, the question was that much sweeter.

Chick Lawnley said that this meeting prevented him from visiting Indiana this week and McAdam was polite enough not to laugh. Todey Creud said, with a straight face, that Floridians were applauding his work to repeal the current federal health insurance plan and Tim Wooley echoed that Kansans were equally on board. Mattie returned with the drink orders and glided out, signaling that the gloves were off and the visitors were free to attack.

Creud, being the nastiest of the three, which was saying something, began by calling McAdam a traitor to his Party and fellow Senators.

"I expect that at your age you've decided that you won't run again so you can stir the pot, grab a lot of attention, and ride into the sunset as a hero. That's a chicken shit thing to do. Where's your sense of right and wrong?"

McAdam couldn't stifle the laugh, even if he wanted to. "Right and wrong? Since when did you ... or any of you ... think about right or wrong? All you think about is where will the money come from for the next election, how can I make myself bulletproof with the big spenders so no one else will attract their support, and how can I make a fortune in the process?"

Wooley jumped in. "And you've never thought about catering to people or companies with bags of money in exchange for a bill here, a vote there? Talk about hypocrites."

McAdam confessed, "Sure, I've been at the trough, although not as much as any of you three, but that doesn't make it right and it has to stop. These pledges that we take to always vote with the Party often put us on the wrong side of what our constituents want."

Lawnley piped in, "They don't always know what's good for them. They're like kids and we're the adults."

McAdam looked at him like, are you all there, Chick? "You must be smoking some local crops from one of your college towns. People in Indiana don't really need healthcare? They really don't care about freedom of speech?"

Creud interrupted, "If you're going to recite your stupid six points, save us the agony. We know about your involvement with the bankruptcy of Gulf States Steel, Nucor, the loss of 1700 jobs, and the Chinese getting all the manufacturing equipment."

McAdam replied, "I fought hard to help Gulf States, but it was too far gone to survive. And I had nothing to do with the giveaway price of their equipment."

Wooley added, "And we also know about you accepting hundreds of thousands of dollars in drugs to treat your wife, in exchange for legislation to help Cotton State Pharma."

McAdam responded more heatedly this time. "Not sure where you got 'hundreds of thousands' but Cotton State

Pharma did supply some experimental drugs to help Anne with her cancer. They did it for hundreds of others, too, and the bill was a good one that passed with bi-partisan support."

The trio kept throwing accusations at McAdam who kept parrying back. At one point, Lawnley suggested that they might be willing to support some aspects of his concern about freedom of speech, acknowledging, off the record, that the President had been trampling on the First Amendment a bit. But Creud interjected that they would only do so as far as freedom of speech is concerned, not Freedom of Religion. McAdam was getting tired. Tired of these hypocrites and ... well, just tired. Getting up from his chair, he tried to end the meeting on a civil note saying that he would consider their points, but Wooley was out for blood.

"You have 24 hours to apologize or make any excuse you want to reverse yourself as publicly as possible, or we will make sure that you won't make it through your term. You will jump ahead of Nixon and Agnew on the corrupt politician list."

Creud added, "There is not a senator on our side of the aisle who won't vote for expulsion, and there are even some Dems who will vote with us because you threaten all of us."

Wooley had to get one more shot in. "And in addition to making you live your last years as a leper, we will smear your wife's name for her complicity in accepting bribes. I hope your children have the stomach for what you are bringing down on them."

McAdam was livid. "I knew you were a piece of shit, Tim, but bringing Anne and my family into this goes far beyond the depths I thought you were capable of."

Creud retorted, "You should have thought about that before you decided to promote your radical agenda."

There were no further replies because a number of gunshots were heard and the terrible three became the terminal three. It all happened so fast and without warning that they didn't even have time to be surprised. The only person surprised was McAdam. He stood there staring at the slumped over bodies of three US Senators, dead, in his living room. Out of the corner of his eye, he saw Mattie Mays walk slowly from around the corner, a gun in her right hand, pointing to the floor.

"I'm sorry, Senator, but I wasn't gonna let them spread lies about Miz Anne and you. You are good people. They are not. I took Miz Anne's gun from the drawer and the next thing I remember is pulling the trigger."

She slumped into a chair and sat there quietly, breathing deeply.

McAdam tried to make sense of what just happened. She's a good woman but three people are dead, and even though it's these three people, it's still wrong. He sat back down and thought about what would happen next. How to deal with it, and then he realized what he needed to do.

"Mrs. Mays, Mattie, I need to tell you something and I need you to do something for me. Promise me that you will."

"Senator, I'll promise you anything, if I can."

"You can and you will."

It wasn't easy, but McAdam explained that he had about 20 days to live. She on the other hand had a lot more time. He made her promise that she would go home and not tell a soul that she had been here while the Senators were here ... and not tell a soul about what she did. He told her that if he didn't die as it seemed he would, she could confess; but if he did die, she could never confess. Mattie Mays appeared to be in a trance, but she agreed, gave him a hug, and left. It was the last time they ever saw each other.

McAdam wiped the gun clean and then put his prints all over it. He collected all the cups and glasses, put them in the dishwasher and turned it on. The phone rang and startled him. He decided to answer it and it was Sally from Doc Turner's office. She had set up an appointment for him to see Dr. Walsh tomorrow afternoon. He told her to cancel it.

He poured himself the last glass of Hundred Acres from yesterday's dinner. Then he sat down in a comfortable chair and called his lawyer, Dean Roberts, who, after hearing the words, "I just killed three Senators," said, "Don't say another word to anyone. I'll be there in 20 minutes."

Although it's the capitol of Alabama, Montgomery still has a small-town flavor, and in legal and political circles it's even smaller. Dean Roberts got an agreement from Richard Edwards, Montgomery's District Attorney, who would agree to reasonable bail for McAdam. Roberts also got an hour's delay for McAdam's trip to the police station for booking, so McAdam could call Rebecca and Thomas. By some miracle and with help from Thomas, he was able to conference them both in. He told them that he loved them. That they would see and hear that he killed three senators. He told them that it wasn't how it might appear and that they needed to know that he didn't kill them. And, he told them that he had less than 20 days to live.

* * *

Quincy, Massachusetts ... Kansas City, Missouri ... and Washington, DC. The news wouldn't break until late evening, but unbeknownst to Vijay, Zoe, or the Senate, tomorrow would be an eventful day.

* * *

Pasadena, California. Vince had just finished his coffee when the phone rang. It was Doctor Parker calling about the Final Notice. Vince gave him an update about his treatments with Dr. Malindra and Parker confirmed that at this point, it was his only hope. Trudi walked into the kitchen just as he hung up and asked who it was. Vince told her a partial truth that it was Dr. Parker asking how his treatments were coming along. Not telling Trudi about his Final Notice made him uncomfortable so he took Miles for a walk.

Trudi told Vince that she was going shopping for tomorrow's dinner and might not be home when he returned. Another partial truth as she was first going to her doctor to discuss the results of the screening mammogram. Dr. Laura Sawyer told her that they also needed to do a diagnostic mammogram to get a clearer picture of the tissue. The screening had highlighted a couple of areas that required a closer look. It may be nothing serious but if it warrants it, they may draw some tissue for a biopsy. Dr. Sawyer said, "Nothing to worry about." Trudi mentally added, "Yet."

After her doctor's visit, she threw herself into shopping for tomorrow's dinner. It was the only positive thing in her life right now.

After dinner, as Trudi and Vince watched CNN, they learned about Senator McAdam and the killings. They sided with those who thought he'd done the world a favor, and Vince wondered if McAdam had a VT2.

* * *

CHAPTER 29 – THE DAYS AFTER

Needless to say, the next day's headlines everywhere were along the lines of, "3 US Senators Killed by a 4th US Senator." And due to the recent publicity that McAdam had received, everyone recognized the name of the 4th Senator.

McAdam would never appear in the Senate again and the GOP leadership, not to mention his lawyer, Dean Roberts, made sure he was not on television again; but that didn't stop the press from presenting his version of the murders along sympathetic lines. The stories read more like self-defense rather than murder. Polls even showed that his favorability marks continued to spike up, even after being accused of murder. Many hoped that a jury would ultimately acquit him. This hope and in some cases, speculation, was brought up often on TV news and talk shows and the sentiment wasn't lost amongst many politicians. Suddenly, McAdam's Six Points became more palatable, even to some hard liners. As proof of that, all three of the replacements for the three dead Senators campaigned on McAdam's platforms.

Dean Roberts had McAdam plead not guilty and their strategy was to delay the proceedings for a couple of weeks to see if the VT2 was as accurate as it was said to be. The machinations of court proceedings being what they are, the VT2 could have been off by a year and McAdam's trial would still be in the future. Roberts, in his statements to the press, consistently stated that his client was innocent and would never be proven guilty. He was correct on both counts.

Quincy, Massachusetts. Vijay saw the newsflash on his iPhone about the shooting of three Senators, but it didn't set off any alarms in his mind. So, it wasn't until he got to the office and Maureen told him that most of the senior team had called about it, that the other shoe dropped. He asked her to assemble as many of the team as possible, but especially Maria, Liz and Don. Fifteen minutes later Maria, Liz, Don, Drew, Patsy and Ganesh assembled in Vijay's office.

"What do we know so far and what does the media know?"

Drew explained that Senator John McAdam received his VT2 two days ago and a 20-day Final Notice yesterday morning. Patsy jumped in and told the story of the call from Dr. Turner and Senator McAdam yesterday morning, and her resetting the Notice periods. Drew, who had been looking at the data said, "That explains these on, off, and on-again Notices."

Patsy went on to repeat Dr. Turner's opinion that McAdam was not a danger. That rolled a number of eyes in the room. Vijay asked, "Patsy, could you call Dr. Turner and see if you can get any additional information?" She agreed, and Vijay asked Maria to give everyone an update about what was being said by the media.

Maria made sure everyone was up to speed with Senator McAdam's recent opinions and the extremely negative reaction from his colleagues and very positive reactions from the media and public. She then explained that the media and public's predisposition to like McAdam had marginalized his crime, with some outlets even wondering if a jury would convict him. He had pleaded Not Guilty and his lawyer claimed that he'd be acquitted. At this point, news of the VT2's role in the shooting was limited to those at VitalTech, Dr. Turner, and the FBI, and it's doubtful if anyone in that room thought that McAdam would ever stand trial.

Liz asked what was known about McAdam's meeting with the three Senators. Had anything been reported about when the meeting was actually set up? Maria didn't know the answer to that but said she'd try to find out. Liz said, "I guess it doesn't really matter because the bottom line is that he got his Notice and he killed them. My guess is that the meeting was already planned, but perhaps the Notice gave him the opportunity to kill with impunity."

Don added that at least McAdam was riding high in public opinion circles, and Ganesh, with his penchant for gallows humor, asked Don if he was going to try to get an endorsement or even run ads with a picture of the Senator wearing the VT2. Kind of like one of those tennis stars and his Rolex. That got chuckles from everyone and a head shake, eye-roll and smile from Vijay. The conversation lapsed for a few seconds and you could see the wheels spinning as the marketing wannabes tried to come up with a headline for Ganesh's idea. Fortunately, Don, the marketing guy, beat them to the punch: "When I want to kill some legislation, I rely on my VT2." The groans were heard all the way down the hall.

Vijay brought everyone back on message. "Liz, does this change anything for us?"

"I don't see why. The only thing that's different here is that it was three U.S. Senators as opposed to regular people outside the public sector. McAdam had a gun. His doctor completed the evaluation and even confirmed it after the Notice was received. We shared that intel with the FBI. What it may do, however, is increase the pressure on the FBI to do something... in other words, politics may intervene and cloud the issue. We have done everything they've asked, so I'd leave it alone and wait for them to make a move, if they do."

"OK, thanks, Liz. Drew, anything to add about the progress so far with the beta test?"

Drew brought everyone up to date with the test results so far and it was all good news. Vijay adjourned the meeting and asked Maria to stay behind. He wanted her to put some extra effort into knowing as much as possible about this incident, so they wouldn't be caught off guard. She agreed and said she'd start by calling Matt, but Vijay said, "If Matt gets a call from you about McAdam, it won't take him two seconds to figure out that McAdam has a VT2 and that he received his Notice. And we need to be careful due to McAdam's high profile and an ongoing criminal investigation."

Maria understood, but countered that it's just a matter of time before it comes out, and "Matt is as much on our side as anyone." She reminded Vijay that with the previous intel feed to Matt, most of the other publications followed his tone and there was a better than even chance they'd do it again. Besides, Matt had wider sources and might be able to help her with info, and he would be much more forthcoming if they worked with him. Vijay mulled it over and agreed but urged Maria to be careful. Right now, he had other things on his mind.

Maria returned to her office and called Matt. "Hi Matt, it's Maria at VitalTech. How are you?"

"Great. How about yourself?"

"Doing well. I wanted to ask you what you knew about the McAdam shooting?"

Matt laughed and said, "A lot more than I did a second ago!"

"Vijay was right. It didn't take you two seconds."

"What?"

"Nothing. Listen. You know I can't tell you anything, but now you have a hint, thanks to me. So, we'd like to keep ahead of this, and I'd appreciate knowing what you know. And when you're ready to run with anything, keep me in the loop?"

"Sure. This was already a fascinating story but now it just got a lot more interesting. A lot of people have been wondering if he'll get away with it and now it's obvious that he will."

"What do you mean?"

"He won't live long enough for it to go to trial, even if he got a 30-day Notice. In the USA, you're innocent until proven guilty at least for the moment – and by law, a defendant has to be able to speak in his own defense. So, the case will die as soon as he does – as an innocent man. It's a fairy tale ending that most people will really like."

"I hadn't thought about it from quite that perspective. So you'll keep me posted?"

"Sure. How about over a drink?" "Are you asking me out?"

"That didn't take two seconds, either."

"When you're ready, name the time and place."

* * *

Vijay couldn't escape the feeling of déjà vu as he stood at the door of Suite 840 at the Four Seasons Hotel, nor did he want to. He knocked on the door and a bathrobe-attired Jennifer slowly opened it. He walked in and the robe slid off her shoulders onto the floor as he hungrily kissed her, caressing her completely naked and wonderful body. She did the best job she could, operating at very close quarters and shuffling backwards, to strip him of his clothes as they slowly made their way through the sitting room toward the bedroom, leaving a trail of a shirt, shoes, chinos and boxer shorts to accompany her robe. For those of you wondering if he was wearing socks – seriously? – the author feels sorry for you but is compelled to say he was.

If the room had been bugged to capture corporate secrets, it was an utter failure, as the majority of audio captured would have been heavy breathing and a number of other unintelligible but completely understandable sounds. The author was tempted to insert *** as a lot of time passed without much else happening; however, the episode ended with an extremely consequential discussion.

Both Jennifer and Vijay were exhausted and hungry. They had also missed "last call" at the hotel restaurant, which either meant going out, or calling for room service and possibly exposing their tryst. Vijay helped make their decision. "Will you marry me?"

The newly engaged couple, attired in matching, plush Four Seasons' robes and nothing else, ate a sumptuous late supper accompanied by a bottle of pleasingly bubbly Veuve Clicquot and discussed their plans. Jennifer wanted to announce their engagement immediately and continue to work at KKL. She would insist on living in Boston and she was pretty certain that J. Edward wouldn't have a problem with that.

Vijay, the scientist and mathematician, discussed the logistics of their wedding – halfway 'round the world; and all he had to do to convince Jennifer of his idea was to describe an Indian wedding.

Despite the late hour in Quincy, it was three hours earlier in California, so she called her parents and told them to get ready to apply for an Indian Visa. The late hour in Quincy also made it possible for Vijay to call his family in Mumbai and tell them the news. They finished their meal and returned to the bedroom to resume the unintelligible noises, interspersed with a number of "I love you's."

* * *

Kansas City, Missouri. Zoe Brouet had heard the news last night and she knew that Dr. Turner had been wrong. And that made her wrong, but what could she have done about it? How could she know that McAdam was meeting with Creud, Lawnley and Wooley? If she had, would she have been able to stop the killing? And the answer to this last question was possibly yes, or maybe that was 20/20 hindsight. But given the hard feelings between most of the Senate and McAdam, and given the stature of the four participants, it wouldn't have been completely out of the question to provide some security for the meeting. One thing for sure was that the problems would become bigger when the VT2 was released in a full rollout. Vijay told her about the strong demand based on a few newspaper articles. If, rather, when the news got out about McAdam, the message would be clear: When you know you will die shortly, you can kill and die as an innocent man or woman. Her gut told her that this might be a game changer.

And then, her desk phone rang, and it was Hawke, her boss, wanting to see her.

Eric Hawke was not happy. He played Cover Your Ass with capital letters and he was an all-star at it. He lashed out at Zoe for being soft on VitalTech and for allowing things to get out of hand. She countered by saying that VitalTech had complied 100% with the court order and was doing everything they could. She asked, "If John McAdam was diagnosed by his doctor, as opposed to a watch, as having 20 days to live, what could we do? Doctors don't have to tell us anything unless they believe the person is a threat. We knew McAdam had a gun and we knew that he received his Final Notice at the same time he did, but his Doctor rated him as a low risk. I even called his doctor to ask him personally."

Hawke asked what the doctor told her, and she repeated what Turner had said, that, "He was more at risk of being killed than killing."

Zoe then said something that made Hawke sit back and think. "The difference between that watch and a doctor's prognosis is that doctors will never give you anything very specific, and, in most cases, they try to give you some hope. Therefore, it's not as definite or real as saying 'you have 20 days to live.' There is no hope when that watch tells you it's over. But there's nothing illegal about it. In fact, since the watch has the capability to predict death, suppressing it may actually be considered illegal."

Hawke's demeanor changed. "I'll talk with legal and see if there is anything else we can do, but you're probably right. And the fact is, we have no idea how many people, if any, have killed someone because they knew they were going to die shortly. You did everything you could. Thanks."

* * *

Pasadena, California. Vince had walked the streets for hours the past night and he was out for so long that Trudi was fast asleep when he got back. His recent searches for the two guys were unfruitful and he feared that he wouldn't find them in time. As he walked, he thought about the reality that he only had 28 days to live. How could it be? He was only 70. He and Trudi were supposed to have a lot more time together to enjoy each other ... time they never had while he was working. What about 70 being the new 50? As his eyes misted, he wondered, "What will she do?" Financially she'd be fine, and everything was in order insofar as wills, insurance and instructions. He hadn't thought about dying before. It was really hard to take in. The VT2 was supposed to be highly accurate and it had given him 30 days, which was now 28 ... or was it 27? He needed to tell Trudi, prepare her, but what if the Rabies treatment worked? He decided to wait a little longer to tell her about his Final Notice sentence.

Vince was up early and was hastily making coffee when Trudi came in. "What time did you get back last night? I didn't hear you come in or come to bed."

"I don't know. Maybe midnight."

"So why are you up so early?"

"Are you kidding? It's pick up the gun day!"

Trudi didn't understand why he was so excited, but she was happy to see him happy for a change. "Aren't you supposed to see Dr. Malindra again to follow up after your last shot yesterday?"

"Damn. Thanks. I can do it after I get the gun."

"I suggest you do it before you get the gun in case someone breaks into the car."

"Do people break into Priuses? ... Good idea. I'll do that."

Fifteen minutes later Dr. Sawyer's office called to request another appointment for Trudi. She thought about the expression "bad news comes in three's" ... "So, there's the rabies, the shooting, and I wonder if I'm about to get the third?"

Vince went to Huntington to see Dr. Malindra, who wanted to draw blood after the last shot as a final baseline.

Vince was too excited to even think about his situation and immediately headed out to Turner's Outdoorsman.

A different woman, Angie, was in the handgun department when he arrived with his receipt. She checked it carefully, checked his ID, and had him sign and date her records. He asked her to take him through the loading, firing and cleaning operations one more time, and as it was early, and the normal crowds hadn't arrived yet, she patiently showed him how to operate his gun. The gun came in a nice box and had full and easy to understand instructions. She asked if he needed ammo or anything else, but he told her he was all set.

On the way home, he kept glancing at the box on the passenger seat, dangerously running outside his lane a few times. He brought in his new prize and tried to get Trudi's interest, but she was too busy getting organized for dinner that evening. Even with Vince's excitement, he guiltily realized that he needed to pitch in and help.

Trudi had decided on an American-style dish, roasted salmon encrusted with pistachio nuts, as the main course. For a starter, she chose Nori-Bean Lettuce Wraps, a vegan dish from her favorite vegan chef, Julie Morris. She and Vince alternated between eating vegetarian or vegan four to five days a week, and chicken or fish in between; and she liked introducing people to things that they might not normally eat.

Vince made sure there was beer for Rueben and white wine for Doris. He suspected that neither Qasim nor Rasha drank alcohol, and he knew the Khans didn't, so he checked to make sure they had a good supply of fruit juices, Perrier and soft drinks. Trudi heard him yelling and swearing in the garage and went running out to see what happened. He had dropped a bottle of orange juice and it had smashed on the floor. She was very surprised that this would bother him so much. He was usually calm, even when things got rocky.

"Are you OK?" she asked.

"No!" he screamed back.

Trudi actually backed up a step at his reaction. She was afraid to ask but did anyway, "Are you feeling OK, honey?"

Vince had regained his composure and apologized. "I'm sorry. Maybe I didn't sleep so well." To some extent, that was true. Vince was excited about getting the gun and he did wake up a few times. "I'll take a nap if there's time."

Trudi agreed and encouraged him to do just that. His outburst worried her, as it was ongoing proof that he was infected.

After lunch, Vince took a nap and Trudi went about prepping for dinner, but her bright enthusiasm for the evening was overshadowed by her doctor's call and Vince's outburst. Vince woke when Trudi emerged from taking a shower as she readied herself for the evening.

"Hello, sleeping beauty." She tried to sound cheerful. "You must have really needed that. You slept for almost four hours."

Vince was groggy from his long nap and mumbled an affirmation. "I'll jump in the shower and shake the cobwebs off."

* * *

The Melhos arrived at the stroke of 7:00. Perhaps it was Qasim's taxi training or maybe Qasim was just one of those people who was always on time. It was hugs all around, after Vince had relieved Rasha of the sacred Syrian cheesecake. Just as they were settling onto the couch, the doorbell rang, and it was the Khans. Trudi led them into the living room and introduced Alma and Ahmed to the Melhos. Vince got their drink orders, three orange juices and one apple juice, and left them with Trudi, who explained to the Khans how she and Vince had met Qasim and Rasha. The doorbell rang again, and Trudi returned with Doris and Rueben, again introducing Rasha and Qasim. "This is the couple we told you about ... heroes, both of them!"

Vince returned and after welcoming the Martinezes, asked if it was beer and white wine or something else. When he returned with their drinks, as well as the predictable red wine for Trudi and himself, they all settled in and began a lively conversation– about their lives, children and latest happenings in the world and neighborhoods; but for the Khans and the Martinezes, all they wanted to hear about was Rasha's school shooting. Trudi excused herself to get dinner ready while Rasha gave everyone a very modest overview. Vince prompted her a few times to tease out some additional details, and Rueben mentioned that he knew Jeff Sykes, the officer who shot the shooter. He said it was universally accepted amongst the local police that Rasha's quick thinking saved a lot of lives.

Doris and Alma grabbed Rasha by the arm as they excused themselves to offer help to Trudi, giving both Ahmed and Rueben another chance to ask about the attack on Miles and Vince, and to get Qasim's view. Vince gave Qasim a look that said, "don't mention the rabies," which he seemed to understand. Qasim downplayed his part and said he did what anyone would, which met with headshakes and doubts. They asked about his job as an Uber driver, which seemed to them a more interesting occupation than simply driving a taxi. Qasim explained the system to them and they were surprised to know that the drivers rated the passengers. The payment system and bonuses were also a surprise. Qasim liked it but confirmed that you needed to work very hard and put in long hours for very modest compensation. He added that many Uber drivers had other jobs as well.

Ahmed asked Rueben about a recent incident involving the Los Angeles Police and a report that speculated about excessive force and over-reaction. Rueben was aware of the incident and it made him a little uncomfortable, perhaps because it involved Middle Eastern victims. He agreed, however, that it was very possible that they over reacted. He explained that the situation was one that might have been part of a terrorist operation and the officers knew that if it was, split seconds separated them and others from life or death. It's not always as black and white as the media makes it out to be. He had confidence in the LAPD's investigation process and integrity and felt that an honest outcome would come out of it. That was more than he could say about some police departments.

Vince was very subdued during the conversations and he seemed relieved when Trudi, Alma, Doris and Rasha returned to tell them that dinner was served. Trudi's Nori-Bean starter was a hit and initiated a conversation about vegetarian and vegan food. It turned out that all of them were, in fact, part- time vegetarians, partly as a result of their ancestral foods – beans, rice, cheese, flatbreads and tortillas –

and partly for health reasons. Trudi intrigued everyone with her knowledge of "super foods" and the outsized health benefits they provided.

The earnest and animated conversation continued over Trudi's signature dish of roast salmon with a pistachio crust accompanied by stir-fried, Indian-style asparagus and sweet potato medallions with fresh ginger and cinnamon. The exotic flavors seemed to lead to the topic of travel bans for people coming from select countries, which included Syria, and to Rasha's and Qasim's relief, everyone disagreed with the idea. The conversation was reminiscent of the one at the Khan's a few weeks ago, but more mellow.

In a blatantly sexually-discriminatory fashion, the dinner plates were cleared by "the ladies" while the men continued the conversation about immigrants. Ahmed asked Qasim if he had encountered much prejudice both in his job and life here in general. Qasim said that there was some, but it was very seldom and mostly minor. He'd had a couple of Uber passengers that were obnoxious, typically at night and with strong smells of alcohol. Rueben asked if he gave them bad ratings and they all laughed. They laughed again when he said, "Yes." But Qasim was now serious. He explained that many of the drivers were immigrants; and when viewed by others based on their appearance, proficiency in English, and accents, it was obvious they were, which sometimes caused trouble. A number of them had passengers who were extremely aggressive, and in a few cases, even waved guns at them. Rueben expressed surprise, explaining that carrying concealed weapons in California was unusual, given the strict control of concealed carry permits. Qasim continued that he felt the rating system served as a warning for all the drivers, and it was his duty to use it to help them avoid potential problems.

Staying with guns but shifting the conversation, Rueben asked Vince if he had gotten his gun yet. This took both Ahmed and Qasim by surprise and Vince, and probably Rueben, too, wished he hadn't mentioned it. Vince said yes and also, to underscore that the purpose was for protection, told them that he had obtained a biometric gun vault that could be opened only by Trudi and himself. This was interesting to the guys and they liked that idea. Vince didn't tell them that he had also obtained a concealed carry holster. Nor had he told Trudi.

They were rescued from the awkward conversation by Rasha's beautiful cheesecake and coffee and tea. Ahmed asked if the cheesecake was vegan or vegetarian and they all laughed. The answer was vegetarian. The admiration for the cake's appearance quickly switched to admiration for its flavor. It was a big hit, although Vince was secretly disappointed when offers of another piece were accepted by everyone, reducing his opportunity for leftovers.

Over dessert conversation, Vince belatedly thanked Qasim for asking his fellow Uber drivers to keep an eye out for the two guys and their pit bull. Rueben asked what they would do if they spotted them. Qasim explained that they were to call him; and as he had done recently when there was a potential spotting, he would contact the detectives handling the case. Vince added, "And he calls me, too."

Rueben asked Vince, "What did you do when he called?"

Vince knew where Rueben was going with this. "Nothing. It just keeps my hopes alive," he replied unconvincingly.

Rueben persisted, "I hope you guys and your Uber colleagues don't get involved with a vicious dog and two deadbeats. Leave it to the police."

Qasim, said, "I agree but our only chance is if the drivers call me first. Most of these guys won't call the police to report a white American. They mostly come from places where the police are not their friends. I have the phone numbers of Detectives Lucker and Reed and they know me. I can call them, and I think they will respond."

Vince slapped his hand on the table and emphatically demanded that he also be called. "I want to know too!" His demeanor and tone of voice raised eyebrows around the table, prompting Qasim to placate him, "Don't worry, Vince. You know I will."

Vince's outburst cast a pall over the group and Rasha began the exodus saying that they needed to get back as their sitter was young and needed to be taken home. The others used the opportunity to make their excuses and the three couples left together, leaving Vince and Trudi to say good night, as their dinner party seemed to come to a screeching halt.

As they walked out to their cars, Rueben pulled Qasim to the side and implored him to only call Vince if he was sure that the police would be there. Qasim understood and assured him that he'd do that.

On their drives home, all the couples discussed Vince and his behavior. He had been withdrawn for much of the night and then agitated at the end. They were worried about him being so much out of character. Back in the house, Trudi was also worried, but she knew why.

While Trudi was, again, cleaning up the kitchen on her own, Vince went to the bedroom and removed the gun from the vault. He quickly checked to ensure there was a round in the chamber, the clip was full, and the safety was on, and promised himself that he and Trudi would take lessons soon. He fished out the hidden holster and wrapped everything up in a windbreaker. Unenthusiastically, he asked Trudi if she wanted any help in the kitchen and when she said no, reading his vibes, he said he was going for a walk and he'd take Miles out and let him in again when he returned.

Before leaving the backyard, he practiced reaching for the gun a few times and then began walking to the area where he and Miles had been attacked. He stopped as he got close and stood still, listening closely for any sounds. A car passed, and he turned back, walking normally, until it was out of sight, and then he returned. Hearing nothing, he took a few more steps. It was very dark, and he was reluctant to leave the sidewalk and enter the brushy area.

After listening a bit more and hearing nothing, he pulled out his cell phone and switched on the flashlight with his left hand while un-holstering his gun and turning off the safety with his right. Carefully trying to avoid sticks, he walked back into the darkness, swinging his phone from left to right, but there was nothing but a fallen log in the small clearing. He returned to the sidewalk, switched off the light, switched on the safety and returned the gun to his holster.

He returned home, finding Miles curled up at the back door, and they both went in for the night. He hid the gun until he could put it back into the vault without Trudi knowing.

* * *

CHAPTER 30 – MORE CONSEQUENCES

Quincy, Massachusetts. Matt had been keeping Maria in the loop with developments related to the McAdam shooting. As the case was very much under investigation, there wasn't much information other than a few ongoing stories about the slain Senators and much wider coverage about McAdam. One reporter managed to get McAdam to state that the three Senators threatened to blackmail him with wildly distorted claims of events that were easy to shout but impossible to prove. They were equally difficult to disprove since there was no substance or factual information to discredit. And he stood by his positions that major change was required to fix what ailed the government, adding that the three dead Senators represented the worst faults, but they were by no means the only ones. As agreed with his lawyer, he never confessed to killing them and either ignored or deflected any questions asking for outright admission of guilt. The public wanted to believe in his innocence – at least in the bandied-about theories of "self-defense" – and his political approval rating grew, making it very difficult for his colleagues to attack him. As experts in the value of public opinion, they either were supportive or chose to keep a low profile.

A few days after Maria's call to Matt, he returned the call and, as promised, named the time and place to meet: 7:00 PM at Cagney's on Washington Street.

She agreed and met Matt at the popular pub. He had identified McAdam's doctor from a story where he was quoted with respect to McAdam's mental state. Using his skills at assumptive interrogation, he had called, identifying himself as Matt Harper from The Boston Globe, who had been working with VitalTech and the launch of their VT2 watch. He had simply asked, "Do you believe that Senator McAdam was at all influenced by receiving the Final Notice on his VT2?" Dr. Turner's response had been, "I'm not at liberty to discuss privileged doctor-patient confidences. However, I've known the Senator for many years and I'd be surprised that even that information, if he received it, would be a catalyst for murder."

Maria had to admire Matt's approach. He hadn't lied but his confidence in what he was asking had gotten the doctor to tacitly reaffirm his assumption. She asked, "So are you ready to go public?"

"I am. I actually spoke with McAdam. He wasn't easy to gain access to but I found a way," which made Maria smile and say, "Surprise, surprise."

Matt smiled and continued, "After a series of questions about his positions, I hit him with, 'Were your actions regarding the three dead senators influenced at all by your health concerns?' "

"Wow! How did he answer that?"

" 'No comment,' preceded by the telltale, but not convicting, three seconds of hesitation. I tried to push but that question shut him down."

"I guess, given his refusal to admit that he killed them, he wants, or his lawyer wants him, to steer clear of even oblique pieces of evidence."

Matt hadn't written his story yet and wanted to get Maria's input and a VT2 beta test update first. She told him that it was all going very well. She realized, too, that based on Matt's research, she believed that the VT2's involvement would remain highly speculative because of the lack of substantiation from McAdam. This was the first time that a user committing a crime, assuming McAdam did, was still alive. And unless he came out and said he killed the three senators because he had nothing to lose (and that would be very unlikely), the VT2's involvement would remain a theory. McAdam would be dead before a trial could begin, and therefore would retain his innocence.

They discussed this, and Matt confessed that it was one of the reasons he wanted to meet with her. He suggested that he could write something that would ask the question about the VT2's influence but it could never really be answered. He was uncertain if that was a story or not. Maria, on the other hand, her memory fresh from what the earlier stories did for the watch's demand, was bullish about a story, even hinting about it. It would help to rekindle the interest that the earlier stories did. Matt said that he would draft something and run it by her. She smiled and asked, "You said this was one of the reasons you wanted to meet. Were there others?"

He smiled and in a brighter room his blushing would have been more obvious. "Ahh, yes. Uhh, I wanted to see you again."

Matt's story and the additional follow-up coverage in other publications across the nation had the desired effect that Maria wanted – maintaining interest and building up stronger demand that, hopefully, could be sustained for the commercial launch:

"DID A WATCH KILL THREE SENATORS?"

Boston, MA. A short time ago it was announced that a new sport watch/health monitor known as the VT2 was in its final test phase before a national launch. The VT2 is unrivalled in many respects, but one feature of this device that is unique is its ability to predict the user's death within 30 days. It is known that a small percentage of earlier test users had resorted to murder after receiving their Final Notice, as the feature is called.

The Boston Globe has learned from undisclosed sources that Senator John McAdam was wearing a VT2 and may have received his Final Notice just prior to the murders of three Republican Senators, murders which Senator McAdam is accused of. McAdam would not comment on this, nor would his physician, Dr. Angus Turner, violate the rules of doctor-patient confidentiality. But the doctor did say, speaking theoretically, that he didn't think that any Notice, as shocking as it might be, would trigger an action of that nature in McAdam.

Still, the question remains. Was the watch the trigger? – Matt Harper, Boston Globe"

* * *

Pasadena, California. Trudi returned from her doctor appointment. Dr. Krishnan, an oncologist, had used a new, less invasive biopsy procedure to take a tissue sample that could be examined in greater detail. Trudi was told that they would call later today or tomorrow with the results, and what next steps, if any, were necessary.

There was a note from Vince that he was walking Miles and there were two messages on their house phone. One was from Rasha asking Trudi to call her. The other from Barb, just saying, "We are all OK." Trudi wondered, "What does that mean?" and tried Barb and Dave's home number, getting a recording. Same with Dave's cell. She tried Barb's cell and she answered but there was a lot of talking noise in the background. Barb told her that there had been a shooting at the school where Dave taught and that he was OK, but the shooting was horrific. Ten or more dead. Barb said she couldn't talk now but they would be home this evening.

As she hung up, visibly upset, Vince walked in and asked, "What's going on?"

Trudi explained, and Vince grabbed his laptop and typed in "Austin school shooting." The only listing originated at KXAN News: "More than 10 dead in East Austin School Shooting. Police have arrested a suspect in today's shooting at Birchwood Elementary School in East Austin, Texas. The suspect, who has not been identified, was apprehended by police as he tried to escape. An assault rifle and at least two other guns were seized. Sources at the school said that a guard, two teachers and at least seven students have been killed and a number of others wounded."

Trudi called Rasha, who was very upset. The school Administrator, Shirley Jackson, had called and told her that she was under pressure to dismiss Rasha because of complaints from some parents. One of the parents had confided to Ms. Jackson that her husband asked her to complain after receiving a call from the NRA, where he was a Ring of Freedom member. Ms. Jackson was trying to wait it out but if other parents came forward, the school Board may force her hand. She added that she was being muzzled and may also face more consequences for speaking out. Rasha asked for Trudi's advice and she suggested that they go to see Ms. Jackson tomorrow. Rasha thankfully agreed.

Later that afternoon, Dr. Krishnan's office called. They needed to see Trudi again.

At 5 o'clock they tried Barb and Dave at home and Dave answered. He sounded pretty normal at first but as he spoke about the shooting, it was evident that he was very shaken by the events. They were talking with him on their speakerphone and Vince asked him directly, "Are you OK?"

Dave replied, "I'm fine. The bullet went through my leg and missed the bone."

"What!!??" they both gasped. "You were shot?" Trudi asked.

"Yes. Didn't Barb tell you?"

"No! She said you were alright."

"I am. I'll be limping for a while but no permanent damage."

They asked him to tell them what happened, and Dave gave them a comprehensive, and sadly, what's become an old story: Gunman comes to the school and kills the guard first, then takes out any adults he encounters who may have guns, and then starts in on the kids. Dave was in the hallway near the entrance and was the second person shot, after the guard. Fortunately, the shot hit him with such force that he went down fast, making the killer think he was dead, or at least unable to intervene. He was able to call 911 as soon as the killer went around the corner. He sobbed as he told them that 9 students were dead and then said something they couldn't quite hear. When they asked him to repeat it, he said that his school Administrator had told them not to make any public statements disparaging the NRA. They could hear Barb say, "That's not my view!"

Trudi told them about Rasha and her situation and they were sympathetic but said the NRA was a law unto itself and it wielded too much power. Trudi and Vince asked if they needed any help, but Dave told them that the wound was so clean ... the bullet missed anything important ... and he really only had a slight limp. If that changed, he'd let them know.

That evening, in what had become all too routine, Trudi and Vince watched the CNN coverage of the Austin shooting. They suddenly sat bolt upright when the local reporter introduced Dave Fuller, a teacher at Birchwood Elementary, who had been shot at the outset of the incident. Both Trudi and Vince beamed seeing their son but realized how different the story could have been. The reporter ended his interview with Dave by asking, "Do you agree with the NRA that arming guards is not good enough and that arming teachers is essential?"

Dave hesitated a second or two and said, "I've been told not to say anything against the NRA, but I will say that if I had been carrying a gun, it would not have helped me today. And I will add that carrying a gun and being a trained anti-terrorist soldier are two very different things; and unless we train our teachers the way we train our military, armed teachers will create more problems than they solve. But that is simply my opinion."

The reporter tried to get Dave to say more but he simply said, "No further comments." Although Trudi and Vince were definitely up for the 'Proudest Parents' award, Vince's questionable mortality weighed heavily. All he could think about was revenge.

Trudi was also being smothered in bad news and went up to take a shower, to wash away the remnants of physical and mental debris from her biopsy.

While Trudi was in the shower, Vince once again opened the biometric gun case and removed the Glock. He then rummaged with his hand to the back of the drawer in the bureau and retrieved his holster. He slipped in the gun and the clip, and positioning them in the small of his back, he put on a lightweight windbreaker and waited for the shower to stop. When it did, he called in to Trudi that he was going out for a walk.

"I won't take Miles, but I'll let him out to do his business before I go."

"OK, honey. I may be asleep when you get back."

330

Vince let Miles out and stood there while the fuzzy little guy sniffed around for just the right place. He realized how much he would miss not being alive to see him, as tears welled up. Miles finished his business and Vince scratched him between his pointy ears and then let him inside this time. He might not be coming back. He closed the door and went for a walk.

He double-checked the gun to ensure there was a round in the chamber and the safety was on. He was resigned to the probability that he and Trudi would never get to take shooting lessons. He reached for the gun a few times and began walking, no destination in mind, but he started by strolling past the area where he and Miles were attacked. As he approached the area he froze in his tracks, thinking that he heard voices. It seemed like minutes, but the voices started again. He walked a few steps closer and listened, keeping on the sidewalk. It was two men, and their voices, if not definitely recognizable as the two from that night, were very possibly the same. He took another couple of steps and could see that there was a flickering light, possibly a campfire, shining through the bushes. He could just about make out the path to the back of the brushy area but was concerned that they might hear him approaching. He un-holstered his gun and turned off the safety.

Coming up the street was an old truck, loud enough to mask the sound of his approach, and as it got closer, he carefully stepped off the sidewalk onto the path. He took another step and then another and he could see two men, who could be his guys, sitting on what looked like a log, smoking something. They passed it back and forth. His eyes grew accustomed to the dark and the little fire was good enough to see that they were passing a glass pipe-like thing back and forth between them. Drugs? He couldn't see the dog but knew from their previous encounter that it might attack and braced himself to shoot in self-defense.

Taking a deep breath, he charged into the small clearing and faced the two guys across the flickering fire, aiming the gun at them. The guy holding the pipe dropped it behind them. In a voice as menacing as possible, Vince demanded, "Where's Rambo?"

The one with the baseball cap said, "He's dead. Who are you?"

"I'm the guy that Rambo bit after he almost killed my dog. And now I have rabies and will probably die, so I thought it only fair that you two join me."

"Hey man. We didn't tell him to do that. He was acting all weird and we was both getting 'fraid of him, too. He tangled with a skunk and stunk real bad but we've had him since he was a pup, so we put up with it. But he started getting weird. Growling and snapping at us. 'Bout two days after that, after he bit you and your dog, he tried attacking us, but he couldn't even stand up good and then he dropped dead."

Vince was not a killer and he believed their story. He tried to stay angry at them, if for no other reason than to keep the upper hand. "Let me tell you something else. That foreign guy you swore at that night has been through more suffering than either of you could imagine. He survived bombings and shootings in his country and after years of being a refugee, he was admitted into this country. He works hard at a job that he didn't take from either of you. He pays taxes and he makes a contribution to this community and country, which is a whole lot more than either of you do."

Vince took a few steps backward to put some more space between him and them, while still pointing the gun at them, and with his free hand, pulled out his phone and swiped up the camera app. He quickly took their picture a couple of times. "I'm not going to kill you tonight, in case my rabies shots work, but tomorrow, I'm going to bring these pictures to all the police in this area. So, you have less than a day to get as far from here as you can. And never come back. Because I will also show these pictures to my friends, and if any of them see you, someone will come looking for you, and they will not be as understanding as I am. Is that understood?"

They both nodded profusely and said yes.

Vince told them to get up and, still pointing the gun at them, marched them to the sidewalk and motioned for them to start walking in the opposite direction of his way home. He watched them until they were out of sight, switched the safety back on, and re-holstered his gun. He was shaking as if it were 20 below.

He walked aimlessly for a bit thinking about what had just happened. Those two guys were responsible for his rabies and impending death. He had a gun so why didn't he use it? And he knew the answer. He had succumbed to the notion of fear, of powerlessness, and of the idea that a gun was the answer. That was why a million seniors had answered the call: The call to arms by the NRA and their puppets in Washington and state legislators across the country.

The shaking had stopped. His head was clear. He knew who he was and that guns were not the answer. He returned home, went in, let Miles out, and sat down on the back porch. Miles lay down by his side and got all the head scratches he wanted. Well, almost all.

* * *

The next day, Trudi picked up Rasha and went to see Ms. Jackson. They knew something was wrong when they arrived and, after politely greeting them both, Ms. Jackson asked to see Rasha privately. When the door opened again, a teary-eyed Rasha strode out. She had been fired. On their way to Rasha's, Trudi tried to get her to open up but Rasha remained quiet. When they arrived, Trudi asked if she could come over tomorrow. She had an idea.

* * *

CHAPTER 31 – THE PLAN

Pasadena, California. Trudi went to see Dr. Krishnan. She was compassionate but didn't beat around the bush. Trudi had early Stage III breast cancer in her left breast. They would need to do some additional testing but since she had annual exams, Dr. Krishnan hoped they had caught it before it spread. If that was the case, the worst outcome was a total mastectomy followed by radiation and chemotherapy. She added that as scary as that all sounded, the long-term prognosis was very good.

Dr. Krishnan told her that it was important to start the process as soon as possible but in this situation that meant a week or two. Trudi told her that she would get back with her soon. She wasn't unnerved by the news. The way things were going, she more or less expected it. Her next stop was to see Rasha. Jack was home, but he was playing outdoors with a toy truck, so she and Trudi watched him through the window as they talked.

Trudi explained Vince's situation and her own. Rasha was beside herself with grief. Here was both her very best friend and her friend's husband facing death! It made her current employment problems seem insignificant. She would do anything to help. But how?

Trudi presented her plan to Rasha. She articulated her very strong desire to make a contribution that would benefit others, but she needed Rasha's help. She emphasized that it would not jeopardize Rasha's own safety but was important to carry out the plan. Her belief that Rasha would be safe turned out to be very naive, but Trudi truly believed it at the time. She made Rasha promise that she would steadfastly claim that she knew none of the details of this plan, but simply went along as a friend to have fun. Because of her strong affection for Trudi, as well as her own recent experiences, Rasha jumped at the chance to help, although it did not make her happy knowing that it might be her last chance to do so. Listening to Trudi's plan, she remained committed but had grave doubts about success.

When Trudi returned home, she asked Vince if she and Rasha could use the NRA tickets and would he pay for airfares and a hotel for both of them. Vince couldn't help but smile that she and Rasha wanted to go.

"I thought you hated the NRA and the NRA has cost Rasha her job?"

Trudi knew she couldn't completely lie her way out of this, so she professed to come clean, explaining that they wanted to attend the convention and then hold up signs to protest what it stood for. There would probably be TV coverage and it would give them a chance to make a statement before they were removed. Hopefully, they could talk with the press, too.

Vince laughed and gave her a hug. "My old Berkeley girl. Sure. If that makes you happy, no problem. When is it?"

Trudi hugged him back, "Friday." She felt badly about lying and about dying. Her plan might work and might also save him the anguish of helping her through surgeries, radiation and chemo. An even worse outcome was that he might not be around too long if the rabies shots didn't help.

Vince booked their flights and hotel, using his old "mileage points" from his travelling days. He also played around with his VT2 App by changing the Final Notice period to 10 days. It was exciting to see the Notice actually disappear. Then he set it for 20 days and it reappeared. It also triggered a call from Dr. Parker. Vince explained what he had done and apologized for the false alert. Parker asked how he was and about his regimen of shots and Vince told him that he actually felt a little calmer and that he was due to see Dr. Malindra for a follow-up tomorrow.

Trudi spent a lot of time with Rasha over the next couple of days discussing plans and researching information on Trudi's iPad.

* * *

Vince dropped Trudi and Rasha off at LAX, Terminal 3, before continuing to Huntington Hospital to see Dr. Malindra. The women had arrived in plenty of time, as security line waits could take an hour or more. Trudi decided to not take any chances with getting her special necklace for the occasion to Virginia, so she checked it in along with her baggage. She hoped Vince wouldn't open the gun vault. Vince had printed their boarding passes and, after dropping off their checked bags, they entered the TSA security line.

It was a fairly light day and they reached the baggage and body scanner in less than 20 minutes. Rasha went through first and set off the buzzers. A female TSA agent asked her to step to the side and scanned her body with a handheld wand. The agent began the scan from the back of Rasha's head down her back and the wand buzzed wildly. Rasha unfolded a document and handed it to the agent who read it, thanked her and finished her scan, albeit with less intensity. Trudi followed without setting anything off.

They had extra time now, so they stopped at Starbucks for a coffee for Trudi and tea for Rasha. They were both excited but nervous about their trip. Virgin America flight 108 boarded through gate 31 and they settled into their seats for the almost five-hour journey to Dulles International Airport, just outside of Washington DC. Trudi tried to sleep but couldn't and decided to pass the time watching The Pink Panther. It always made her laugh, and it did again on this occasion, although not quite so much. Rasha read the Study Guide for the U.S. Citizenship Test, although there were still two to three years before they could reach the point of taking the test. She had already read a few other books to help her prep and the fact that she could read English was a big advantage.

The time passed quickly, and they arrived at Washington Dulles Airport on time, seemingly sooner than they thought. Vince had once again donated some of his hoard of Marriott points from his travelling days, and they were booked into the Washington Dulles Marriott Suites Hotel in Herndon, Virginia. The hotel was in a small shopping center with many restaurant choices. When they checked in, the agent told Trudi that they had received a large package and it was in their room. The two friends were tired but stretched their legs and grabbed a light dinner at a nearby Turkish restaurant. Rasha assured Trudi that the food was not authentic, but that the waiter was, and the meal was satisfactory.

The following morning, they woke up late, as their body clocks were three hours off. Their suite had a small dining area, so they ordered breakfast from room service in order to discuss their plans in private. Trudi repeated again the promise she had exacted from Rasha earlier, that Rasha knew nothing about Trudi's plan and had no idea how she had smuggled a gun into the NRA event. They had gone over the plan often, and this discussion was simply a repeat of the others.

They had the whole day to themselves, so they booked an Uber and went into DC to see the nation's capital. It was a beautiful day, so they decided to take a Hop-On, Hop-Off double-decker bus tour. In one-and-a-half hours they could see the White House, U.S. Capitol, Washington Monument, FDR Memorial, Martin Luther King Jr. Memorial, Lincoln Memorial, World War II Memorial, Vietnam Veterans Memorial, Korean War Veteran's Memorial and the Supreme Court of the United States ... but they had time, so they used the hop-off, hop-on option to explore a bit more. Rasha was enthralled with DC and Trudi had only been there once before, many years ago. It was the perfect activity to keep from thinking about the evening's task, and the day was so magnificent that Trudi truly enjoyed it.

Back at the hotel, they showered and got ready for the big NRA function. Just as they had practiced, Rasha strapped the gun onto her inner thigh, using the holster that Trudi bought (unbeknownst to Vince) but now modified expertly with a Velcro thigh belt that she had made. Rasha wore a thin head cover that was much more a fashion statement than religious apparel. Trudi carefully unwrapped her special necklace – a "biker chick" piece of jewelry made entirely of real bullets – and placed it around her neck. It was heavy but strangely comforting. Nervous but committed, the dynamic duo set off in an Uber for the 25-minute drive to the NRA headquarters. The driver didn't comment about the empty folding wheelchair that they carried.

When they arrived, Rasha helped Trudi, who "miraculously in reverse" became handicapped, into the wheelchair that the driver retrieved from the trunk. They joined the sizeable number of people attending, most of whom appeared to be seniors. As they reached the entrance, they realized that part of their planning was incorrect, and they smiled at each other as they entered the building without going through a metal detector. The only control was collecting the tear-off stub of their invitations.

As they made their way to the ladies' room, they were a bit startled to see a number of people openly carrying guns. Even though this was NRA HQ, they had never seen guns openly flaunted like this. When they came out, after loading the clip with the live ammo from the bullet necklace and transferring the gun to Trudi's purse, they observed the crowd – possibly numbering a few hundred. Waiters were openly carrying, too, but only champagne, juices and canapés, which were being gobbled up by the mostly older crowd. Trudi was tempted to ask for a glass of champagne but decided it wasn't a good idea. Besides, celebrations should be for successful operations, so she could wait. They looked into the large auditorium and noted with smiles of satisfaction that there was an open area for wheelchairs at the front, near the stage. A number of people had begun to sit down near the front, so Rasha slowly wheeled Trudi down to the wheelchair area.

They chose a spot at the very front next to a young man in a wheelchair who looked almost sedated, staring straight ahead. A woman who might have been his mother was seated next to him in one of the folding chairs provided for attendants. Trudi and Rasha smiled politely to acknowledge them, then Rasha locked Trudi's wheels and brought a chair over for herself. Being in the front meant they had to turn around to gauge the progress of the room filling up, which made them directly face people looking toward the front. They didn't like that, so they looked straight ahead or glanced sideways, but avoided making eye contact with each other. Trudi was enormously grateful for the risk that Rasha was taking; and Rasha, in turn, admired Trudi's bravery.

Small talk between them seemed absurd at this point so they both went into their own thoughts, hopes, regrets and fears as they passed the time. Trudi was nervous and fearful in ways different from Rasha. She was afraid of failure, afraid of pain if she were shot, afraid of jail, and afraid of staying alive to face her own health issue on her own. Rasha was afraid that she would be caught and that she wouldn't see Jack or Qasim again; that she would be deported. She wasn't afraid of getting shot. But both were unwavering in their hatred of the NRA and what the NRA had done and wanted to do ... all for the sake of greed. And for both, the wait seemed an eternity.

The steady flow of people entering the auditorium must have slowed to a trickle and an announcement was made for everyone to please take their seats. A number of younger-looking, casually dressed men took positions around the back and sides of the stage perimeter in front of a backdrop reading *"NRA CELEBRATES 1 MILLION ARMED SENIORS".* Some wore shoulder holsters over their casual shirts. Trudi could also see a gun in the waistband of one of the men, standing sideways to her.

The lights in the seating section dimmed a bit and a spotlight illuminated the podium. A young woman stepped to the podium and the large screen backdrop changed to: *"Betty Lou Harris, Vice President-Public Relations, National Rifle Association."*

"Good evening ladies and gentlemen and good evening, seniors!" The audience clapped and whooped a bit. "We're here tonight to celebrate the millionth senior to buy a gun under our NRA Armed Senior program. We appreciate that aging isn't easy; in fact, some say, getting old isn't for sissies!" She paused for a laugh and applause. "But we say, 'Never fight if you can avoid it, but when you must fight, Don't Lose!' " Cheering and clapping ensued.

"I want to introduce a good friend of the NRA and by extension, a good friend of yours. A man who fights to protect our constitution and protect against liberal actions to take away our guns. Ladies and gentlemen, I give you Dave Pratt, United States Representative for Virginia."

The caption on the large screen changed to *"Dave Pratt, U.S. Representative for the State of Virginia,"* as a smartly dressed man walked rapidly to the podium. There was a good round of applause, but Trudi didn't pay much attention to what he was saying as she slowly unzipped her purse and wrapped her hand around the surprisingly cold gun hidden inside. She switched off the safety as she had practiced many times over, ensuring that her finger stayed outside the trigger guard. She focused on her task; stay focused, aim, squeeze slowly and repeat. Finally, she heard him say that he was "pleased and honored to introduce a man he had known for a long time, a good friend and a good friend of Americans, Dwayne LaPlant."

The screen changed to, *"Dwayne LaPlant, Executive Vice President-Marketing, National Rifle Association."* LaPlant strode confidently to the podium as the audience stood up and gave him a tremendous hand. Trudi had a clear shot, and this was a time they had discussed that might provide an excellent opportunity. Waiting until he reached the podium, she reached out with her left hand, and concealed by her chair, gave Rasha's right hand a firm squeeze, never taking her eyes off LaPlant. Then she slowly pulled the gun from her purse and began to lift up her arm when one of the casually dressed men on stage shouted, "SHOOTER!" and drew his gun, aiming it at Trudi. Seeing this, Rasha grabbed the back of Trudi's wheelchair and pulled it over backwards just as the shooter on stage pulled the trigger. His shot ricocheted off one of the steel footplates of the overturned wheelchair, hitting the young man in the wheelchair next to them. Blood spurted from his leg, which seemed to jolt him into action and he reached under his seat and pulled out a gun, firing back and hitting the shooter on stage. Another shooter on stage fired back but missed the young man and hit someone else in the audience. The young man shot back again, and others joined in. Rasha held Trudi down, scooped up the gun and put it back into Trudi's open purse.

Gunshots rang out all over the auditorium amidst screams and yelling, and it seemed like many minutes passed

343

before a loudspeaker announcement demanded that "EVERYONE CEASE FIRE!" A final shot was heard as the announcement stopped and full lighting came on. Rasha righted Trudi's chair and helped her resettle into it. They could see a number of people sprawled out on stage and a lot of screaming and yelling in the audience. The guy who shot at Trudi was down along with some others, and there were a number of people kneeling down and helping a person or persons near the podium. The young man next to them had been wounded again, in addition to the ricochet shot. But he was smiling. Someone on stage made an announcement that everyone who was not injured should slowly move to the side aisles and make their way out of the auditorium, to allow paramedics to attend the wounded. Before leaving the building, everyone would be interviewed by the police who would be asking for identification, contact details, the main section of their invitation, and their Row and Seat number ... "so please make a note of it before you leave your seat." Also, their guns would be taken from them for ballistic tests.

Stretchers were brought out onto the stage and a number of staff lifted two men in suits onto the first two stretchers. They were Dave Pratt and Dwayne LaPlant.

It took a long time before Trudi and Rasha arrived for their interviews. On their way out, Rasha said to Trudi in an exaggerated voice, "It seemed like the man on stage shot the young man next to us, so I pushed over your chair to get you out of the line of fire. I'm sorry if I hurt you." In fact, Rasha's quick action undoubtedly saved Trudi's life. When that first shot ricocheted off the footplate, she hadn't taken in what happened. There was a loud ping sound followed by the dull thud of the bullet hitting the young man next to her. When she looked over at the footplate of the overturned chair, she could see that it was about the same height as Trudi's mid-section or chest would have been.

Trudi looked back and said with a smile, "Yes, that's what seemed to happen, and thank you." When Trudi was interviewed and asked if she had a gun, she took her gun out of her purse and gave it to the female police officer. The officer asked if she had a concealed carry permit. Trudi answered honestly, "No I don't. I didn't think I needed one in Virginia."

The officer was wearing gloves and looked at the gun, smelled it and said, "This hasn't been fired, has it?" When Trudi confirmed that, the officer said that they would need to check it anyway and that she would get it back within a week if it didn't match any bullets. She also said that Trudi might need to respond to a complaint for carrying a gun without a concealed carry permit. She could be charged with a misdemeanor. The officer then ran a wand over Trudi to check for any additional weapons, and finding none, thanked her and said good night.

When Rasha was interviewed, she answered "No" to the gun question and when she was wanded, the machine squawked like crazy. The female officer patted her down and Rasha showed her the doctor's letter. She too, was thanked and dismissed. Outside there were ambulances coming and going and police cars all over the place. They called an Uber and while they waited, Trudi called Vince and told him that he should watch the news, they were both all right, and he should call Qasim. Fifteen minutes later they were on their way back to their hotel. They said nothing during the 25-minute ride.

Back in their hotel suite, Trudi raided the mini bar and opened a small bottle of wine and wished it were larger.

Rasha opened an orange juice and wished she drank. They turned on CNN and there it was in a big bold red banner, "Carnage at the NRA." Vince's "friend," Wolf Blitzer, was talking over a live video feed showing the chaos at NRA's headquarters. "We can confirm that Dwayne LaPlant, Executive vice president of the NRA and U.S. Representative for Virginia, Dave Pratt, have both been killed. It is believed that 11 others have been killed and scores injured as a veritable firefight seemed to break out at an NRA celebration at their Fairfax headquarters. Details are still sketchy, but it seems to have started with a shooting exchange between an NRA staffer and an attendee at the event, who may have drawn a gun. Other NRA staffers and guests then began firing, although it is not known why. Guns are permitted at the NRA headquarters, which is consistent with their belief that more armed people make it safer. Seems like that backfired tonight. Let me switch over live to Tim Larker, who was covering tonight's NRA event. Tim?"

"Hello, Wolf. It's a very chaotic scene here as paramedics are dealing with the dead and wounded and police are trying to process out all the attendees to get their identity, contact details, and guns if they have them. There were a lot of guns in there tonight and a lot of seniors. I really don't know much more than you already said in your introduction, but I have snagged a few attendees that can tell us what they saw. This is Helen Matthews from Little Rock, Arkansas. Helen, tell our viewers what happened in there."

"Well, it was just gettin' started and one of the young guys on stage shouts, 'Shooter' and fires off a shot toward where the wheelchairs were. Then it seemed like a shot came back out from there taking that NRA guy out, so another guy on stage shoots into that area and a couple shots came back

346

from a bigger area and then more shots from everywhere. I got down on the floor until they announced everyone to cease fire."

"Thanks Helen, and this is her husband Norman Matthews. Tell us what you saw."

"Sure thing, Tim. It was a veritable goat (**bleep**) if I ever saw one. Funniest goddamn thing I've ever seen. (**bleep**), I kinda wondered if it was staged to show how if everyone was armed, bad (**bleep**) wouldn't happen. Hell, I even shot my gun into the ceiling a few times just to get in on the action. But on the way out, it looked like some people were hurt real bad, so I guess it wasn't fake."

"Thanks, Norman and sorry Wolf, if any of that colorful language slipped by. We'll be staying right here to bring you further developments as they happen. Back to you, Wolf."

The two women hadn't said a word during the broadcast, but they looked at each other and hugged. Tears ran down their faces as they realized what they had made happen. Trudi said she wanted to call Vince. He answered right away and said he had just watched the CNN broadcast. Trudi assured him that they were both fine and that she would give him a detailed report when she got home tomorrow. Vince said that he had a report that he needed to give her right now. "The rabies vaccine appears to be working." Trudi was overcome with joy and then Vince added, "And now I'll be able to take care of you and we'll fight your battle together. Yes, I know all about it. I love you, Trudi. Come home and let's get rid of that damn gun!"

Reports the following day in all the national media would add additional accounts and details about what went wrong at the NRA. But the most critical details about what happened came from one of the wounded attendees, Eddie Meakin, of Tallahassee, Florida, in an interview with Wolf Blitzer:

"Mr. Eddie Meakin of Tallahassee, Florida, attended the event with his mother, Dorothy Meakin. Mr. Meakin is 28 years old, an Army vet who was discharged 4 years ago after serving one month in Iraq. He has been receiving behavioral therapy since then and his medication confines him to a wheelchair. According to Mr. Meakin, one of the NRA staffers on the stage shot him in the leg – for no apparent reason – and Meakin removed his gun and fired back, possibly killing the staffer. Another staffer then shot Meakin in the shoulder and Meakin returned fire, possibly killing him as well.

"Mrs. Meakin confirmed what her son said and added that Eddie is deeply disturbed and is generally very removed from any social interaction. The only thing he seems to enjoy is sitting in his wheelchair and shooting at targets. "He's a very good shot."

* * *

THE END

EPILOGUE

Montgomery, Alabama. Exactly nineteen days after the murders of his fellow Senators, the senior Senator from Alabama, John D. McAdam, passed away peacefully in his sleep at The Retreat. His funeral produced a huge outpouring of attendees, including most of his fellow Senators, from both parties, a majority of U.S. Representatives, the Governor of Alabama, his daughter Rebecca, son Thomas, and his good friend, Mattie Mays. Senator McAdam died an innocent man. Which, in fact, he was.

* * *

Kansas City, Missouri. The FBI's legal department decided that there was no way to stop the inclusion of the Final Notice in the VT2. In fact, they conceded that VitalTech's cooperation was generous under the law, and if all potentially dangerous situations needed to be reported, the FBI would need to monitor divorce courts, airline baggage offices, help line headquarters and even schools at report card times. Zoe currently heads up a special team of Agents assigned to monitor Final Notice recipients. It's a huge task and growing.

* * *

Quincy, Massachusetts. The VitalTech team was stumped about a VT2 user in Pasadena, California, whose Final Notice had been rescinded. In follow-up discussions with the user's doctors, they learned that the user had been diagnosed with rabies and that the vaccine, although given late and after the disease had established itself, appeared to work, thus causing a reversal of the Final Notice. After thorough discussions both within VitalTech and with other physicians, the conclusion was that when it comes to medicine, there is never a 100% certainty.

VitalTech's IPO was an outstanding success. Not as big as most of the social media ones but even better than J. Edward expected, and he had big expectations. In fact, J. Edward acquired VitalTech, making Vijay much more than an "on paper" multi-millionaire, and the Patels in India (at least three of the million-plus clan) have dramatically improved their standard of living.

Over 2 million VT2s were sold – in the first quarter alone – following its release. So, if you're a bully ... an irresponsible politician out for him/her self ... or anyone that lies, cheats and steals, leaving in your wake, physically, emotionally and/or financially damaged people ... watch out!

On the other hand, reports continue to flow in about amazing acts of generosity. Cars, furniture and even houses have been donated to worthy causes from people, literally days before they passed away; and many cities are reporting that their homeless are looking better dressed, even chic, as women and men share their closets just days before they will never need their clothes again.

Jennifer stayed on at KKL after announcing her engagement to Vijay. They held a five-day wedding in Mumbai which was attended by the parents of the bride and groom, Vijay's brother, Sanjay (who is the plant manager at the VitalTech manufacturing center) all of Vijay's senior team from VitalTech, plus Matt Harper as Maria's date, and J. Edward. Zoe Brouet was invited but was too busy tracking high-risk VT2 users to attend.

Vijay and Jennifer have also announced two new projects. One is a foundation focused on promoting gun safety and responsible gun ownership; and the other is their first child.

Vijay was never able to completely come to terms with the unforeseen consequences of the Final Notice, so, not surprisingly, he is working on a new medical/technical project with a small team of scientists. It involves pushing the VT2 technology further to analyze serotonin-cortisol levels to identify depression and anger, and possibly flag likely Final Notice aggressors. Zoe is hoping he cracks it.

* * *

Pasadena, California. Rasha Melho was offered a job to head up the Foreign Language department at a private prep school in the area and Qasim started his own taxi company and now employs 20 people who might have been drawn from the United Nations. It gives him more time to spend with Jack, especially now that Rasha works full time. Both are on course to set new speed records to become U.S. Citizens, and they remain great friends of the Fullers.

351

When Vince went to see Dr. Malindra the day Trudi and Rasha flew to DC, Dr. Malindra mentioned that his last blood test was interesting but inconclusive. He drew some new blood samples as well as saliva and tissue samples. The following morning, Vince's VT2 Final Notice disappeared. He reset it for 30 days and it still showed nothing. Later that day, Dr. Malindra called to say that it appeared that the rabies vaccine was working. Vince replied, "I know."

Vince had also taken a call from Dr. Krishnan following up with Trudi. She explained Trudi's situation and felt optimistic about the outcome.

Trudi, with Vince's help and support, took on cancer with the tenacity you'd expect from her, and she's on track to beat it. She still has a major obstacle, however, as Vince now knows how devious she can be.

Trudi confessed to Vince her role in the NRA shoot-out, after returning home from Virginia ... as well as her clandestine shooting lessons and practice at the Firing Line shooting range in Burbank. Vince was speechless ... blown away ... and it took a few seconds for him to decide if he should laugh or cry; so, he just took her in his arms and said, "I love you!" And then they both laughed and cried. And Vince, for his part, told Trudi about his confrontation with the two guys and how he realized that he couldn't kill them. He was surprised when Trudi responded with a big hug and kiss. But he never did tell her about the thug in the parking lot. In the end, however, they both emphatically agreed to get rid of "that damn gun" the moment it was returned by the D.C. police.

Trudi also began working on a new song, Crazy Eddie Got A Gun (That's What The NRA Has Done). Visit

www.finalnoticebook.com for the lyrics and a link to a free download.

Vince now takes Miles to a nearby dog park where Miles and his new BFFs, Yogi, Gaja and Olina, romp and play each day. Miles seems 10 years younger, and he can still bark with the best of them.

* * *

Fairfax, Virginia. The police and the FBI concluded their investigation after weeks of depositions and ballistics tests. It was determined that Eddie Meakin killed the two NRA staffers. Corroborating testimony from most of the attendees, as well as Mr. Meakin, confirmed that the gunfire originated from the stage by NRA staffers. The District Attorney decided that a crime was not committed, and that Mr. Meakin acted in self- defense.

Dwayne LaPlant was killed by a single bullet fired by Ida Smothers, 91 years old, from Culpeper, Virginia. Mrs. Smothers is legally blind and when questioned why she shot Mr. LaPlant, she asked, "Who?" Apparently, she felt a bullet whiz by her head, so she just started shooting back. Her shot hit LaPlant in the middle of his forehead. Charges against her are pending.

Dave Pratt's death was ballistically linked to the NRA staffer on the stage who was killed by Eddie Meakin. The shot hit him at the back of his head.

Most of the other deaths were found to be caused by gunfire from NRA staffers.

* * *

Washington, DC. The "visionary" thinking and agenda of John McAdam was embraced by both the GOP and Democrats and our political system is functioning as never before, with amazing progress seen on many fronts, driven by our new female President and openly gay Hispanic vice-president. Significantly, too, ISIS has disbanded, as have all the other terrorist organizations, due to a labeling change. It appears that no one wants to join a Cowardist organization.

* * *

Remember, this is a work of fiction.

AUTHOR'S NOTE

And finally, on a more personal note, my legal affairs are in order and instructions written. I'm at ease with my relationships and connectedness, my bucket list is under control, and it's highly unlikely that I would clean out the refrigerator, dust the furniture, wash the floors or do the laundry, if I were to get my Final Notice. And so, I might have time to right some wrongs (without a gun!) and do some good... but I'm not waiting!

Seriously, my intent in writing this book was to highlight a few of the many critical issues facing our country today, and if you are reading this now, I am probably preaching to the choir. Our country needs to re-examine our attitude toward seniors ... put a stop to profit-driven legislation that puts gun sales before human lives ... and elect politicians who set the right tone of civility, as well as uphold our constitution.

And finally, we can't afford to lose our role as the beacon of hope for the world's best and brightest. Let's keep that welcome mat out.

* * *

While Final Notice is a work of fiction, what is not fiction is the help and support I have had from friends and family, especially my partner in life, love and happiness, Jackie Morris, whose singing has been a joy as I plot and write. Equally important has been her advice and editing. Thanks, too, for some great ideas from my daughters, Heidi and Amy, and to my dog, Yogi, whose enthusiasm never flags and who has never been critical of any of my writing.

I would also like to thank my team of alpha and beta Readers who have given me new ideas, great suggestions and (mostly) gentle critiques: Bud R., Gary G., Leda S., and Pat D.

* * *

For additional updates and links to progressive organizations that support gun control, visit: www.finalnoticebook.com.

THE VERY END

FINAL NOTICE QUESTIONS FOR BOOK CLUBS

Following are some suggested discussion questions for book club moderators. The author is happy to engage in discussions, as possible, and I would love to hear about them. I can be reached at van@vanfleisher.com.

1. Overall, do you think that the author was too one-sided or was he fair in his dealing with: seniors, immigrants, guns, the NRA, and politics?
2. Would you want a VT2, how would you feel about knowing when you will die, and what would you do with your last days?
3. Based on the premise of the Final Notice, do you feel that guns are the problem?
4. How did Vince and Trudi's views on gun ownership change during the book? What caused the changes? Were their feelings and actions believable?
5. How did you feel about the issues of immigrants and immigration as discussed in the book?
6. What are your thoughts on the role and treatment of seniors as discussed in the book and in your own experience?
7. Did you like the author's writing style?
8. Would Final Notice make a good movie? What actors would play the main characters?
9. What are your views on the underlying theme of ethnic prejudice?
10. How did you feel about the book's ending?
11. When Trudi lifted the gun, what did you think she would do?
12. Who were the most likeable characters? Least likeable?
13. Did Final Notice influence your views on guns?
14. Did you feel that the various characters exercised adequate personal responsibility and that the NRA, VitalTech and the FBI displayed sufficient corporate responsibility?
15. Your overall rating: 1-5 stars.

91658712R00224

Made in the USA
San Bernardino, CA
23 October 2018